SPECIA'   **'ERS**

THE ULVEF
(registered ‍

was established ‍ to p‍
research, diagnosis and treatment of eye diseases.
Examples of major projects funded by
the Ulverscroft Foundation are:-

- The Children's Eye Unit at Moorfields Eye Hospital, London
- The Ulverscroft Children's Eye Unit at Great Ormond Street Hospital for Sick Children
- Funding research into eye diseases and treatment at the Department of Ophthalmology, University of Leicester
- The Ulverscroft Vision Research Group, Institute of Child Health
- Twin operating theatres at the Western Ophthalmic Hospital, London
- The Chair of Ophthalmology at the Royal Australian College of Ophthalmologists

You can help further the work of the Foundation
by making a donation or leaving a legacy.
Every contribution is gratefully received. If you
would like to help support the Foundation or
require further information, please contact:

THE ULVERSCROFT FOUNDATION
The Green, Bradgate Road, Anstey
Leicester LE7 7FU, England
Tel: (0116) 236 4325

website: www.foundation.ulverscroft.com

Actress, musician, journalist, and TV and radio presenter Clemency Burton-Hill was born and raised in London. She is a contributing editor for the *Spectator*, has written for many UK publications, and appears regularly on arts and current affairs programmes, including *Question Time*, *Andrew Marr*, and BBC Radio 3, 4 and 5. In 2013 she was chosen as a judge for the Costa Book Awards.

You can discover more about the author at: www.clemencyburtonhill.com

ALL THE THINGS YOU ARE

When New York journalist Natasha Bernstein loses her job and discovers her fiancé has been keeping a dark secret, her world collapses. Turning to her family, she takes inspiration from her formidable grandmother Esther, who runs a community centre in downtown Manhattan. As she starts to rebuild her life, Natasha's friendship with Rafi — the enigmatic architect working on Esther's centre — restores her sense of wonder at the world, and her faith in who she is. But when Rafi and Natasha take a trip to Jerusalem, they are plunged into a story far deeper than their own, and must ask themselves: what are they ultimately prepared to fight for?

CLEMENCY BURTON-HILL

◆

ALL THE THINGS YOU ARE

Complete and Unabridged

ULVERSCROFT
Leicester

First published in Great Britain in 2013 by
Headline Publishing Group
London

First Large Print Edition
published 2015
by arrangement with
Headline Publishing Group
An Hachette UK Company
London

A catalogue record for this book is available
from the British Library.

ISBN 978–1–4448–2326–4

To the memory of my great-grandparents,
Abraham and Sarah,
who left everything behind.

Once the realization is accepted that, even between the closest human beings, infinite distances can still exist, a wonderful side-by-side living can emerge, if they succeed in loving the distance between them, which makes it possible for one to see the other whole against the sky.

Rainer Maria Rilke

Part One

1

September

There was usually one, she had learned over the years. Taking a sip of water from the glass on the lectern, Esther Goldfaden scanned the auditorium to better study the face of the person who had just spoken. It turned out to be a young woman, dark-haired and intelligent-looking; somewhere around the age of her grand-daughters, she guessed. The woman was still holding the microphone in her hand, close to her mouth, as if poised to come back on whatever answer Esther should give. A steward hovered anxiously on the aisle nearby: there were a number of other raised hands in the lecture theatre.

Esther carefully set the water glass back down and smiled at her interlocutor. 'Thank you for your thoughtful question. It's certainly a very interesting one, and a complex one . . . '

Earlier, in the cab down to Battery Park, she'd thought that perhaps she wouldn't do these kinds of events much more. People must surely have got tired of her story; she

3

knew she had. But this museum was a wonderful organization: not only a resource for academics but a place to which interested people might come, learn and reflect. She liked and respected its director, a bright, perceptive woman named Maggie Adler whose temperament, Esther felt, had the capacity to make people feel more optimistic about humanity, not less. Esther invariably enjoyed the experience of speaking here. Today, though, she was unusually tired, and had found the session draining.

And now, this question. *Why have you never been?*

'Mine is a very personal response,' she said, ever so slightly adjusting her chair on the stage. 'I understand that others feel differently, and I deeply respect their positions, as I hope they respect mine. But you must also understand that for me, my homeland was the village of Zholkva, near Lvov, in eastern Galicia, until it was here in the United States. I had never once set foot in the Middle East. Israel was not my home, it never was. It was not a political stance I took, deciding that I had no need to visit. It was purely a personal one.'

She nodded over at the steward, as if to say: next question.

'But I read an interview you gave a few

years ago in which your decision not to go did seem political,' the woman countered. She was holding a Dictaphone in her other hand, Esther noticed for the first time. 'In which you expressed what sounded like pretty strong views about Israel that some of your fellow survivors might reasonably see as objectionable. So I guess I'm just trying to get to the bottom of whether there is any . . . any *causal* connection between your experiences during the Holocaust and how you got to your position on Israel today?'

Esther maintained her smile.

'First of all, I should just like to clarify: I have no 'position' on Israel today. Choosing not to live in a place, or even not visiting it, does not equate to a position, not as I understand it.' She was buying time as she steeled herself, gearing up for the phrases she had rehearsed so many times. It wasn't that the sentiments were not genuine or hers, they absolutely were. But in such moments she often found it easier to cling to the lifeboat-like words of a familiar script rather than access the emotions themselves, lurking so many fathoms below. 'I hardly need to restate my belief that it would be facile, not to mention perilous, to compare Hitler's Holocaust to any other inhumanity man has inflicted on man. But I have also always held

5

that my experiences during the war, what happened to my family, were tragedies specifically personal to *me*. I have never thought it appropriate to use those experiences to make any wider point.' She cleared her throat. Why did she feel so fragile today? 'Nevertheless it is *also* true that the experiences of my life have made me aware of the suffering of others, many of whom are being denied their fundamental rights all over the world. And I have always believed, as deeply as I believe anything, that any argument about human rights becomes discredited unless those rights are to be extended to every human being everywhere.'

'So you are saying that Israel doesn't extend those rights?' Triumph had crept into the woman's voice.

Edging towards exasperation, Esther held up a hand. 'Please! I am not saying anything of the sort. I am no expert on Israeli policy today. I can tell you a lot about the bureaucratic hurdles facing homeless and disenfranchised New Yorkers, if you are interested in that?'

There was a ripple of laughter, which pleased her: she was always keen to remind audiences that her life's work and focus was down at the community centre on West Street, not really in lecture theatres like this one.

The female journalist continued undeterred.

'But in the same interview you said, and I
quote, that the Israel-Palestine conflict 'is the
greatest moral issue of our age'.'

Esther inclined her head. 'Did I? Well, I am
sure it is. And I believe, as I am sure many
people here in this room believe, not as a
Jewish woman but merely as a rational
human being, that it would be a tragedy, a
tragedy, were Israel's treatment of others to
fatally undermine the moral foundations of
its own existence. Not to mention its own
long-term security interests.' A smatter of
applause broke out in pockets of the
audience. 'And as I have *always* maintained
whenever I am asked about this most difficult
topic, I am deeply wary of any attempt to
make causal links or comparisons between
the systematic annihilation of European Jewry
by Hitler and the conflict between Israelis
and the Palestinians today. One must never
be posited as justification for the other; nor
can they possibly be compared.'

Over more applause, Esther glanced
reassuringly at Maggie, as if to assuage any
concern at the direction the Q&A had taken.
She nodded again at the steward and
indicated with her forefinger a man seated
towards the middle of the auditorium, who

had patiently kept his hand up during this whole exchange. 'And *now* I think we really must move on!'

But still the bespectacled woman had not relinquished the microphone. She said, 'And what about Emanuel?'

Esther squinted at her.

Her soul.

It took her a moment to regain her composure. She swallowed, heaved his name from her heart onto her lips. When it came out, it was almost a whisper. '*Emanuel*. What about him?'

How they loved to bring it back to him, these audiences. Beyond the fact of her being a survivor, and the widow of a celebrated playwright, Esther Goldfaden, neé Loew, was also a figure of fascination at such memorial centres as this because of the letter that had been discovered at Buchenwald in 1945. The original was in the archives at Yad Vashem, along with so many other diaries, letters, small correspondences; the evidence in ink and paper of humans still clinging to the possibility of their lives — humans who mostly had not survived. But there on that frayed and tattered sheet, by now almost translucent, was Esther Loew's confident nineteen-year-old Yiddish hand: faint and illegible in places, but thrillingly alive. Many

American holocaust museums had facsimile copies, like the one in the glass case upstairs. Usually, it was the thing people most wanted to talk to her about.

And most of the time she didn't mind. Sometimes, on days when she was feeling stronger than today, Esther would even paint for them a picture: of how she and the cobbler's son from a neighbouring village had met each other just once, teenagers, at a winter dance in Lvov during the war. And how they had not known each other's names; but had known something else. 'No sooner met but they looked; no sooner looked but they loved,' she would tell her rapt audience, quoting one of her favourite Shakespearean characters, before going on to explain how, almost a year later, as she ran to the neighbouring village to get her father's boots repaired because their own cobbler was sick, she had collided with the boy once again and he had said her name.

She would tell them how, after the Nazis broke the Molotov-Ribbentrop pact in 1941 to take Lvov, their villages had both been subsumed into the ghetto that winter. And how for a while, despite the whispers about the horrors happening outside the ghetto walls, her time there had been in its way a miraculous thing. Because it was there in the

9

ghetto, that freezing winter, that she and Emanuel had answered each other's souls: two young people twining together as they made love and plans; plans for tomorrow and plans for the future. Plans for such simple happinesses: children, music, food, books. Each other. After this was all over. One day.

And Esther would describe to audiences that last evening in the ghetto, before the Gestapo arrived. 'We met, we made love, and then we ate a last meal at our favourite café: a traditional Galitzianer sweet *kugel* with *lokshen*. I can still taste it to this day. We had a plan: he was going to go underground that same night, into the forest with some friends of his, to join the resistance movement slightly further east. And I was going to escape with my family. My father had these government contacts, or thought he did; there was a neighbour enlisted to help us escape in the middle of the night. Emanuel and I knew we would meet again somehow. We made our plan. It was simply unthinkable we should not see each other again.' It was all unthinkable, of course, everything that had happened next. Often her audiences already knew the outline of her biography, and she need not say the words. *My family and I fled our house in the middle of the night, leaving everything, all our possessions. We thought we would*

10

return, of course we would return, but we were taken at the border. My father had been betrayed by his contacts. He was shot dead in front of our eyes. And then my mother, my brother, my sister and I were sent to Belzec, and from there the Janowska camp, and from there I went to Buchenwald . . . And of all of us, I was the only one to survive.

Sometimes, if it felt appropriate, if her heart could bear it, she would go on to tell them how she had later found out that she and Emanuel had missed each other in Janowska — he too had been betrayed by those he trusted — by days; she already on a transport to Buchenwald by the time her love walked through those same gates. Or how, many years later, with her husband Max's help, she had discovered that her darkest terror had been realized: not that Emanuel had perished — for that much she already knew. But that he had also been interred at Buchenwald, for *seven months and twenty-two days* during the period that she was also there. That they had been in that same place without ever once passing — for they would surely have known each other if they did, even with the bare skulls and the lifeless eyes, the jutting bones and the tattooed limbs. That, finally, was the most unbearable thought of all: that he had been there.

Emanuel had died, they discovered, in the Buchenwald gas chamber in the springtime of 1945, just three days before the camp — and she — were liberated. April indeed the cruellest month.

That he had been there.

Today, in her vulnerable state, Esther had deliberately avoided mentioning his name in her talk. But now, thanks to this persistent woman, here he was in the room again anyway; the very core of her life: beautiful and freckled and nineteen and smelling of boot-polish, and saying her name . . . How had he ever discovered her name?

The woman cleared her throat. 'I mean, if you had known, for certain, say, that Emanuel had survived and made it to Israel, would *that* have changed your mind? Would you have gone then?'

There was a rumble of disapproval around the auditorium now. 'I really don't see how that is relevant!' a man called out. 'It might be polite at this point to let someone else ask a question!'

Esther smiled at her protector, but held up a hand. Another thing she had come to understand was that, while some people would always dislike or resent or find distasteful or inexplicable her opinions — she had even been called a 'self-hating Jew' on a few memorable occasions — most of the audiences she addressed at places like this were fiercely protective of her. As if simply by dint of surviving what they felt was un-survivable, she had impunity to think or behave in any way she liked afterwards. Max had treated her that way too: Esther had had to be vigilant not to become spoiled under his tender and sometimes over-indulgent watch.

She leaned forward and found the female journalist's eyes. 'What is your name, my dear?'

The woman seemed taken aback. 'My name? Uh, Anna Mayer.'

'Tell me, Anna, have you ever done anything truly *mad* for love?'

'Uh . . . I . . . I don't — '

'Well, *I* haven't,' Esther confided, 'not *truly* mad, not mad enough, because after 1942 I never again had the opportunity. But trust me, if I thought Emanuel had survived, if I thought there was *any* hope of him being there, I would walk to Israel tomorrow to find him. Then again, I would walk to the moon to find him.' She looked up. 'Okay. I mean it. Next question, please.'

★ ★ ★

At the back of the auditorium, Natasha Bernstein was watching her indefatigable

13

grandmother with a mixture of emotions. Pride, of course, and the deepest admiration. But also a reminder of how strange it was. To be here among people who hung on Esther's every word, who had been all the way to Israel or Galicia to study her papers and her correspondence from the war, and who had written articles and academic pieces about her experience, was to be powerfully reminded that Esther was so much more than just their grandma. It was easy to forget that sometimes.

And there she was, moving brightly through the crowd behind her chrome walker: chatting to well-wishers, signing things, even posing for a photograph with an elderly woman, perhaps another survivor, who was accompanied by what looked like members of three more generations of her family. Esther, Natasha thought, as she watched these strangers bask in her grandmother's magic, was so like her sister Rachel: a dispenser of light, to whom others must helplessly gravitate. She noticed her grandmother heading towards the journalist who had interrogated her so relentlessly earlier, and then, after a brief chat, leading the woman right towards the door where Natasha was standing.

'Tash, sweetie, I wanted you to meet Anna Mayer from the *Journal*.'

Natasha realized she knew the byline. If the grand-daughter in her had felt infuriated by Anna Mayer's approach during the question time, the reporter in her had to admit a grudging respect; she was pretty sure she would not have been so tenacious. 'This is my eldest grand-daughter Natasha. She's also a journalist.' Esther beamed. 'At the *Times*, no less.'

Anna Mayer's brown eyes sharpened. 'Oh really? How long have you been at the *Times*?'

'Three years, almost.'

'What's your beat?'

'She writes the most wonderful human interest stories,' Esther cut in. 'Really interesting things about the political or economic situation but with human beings at their heart.'

Anna smiled tightly at Natasha. 'Oh. You too?'

Ordinarily this exchange would have sent up in Natasha a flare of anxiety: unlike Esther she did not move so easily towards her rivals. But not today. Her fingers in her jacket pocket closed around her phone; she longed to pull it out and read again the text that had arrived from her editor John Deegan a short while ago.

Nothing confirmed yet but looks like yr story might front. Hang tight. JD.

Today, then, with a front-page story in the offing, she was immune.

'That's right,' she nodded. 'Me too.' She held out her hand. 'Nice to meet you, Anna. That was a great question you asked.'

'Try nine questions,' Esther corrected with a smile. From her pocketbook, she handed Anna Mayer a card. 'That's our centre. It's up on West Street. If you'd like to talk further about anything, Anna, please come and see us for coffee anytime. I'd be delighted to show you around.'

Outside on the sidewalk, evening had arrived. The sun was sinking lazily over the river, catching the light on a gazillion glass windows and casting downtown in shades of rose and gold. It was beautiful: New York at its storybook finest. Natasha helped her grandmother to the corner to wait for a cab.

'You did that on purpose, didn't you?'

'Did what?' Esther was all innocence.

'Just completely disarmed that woman. Moved towards her, drew her in, *neutralized* her. Just like that.'

Esther smiled. 'I simply asked her for a cup of coffee. We'll see if she calls.'

'I think she'll call.'

From the direction of the ferry terminal a cab appeared, its light illuminated. Natasha flagged him down. Then embraced her grandmother. 'I love you. Well done today. I was so proud of you. That can't have been easy.'

Esther held up her papery cheek for a kiss. 'Thanks for coming, sweetie. You sure I can't drop you over on Kenmare?'

Natasha shook her head. 'I'll walk. It's such a beautiful evening.'

'Well then, I'll see you at Rosh Hashana on Friday, won't I?'

'Of course.' Natasha helped Esther into the back seat and shut the cab door as Esther gave the driver her West 12th Street address.

Just as the car was about to drive off, Natasha called to her through the open window.

'Oh, and *Bubbe?*'

'Yes, my darling?'

'Don't forget to buy the paper tomorrow . . . '

2

Page One! It was still the most exciting thing in the world. On the subway, as more and more people folded themselves into the carriage at 34th Street, she saw another handful of people reading the *Times*, in print or on their devices, and felt the thrill. Its ink was even now transferring itself onto the fingers of the straphanger jammed up next to her. She glanced over his shoulder. There it was: below the fold, but there. Her first lead byline since she'd broken a story about a gubernatorial campaign-funding scandal back in January. She had worked so hard for this one; had been reporting it for months. The payoff felt unbelievably sweet.

When she arrived at her cubicle a short while later, the phone on her desk was ringing. She reached to grab the receiver and missed it by seconds. A colleague, headed to the nearby mailroom, popped his head over the divider to tell her how much he'd enjoyed her piece. She thanked him and powered up her computer to discover a stack of emails whose subject lines conveyed similar sentiments.

It took her a moment longer to notice the message lodged amongst these from Monica Wagner, editor of the Metro section, under whose overall watch Natasha filed. She clicked. There was nothing in the body of the email.

From: mwagner@NYTimes.com
To: nbernstein@NYTimes.com
cc: jdeegan@NYTimes.com
Sent: September 03, 06:27am ET
Re: URGENT — please come see me in my office as soon as you get in. M

The phone on her desk began to ring again.

'You're in. Did you see Monica's email?' It was her editor, John. Natasha had known him since college, when he'd taken her on as a research intern during her senior year whilst he was on sabbatical writing a book. He'd become her mentor, advising her to turn down the graduate scholarship she'd been offered at Columbia J-School — 'this is a trade, real journalists learn on the job' — and helping her secure an entry-level reporting position at the *Boston Globe*. Knowing how she longed to get back to her hometown and the one newspaper she'd fantasized about working for since childhood, when the *Times* Metro section vacancy had come up almost three years ago, John had lobbied Monica Wagner for months on her behalf.

'Just this second. Everything okay?' Absently she clicked open a few more emails and, uncapping a ballpoint with her teeth, scribbled a name and number onto the yellow legal pad in front of her.

Somewhere just out of her view, John Deegan hesitated. Then he said, 'I think you should probably get over here right away.'

Natasha stopped, removed the pen lid from between her teeth. It was, admittedly, curious for section editors to invite reporters to their offices; a more typical interaction might be a yell across the newsroom's backfield or a relentless volley of on-screen instant-messages. Only twice before had she had a personal summons like this. The first was early on, after a regrettable fact-checking oversight. The second had come after her coverage of the original Occupy protests, when she was still a relatively anonymous general-assignment reporter in the *Times* Brooklyn bureau. Things had changed quite rapidly for Natasha after that particular trip over to Monica's office. She was soon shipped over to the newsroom on Eighth Avenue and given the chance to write more. Gradually she had carved out a personal beat that she loved. As Esther had crowed to that woman last night, her stories, if relatively small and tucked far into the Metro section, tried to feel for what was human behind the economic and political phenomena that had dominated front pages since the financial crisis, and continued to hold the world in their grip. Out there in that teeming iridescent city, the epicentre of it all, it was still occasionally possible to glimpse something that might redeem. Natasha was the junior reporter tasked with digging it out.

Today's piece, which Monica had let her run unusually long, took a pressing issue in federal housing policy and examined it through the prism of one female Staten Islander's plight. Natasha had spent weeks profiling Letisha Clark: a terminally unemployed single mother, victim of the hurricane, seriously ill and yet unable, because of classic bureaucratic hurdles, to claim Medicare benefits. Destitute but dogged, the sort of character this city — this nation — ran on, Clark had been campaigning with improbable articulacy to be allowed to move, for nominal rent, to one of the long-vacant apartment blocks in a nearby neighbourhood that had not been affected by the storm. With a powerful central narrative, days of rigorous data-crunching that had made Natasha's brain ache, and some pretty heavyweight interviews, including Senator Gillibrand and one of Mayor Bloomberg's closest aides, she was hoping this might just be the piece that finally elevated her from lowly 'probationer' — so-called after the clause in her contract that stated that she might be released at any point within the first three years of her *Times* appointment — to unionized staff reporter.

Natasha found John at his desk, his grey eyes inscrutable.

'Hey,' she said. 'Everything okay? How was your Labor Day?'

'Come with me.' He nodded towards the team room on the adjacent corner, a glass-doored space used for small conferences or private conversations. Private only so far as it was closed off; the floor-to-ceiling glass did not stop the potential for gawking. 'We won't be here long,' he said as he slid the door shut behind them. 'Mon's expecting us any moment. But this is a big deal. I thought we should talk first.'

Natasha nodded. Somewhere from the depths of her subconscious a thought bubbled up giddily before she could quite quash it. *Oh please say it!* she implored silently. *Say it! After all your hard work these past three years, it's your time! There's a proper union contract waiting on Monica's desk. Welcome on board!*

'Mon received a call from the DA in Staten Island in the early hours of this morning. They'd read your piece on Letisha Clark with some interest.'

She tried not to smile at John's sly almost-compliment.

'It seems this woman was being tapped for, amongst other things, multiple benefit fraud, embezzlement, impersonation . . . ' John pulled out his phone with a frown and scrolled. 'And perjury.' He glanced back up. 'Perjury. Seems they've been tailing her for over six months and were about to bust her when we ran this piece. The DA only called Monica because they know each other personally. We're lucky they tipped us off at all. It gives us the chance to go into serious damage-limitation mode before anyone goes to the *Journal* or the *Post*, let alone the folk at *Gawker* and co.'

There was a pause. A profound, interstellar silence descended upon the room. Natasha could feel, she was certain, the world lurching on its axis.

'*What?*' she gasped.

John folded his arms.

'But wait, I don't . . . ' She struggled to reorder her brain around the existence-altering words her editor had just uttered. 'You're saying Letisha Clark was lying *the whole time?* About everything?'

'Listen, I'll try to stick up for you as best I can. But Monica is steaming. Masthead were all called in early and have been in meetings about it for hours. You can imagine how it's gone down.'

Disbelief constricted her throat as the panic inched slowly but surely up her chest. 'But are you . . . are they sure this is really true? I mean, I interviewed her on multiple occasions. She showed me everything, the records, the Medicare and the welfare and the official letters after Sandy, and it all seemed so legit, I just cannot . . . '

She tailed off. It would do her no favours, she knew, to come over as either defensive or naïve; at this point such attitudes would only discredit her further. She racked her brain. Had she ever run the proper Lexis searches? Why hadn't she called the FBI for a triple-I, the interstate identification index? Shit. It was true: she hadn't even found out whether there was a rap sheet on this woman. Her gut began to churn.

'Tash, we've talked about this before,' John was saying, quietly and not unkindly. 'Having a credulous ear and an empathetic heart is not the worst crime a journalist can commit. But this is unfortunate. As you know, the timing could not be much worse.'

She glanced at him. Of course she knew. After a few relatively stable years following the seismic events of 2008 when multiple crises — the recession, the haemorrhaging of print-ad dollars, the rise of the internet — had seen newspapers laying off journalists by the dozen, there had followed a less vicious voluntary buyout phase, when they had all been able to breathe again, however tentatively. But now that era seemed also to have run its course: these days the prospect of layoffs once again hovered over newsrooms across the country like an ominously gathering fog. John hardly needed to point out that Natasha, technically still on probation, was going to be especially vulnerable.

'What do you think they'll do?' she murmured. She tried to recall what usually happened in similar circumstances. She hadn't plagiarized anyone, she hadn't screwed the company, fiddled expenses. They'd issue a correction, an apology to the readers . . . A thought occurred to her and she began to gabble at him. 'Doesn't this maybe confirm what we're saying in the piece anyway? I mean, even if this woman was lying, shouldn't we be looking at *why*? The facts are the facts — in eighty-seven percent of so-called employment opportunities in this country you are not eligible to apply for a job unless you are already *in* employment; in seventy-two percent of cases where — '

'Natasha.' John held up a hand. 'The statistics are irrelevant. Letisha Clark was a straight-up fraud and we should have been diligent enough to identify that and drop the whole idea, not dedicate a page one story to her oh-so-poignant plight.'

At John's acid tone, Natasha shrank back in her chair, conscious of the newsroom buzz beyond; the very space she would have to walk through shortly to get to Monica's office. Here in this great grand skyscraper of environmentally progressive glass and lipstick-red walls, where the cubicles extended to a little over waist height, the unusual sight of a reporter being hauled into an editor's office could pique everybody's curiosity for a moment, no matter how busy they were.

'They wouldn't bounce me for this, would they?' she said softly.

With the minutest of shrugs, John pushed open the door. 'I doubt it,' he said. 'I guess we'll have to wait and see.'

* * *

'I've got too many people working hard and not screwing up,' Monica Wagner was

26

reminding everyone assembled in the executive editor's office. 'So although we all think you're a talented reporter and this an unfortunate mistake, I'm afraid, Natasha, I don't see how we have any choice.'

The room seemed to scud, vertiginously, as the glare from neighbouring Midtown skyscrapers ricocheted off steel and glass to hit the rows of trophies and Pulitzer certificates lining the back wall. Natasha blinked back an ill-timed but unmistakable sting of salt. It was Friday morning. Three days had somehow passed, in excruciating increments, since she'd been apprised of Letisha Clark's fraud and her own calamitous error. The paper had quickly moved to own its mistake by issuing a prominent editor's correction and apology, and assigning a leading correspondent to investigate the new aspects of the story and re-report it, but this had not stopped the more vitriolic nooks of the blogosphere going to town. It had been easily the toughest week of her life.

And now it was Friday, and she was hearing the words she had most dreaded.

No choice.

She glanced over at John, who did not meet her eye.

'No choice,' she echoed.

'I'm sorry,' Monica said. 'But we are going

to have to let you go.'

Natasha squinted in the incongruous sunlight. 'Let me go,' she repeated.

'That's right.'

Murderer's Row, the junior reporters called this stretch of executive offices. And now the clamour of silence. The faint shifting of eyes around the room. The dim noise of a telephone ringing in a Masthead office next door. A desk clock ticking. Murderer's Row.

'Can I say one thing?' she croaked.

The executive editor Mary Crawford had up until now been largely silent; her presence here being something of a formality. Now she finally spoke, and when she did, her voice was kind. 'Of course, Natasha. Go ahead.'

'I know — I mean, I *really* understand — that I made a terrible mistake, one I'll regret always. But it was an honest mistake, and — '

'Natasha, nobody is under the impression that you did anything dishonest here,' Monica interrupted.

'No, and thank you for that, but the point is, I do think this goes to the core of how we report stories on this newspaper.' Her heart began to race and she became aware of their inquisitive expressions, but on she ploughed. 'In hindsight, of course, I can see that my background checks on Letisha fell woefully

28

short. But unless we're going to assume by default that all of our subjects and sources are criminals and investigate them before we even let them open their mouths, maybe we always run the risk of this happening?' She tried to steady her voice. 'And I hope it doesn't sound like I'm in any way trivializing my mistake, but I can't help thinking this is a risk the paper should be prepared to take.'

Mary Crawford inclined her head. 'Duly noted, Natasha. And for what it's worth, I agree. We'll be sorry to see you go.'

Natasha closed her eyes. The cell phone on Mary Crawford's desk beeped, shattering the charged atmosphere of the room. She took a moment to check it. Nobody else moved. Monica had her arms crossed over her chest; John was staring down at his shoes. Eventually Crawford said, 'Excuse me.' She stood up and extended her hand. 'I know the next few months are not going to be easy, but I want to thank you for everything you've done here at the *Times*. We really do wish you the very best of luck.'

At the periphery of her vision Natasha saw John putting his head briefly in his hands, and felt a crashing wave of guilt. He'd championed her so long, invested so much energy and time in her career and *this* was how she'd repaid him. She barely even heard the three senior editors discussing the formalities of what would happen next: that she should clear her cubicle, say her goodbyes and, once finished, head upstairs to Human Resources on the fifteenth floor to sign off on all the necessary paperwork.

Fired, Natasha repeated to herself as she sleep-walked out of the HR offices a short while later, papers signed, deed done. Like any journalist in this climate, she'd worried about the things preoccupying everyone: losing readers to the paywall and to online news aggregators and the more intelligent blogs. On a personal level she'd fretted about her probationary contract, missing stories, losing traction. But never this. Unemployment. That word that had haunted the news bulletins, the jobless reports on the first Friday of every month over the past few years; reports that ironically she had herself referenced so often. *Unemployed!*

As she waited for the elevator to arrive, convinced that every eye must be on her and know her shame, Natasha wondered how she would find the words to tell Josh that the hotshot *New York Times* reporter he thought he was marrying was now jobless. And her friends, who still took such childish delight in her byline and who had been among the first to send congratulatory messages when her

Letisha Clark story had fronted Tuesday morning. Not to mention her parents, her poor father, who had maybe never been more proud about anything than when his eldest daughter had written her first story — an inglorious 350-word report buried deep within the Metro section — for the pages of his beloved 'Grey Lady' newspaper. She still remembered receiving Frank's phone call that morning, and how he had insisted on taking her out to celebrate with martinis and cheeseburgers at Elaine's that very evening, just him and her.

The elevator appeared and Natasha stepped into it with renewed despair as she remembered that, in just a few hours, she would have to face not only her father but her whole family: it was Rosh Hashana, her mother had probably been cooking all week; it was non-negotiable. Employed or unemployed, there would be no getting out of dinner, no matter how wretched she felt.

On the fourteenth floor, the usual crowd piled in from the *Times* canteen and the doors were just about to close when a figure dashed towards them. Somebody stuck their hand in front of the sensor and the guy just managed to leap in before the door closed. He nodded a cheerful thanks around the car. In his jeans and sneakers, something about him stood out from the businessy-casual *Times* crowd and from those riding down from the corporate floors above. Trying to distract herself from the tears that were gathering behind her eyelids, Natasha noticed that he was very tall, with a great shock of curly black hair — what her family would affectionately call a Jewfro.

She shut her eyes and wondered why they weren't going any faster. An illusion, presumably, born of her desperation to be out of here. She clutched her bags, now crammed with the contents of her third-floor cubicle desk, and waited for the doors to glide open on Renzo Piano's spectacular glass lobby, with its oasis-like internal garden. The lobby and the garden she would no longer marvel at every day as she beeped in through the lollipop-red turnstiles. Because she would no longer work here . . .

Breathe, she reminded herself. *The world has not ended. You only lost your job.*

It seemed as though whole minutes had passed when the elevator finally staggered to a halt. It took Natasha a moment, after she opened her eyes, to realize that they were not in the lobby at all, but wedged between floors.

'What?' people began to exclaim. 'Oh, come on . . .'

'Are we stuck?'

'Oh, crap. You know what, I think it was acting up this morning, this elevator . . . '

'So why didn't they — '

'Has someone pressed the alarm button?'

You are fucking kidding me, Natasha breathed. *Today?*

'HELLO?' A woman squeezed optimistically into a lilac pantsuit was yelling into the intercom. 'Hello, we're STUCK IN THE ELEVATOR. You gotta help us!'

'Easy, lady,' Jewfro guy murmured, sotto voce, right next to Natasha. 'Nobody's going to die in here.'

In normal circumstances she might have laughed.

A faint voice finally crackled up through the speaker. 'Hello, this is the building super. You in some kinda trouble?'

'You bet we are!' screamed the woman. 'We are stuck! You have to help us.' The elevator gave a reassuring lurch, as if trying to appease her, but did not move.

'Okay, lady. I'll try my Yankee best. You just hang tight, okay?'

'It's not like we can do anything else!' someone muttered. Pantsuit lady continued to make hyperventilating noises before announcing that she suffered from severe claustrophobia and was about to throw up.

'Would you like some water?' Jewfro guy asked kindly, pulling a bottle from the brown leather satchel that was slung over his shoulder.

She eyed him with suspicion. 'Uh, no thanks.' With a meaty forefinger she began jabbing at the emergency call button again. 'Hello? *Hell-o?* Can you call the fire guys? We're STILL STUCK.'

Around the elevator people were pulling out their phones, checking for signal, talking about how late they were going to be, bitching generally about the maintenance in the building. One guy cracked that he'd recently watched a movie on Netflix about five strangers stuck in a lift, one of whom turned out to be the devil. Some laughed. Mesmerized by the irony that this should be happening today of all days — *ha! You're fired, but you can't actually leave the building!* — Natasha stood in silence, trying and failing not to cry. Unlike her sister Rachel who, along with the cheekbones and the metabolism, had inherited wholesale from their mother a knack for drama, Natasha had a deep aversion to making a scene. She dug uselessly in her overstuffed bag for a tissue, aware that everyone was staring at her, including pantsuit lady, whose own woes seemed to have temporarily subsided in the face of Natasha's tears. Somebody wordlessly passed her a fresh Kleenex, which she took gratefully.

Jewfro guy seemed to have taken control and was communicating with the building's superintendent in calm, clear tones. After an eternal-seeming interlude, the elevator cranked into action and eventually juddered its way down the remaining floors. And then they were out. Bonded by what they had endured together, shaking hands and joking about how it was the only way to get a bunch of strangers in New York to talk to each other, the triumphant group surged as one into the orange-panelled lobby.

Hanging back, Jewfro guy touched Natasha on the arm.

'You sure you're okay? I mean, it wasn't much fun in there, but that seemed a pretty extreme reaction.' His eyes, she noticed, were startlingly sea-coloured. They reminded her of somebody she could not quite place.

He was surely teasing her.

'I'm okay. Just having a bad day, is all.'

He looked sympathetic, and now it struck her, although it did not make any sense, that the person he reminded her of was her sister.

'Well, I'm sorry to hear that. Sure hope it improves.'

It was, it had to be: the unlikely

combination of olive skin, greenish-blue eyes and black hair; so unexpectedly like Rachel's. She wondered again where he was from; whether he worked at the *Times* or was just visiting someone in the building. In other circumstances she might even have asked.

Today, though, with the barest of thanks for this kind stranger's concern, she pushed through the bright red turnstiles one last time and headed out of the lobby into a steaming Eighth Avenue. She did not look back.

3

'Honey, can you get that?' Rosalind Bernstein yelled. Throwing a glance at the clock as she switched dishes from sideboard to oven, she registered that whoever was at the door had arrived early; the only crime more offensive, in her book, than arriving late. Wondering who it could be — certainly not either of her children, nor her mother, she'd bet — she heard Frank, who was busy setting the table, go to answer the front door and exclaim in delight.

'*Ad!*'

'Frankie!'

Ros smiled to hear joy in her husband's voice again. It had been a rough week for Frank, what with Tash's news on Tuesday, although she was certain that trouble would all pass soon, and a deposition that had gone badly. His half-brother Adam had not visited New York in ages, but now that his daughter Shira and her family had relocated to Brooklyn, Frank was hoping to see a lot more of him over here. Frank could sometimes be a little apprehensive around Adam, over-compensatory, especially here in this house, but from what she could hear they had slipped right back into some ancient fraternal mode and all was well. Momentarily, both men appeared at the kitchen door: dear old Frankie in his striped cook's apron over patched slacks and an ancient but beloved sweater; his younger, taller brother in an expensive-looking tan suit. Adam bore an enormous bunch of calla lilies — her favourite; that was so like him — and a bottle of champagne. Placing them on the side-board, he opened his arms to her. Ros wiped her hands on her apron as she went over to him and they embraced.

'Rosa, Rosa. *Shana Tova!* You simply get more beautiful every year!' he smarmed, in his accent that was part-Israeli, part-New York. Adam had been just twelve when Otto Bernstein had relocated himself, his second wife Sara and their son to a villa in Katamon, Jerusalem, leaving Otto's elder son Frank, who was by then twenty-six and practising law, the brownstone on the Upper West Side. Otto had purchased the townhouse eight years previously, having worked his way up the island from the tenement on Broome that he and his infant son had lived in after they arrived at Ellis Island in 1943, hollowed and harrowed by what they had escaped. As Adam winked over at Frank, with his usual patter about how he'd never understand how his ugly *meeskite* of a brother had landed such a beautiful *sheyne meydel*, Ros swiped at him with her oven glove.

'Oh Adam, you old charmer, we've missed you. You shouldn't have.'

'So what can I help with around here?'

'Nothing.'

'But I'm early! I know how you hate that. There must be something I can do.'

'There is,' she smiled. 'You can go sit down next door, pour yourself a goddam drink and make yourself at home.'

As soon as she said it she regretted it: she sensed Frank bristle, infinitesimally. Adam, though, merely headed obediently through to the drawing room. Frank was still sensitive about the fact that he'd been left the Manhattan house while Adam had had no choice but to follow his parents to Israel and a drastically different life. She remembered Frank telling her years ago about the terrible morning when they'd all left New York; how a pyjama-clad and traumatized but surprisingly strong-willed Adam had barricaded his bedroom door — the bedroom that would later become Tash's — and refused to leave until his revered older brother had negotiated with him from the landing. Adam had eventually got on the plane: something to do with 1968 World Series baseball cards and a precious Mickey Mantle/Denny McLain/Hank Aaron trilogy, if Ros remembered correctly.

Adam had of course turned out just fine. Having followed his older brother into the field of human rights law after his stint in the army, he was now one of the most successful and prominent liberal lawyers in Israel. His wife Yael had left him about ten years ago, which had been pretty ugly for a while; and their once-wild, now rather *frum* daughter Shira had certainly given him some headaches over the years. But Adam seemed to have weathered such storms with little visible damage, and she was glad of it. She liked and admired her brother-in-law very much.

The doorbell went again. *'Shana Tova!'* Ros cried, when she heard Shira and Dror arriving with their two toddlers and the baby. 'I'll be through in a minute!' Their neighbours and great friends Barry and Lisa Rosen arrived soon after, followed by the Federmans, and before long, old Mr Henkel from down the street, on whom they always took pity during holidays. She heard Adam open the door to Josh. More *Shana Tovas* all around, and then Josh came directly through to the kitchen. Ros almost rolled her eyes when she saw that her future son-in-law had also picked up champagne and a bunch of calla lilies, but caught herself just in time.

'Thank you, honey. That's very sweet of you.'

She packed him back off to the living room with a few dishes of things to keep everyone going until they all sat down. Not that anybody was going to starve tonight. Earlier in the week she had sworn she would not go crazy this time, but the appetizer dishes seemed to be amassing in serried ranks on her kitchen counter — roasted apples and honey for the new year, black-eyed peas, baked pumpkin pastries, leek fritters, roasted sweet beets, a fat and glossy challah, chopped liver, egg mayo. Not for the first time in her life did Rosalind wonder what it bought, all this food and theatre: whether this great enactment of a coming together and feeding each other did in fact draw everybody closer; clinch something. For all she inhabited her role with weary good grace, allowed the Jewish-mom clichés and the mocking from her daughters, neither of whom could boil an egg, she did wonder what it was all for.

Deep down, of course she knew. It was for Esther. Esther, who also had barely toasted a bagel in her entire adult life and would have been the last person on earth to profess to care for such things. But if Ros stopped this

41

today: if it all went away, no more Seders, no more Rosh Hashanas, no more any of it, what happened? Could the centre still hold? Did they survive?

Ros poured herself another glass of Adam's champagne and checked on her brisket. The only people still to arrive were her mom and her girls. Which was typical. Still, she felt a glow of satisfaction at the prospect of having both children in the same room again this evening. Her daughters were masters of the slapdash excuse: both had tried to exempt themselves tonight; both had failed. 'Nonsense,' she had told them. 'It's Rosh Hashana. Of course you're coming.' And that had been that: end of conversation.

Because it had been too long, she thought to herself. Too damn long.

★   ★   ★

'Rach?' Natasha almost did a double-take as she collided with the familiar figure who was also exiting the subway at 79th Street in a hurry.

'Oh, hey.' Rachel Bernstein gave her sister an awkward little wave.

Natasha felt the molecules of the evening shift around them. She tried to keep her voice even. 'You're here,' she said.

42

Together they angled, these two sisters, automatically towards Broadway and their childhood home; a route they must have walked a million times together over the years, although Natasha could not remember the last time.

'Don't look so surprised. They're my family too.'

'Really?' Natasha didn't quite say, as she absorbed the full effect of her sister up close. It had taken a titanic effort tonight to get herself out of the ratty crimson track pants that dated from her freshman year at college and the much-washed hoodie she'd been sloping around in all afternoon. After leaving the *Times* she'd spent the day shuttling between paralyzed shock and weirdly frenetic despair. Only the thought of Rosalind's disappointed face had got her up off the couch and into the shower, to attempt something of a resurrection through the blusher brush, the hairdryer and a dress she knew her mom liked. Her sister was make-up-free as always and wearing ripped black jeans, scuffed biker boots and a faded yellow T-shirt. But would surely meet no recrimination from their mother, because she never did.

'And, not that anyone's keeping tabs, I was here a few weeks ago too,' Rachel was continuing, sweetly, as they zigzagged towards 83rd and West End. 'I think you and Josh were at a wedding or something? Speaking of which, will Mr Liebowitz be gracing us with his presence tonight?'

There it was. Already. Natasha had neither forgotten nor forgiven Rachel's comments or the argument they'd had after Natasha and Josh had returned from Rome last spring, newly affianced.

'He will. And what about Skye?' she batted right back. 'Are we finally going to have the pleasure of meeting her tonight?'

'She's away doing this prisons Shakespeare tour thing this week.' Rachel shook her head. 'I should be there too, helping out. But, you know, Mom called. Said you'd had a bad week?'

They turned west at the corner of 83rd and Natasha glanced sideways at her sister, searching for something in her features that might betray a note of sarcasm, even satisfaction. And found none.

'I read that piece and I thought it was great,' Rachel carried on. 'Genuinely moving. I'm really sorry to hear about what's happened.'

Natasha stopped, just as the two of them reached the stairs leading up to the house in which they had grown up. 'Wait. You *read* it?'

Rachel was fishing in her bag for her door key. 'Of course I read it!'

Natasha, also unthinkingly doing the same, tried to respond in a way that wouldn't betray her shock that her sister had read *anything* she'd written lately. Rachel had been her first editor, always, from the pieces Natasha had written at high school to her earliest professional dispatches at the *Boston Globe*. But after she'd moved back to New York and started working at the *Times*, there had been a slow drift. Their lives, once so consonant, seemed to have fissured. Against Natasha's heartfelt advice, Rachel had dropped out of Tisch in her sophomore year ('NYU's more of a corporation than a school,' Natasha remembered her saying at the time. 'Do you know they're about to overtake the Catholic Church as the largest real-estate owners in New York City? That's just not a race I want to be in, thanks very much.') For a couple of years she had squatted with a rotating cast of characters in an abandoned elementary school in Bushwick, moving from one social project to another. And for the past few months she had been living in an 'intentional community', way, way down on the Lower East Side, deep amid the sketchiest housing projects and the highest chain-link fences on streets that even the most penniless of New

York-seeking hipsters disdained. She worked in a cult vegan café called Pulse on Avenue B and taught drama and English at two South Bronx charter schools. According to Frank, who had revealed this information to Natasha with some concern as they'd waited in line for hot dogs at Citi Field one afternoon last season, Rachel had earned about fifteen thousand dollars last year: a simply fantastical number for most functioning inhabitants of this city. Her sister's life and lifestyle seemed increasingly hard to imagine.

'Well, thanks,' she mumbled. 'That means . . . that means a lot.'

Both girls reached up then to fit their keys into the lock, just at the moment when the door opened anyway. And there was Rosalind Bernstein, magnificent always, welcoming her brood with a vigorous 'At last!' and a string of new-year greetings that somehow managed to acknowledge her love and be wearily cross at their timekeeping while pulling them simultaneously into the tightest embrace.

From the hallway behind Ros came the smell of freshly baked bread, roasting meats, holiday candles and her mother's signature scent — the fragrance of all the days of Natasha's life, she realised. It caught her unawares and worked some spell: despite the torments of the day, the week, she felt her guts uncoil a fraction. As Ros released her daughters and immediately started fussing over her youngest, Natasha took their jackets and headed back to the utilities room. There, among the much-trafficked Bernstein para-phernalia — the books, the old snow boots, the busted vacuum cleaners, the countless random *tchotkes* and ancient school folders and piles of sheet music, the old sneakers and the coats — she found a peg that was not quite overflowing and hung them up. *Home*, she thought simply, catching sight of the marks on the door frame — red for her, blue for Rachel — that told in abstract stripes the tale of two sisters literally growing up: red high up above blue at first, the lines drawing ever closer as blue caught up, then so close that for a few years they were almost one, an interchangeable purplish streak, and then, as blue overtook red, the distance between them wider and wider until, in 1999, with four inches between them, the lines froze.

On her way back to the living room she popped her head around the kitchen door, where she discovered her father yanking the cork from a bottle of red.

'Oh, *hey*, honey!' cried Frank, depositing the bottle on the sideboard to better throw his arms around her, also hugging her so tight that she had to, as their time-honoured skit

47

went, splutter and choke in mock protestation. When he finally drew back, he looked her up and down and his face, ever a telegraph of his state of mind, altered instantly. 'Oh, sweetie.'

Natasha touched her fingers to her collarbone in response to his glance. Partly because of the occasion, partly because it always felt like a talisman of sorts, this afternoon, after returning home from the *Times*, she had impulsively unlocked from the safe in their apartment her late grandmother Adela's necklace. Her grandfather Otto had managed to save this token, along with a thin gold bracelet that was now in Rachel's possession, after the family had been deported. The pair of golden trinkets, meaningless on one level, were precious signifiers of something vital but unspeakable. Natasha didn't need to tell her father what the necklace meant to her.

There was a pause.

'So how's it going?' Frank asked, with a recovered brightness that could not quite disguise his concern. 'Any news?'

Natasha felt herself waver. Josh knew what had happened at work this morning, but she'd been planning on not telling anyone else yet, at the risk of ruining the festivities. Not only was she aware how important such evenings were to Ros; tonight her uncle Adam was over from Jerusalem and she knew Frank would be eager that nothing cast a shadow.

'They fired me, Dad.' The words escaped regardless.

Frank Bernstein's mouth fell open. 'They *fired* you?'

Grimly, she nodded.

'Oh, Tash. Oh, *sweetie*. Those shmucks. My God.' He shook his head. 'I can't believe it! My God. Honey, I don't know what to say . . . '

And Natasha saw that her honest, earnest, generous, workaholic marvel of a father did indeed have no idea what to say.

'It's okay,' she said. 'Let's not talk about it tonight.'

'I just can't believe it! What were the grounds — '

'Please, Dad.' She laid a hand on his arm. 'Please. Let's not talk about it. It was my fault, I deserved it. But can we just try and forget about it for now.'

'Can they even *do* that?' Frank was frowning as he sloshed out a glass of wine, which he handed to his daughter before draining his own. 'Maybe I should look into the legal situa — '

'Dad!' she warned. 'I mean it. I'll fall apart.

Enough.' She took a deep slug. 'How are you?'

'Well, we're okay, I guess. D'you get my email about next weekend?'

'The Mets-Orioles game?'

'You in?'

'Of course.' She gave him a smile over her glass. 'We'll always have the Mets.'

'Oh, honey.'

'Oh, honey *what?*' demanded Rosalind as she bustled back into the kitchen with Shira's baby Naomi in her arms.

'Nothing!' they chorused.

Rosalind looked slowly from husband to daughter, as if to try and read what might be legible in the space between them. But she didn't push it. 'Hey, Frankie, what I say about going easy on the booze tonight, huh? And don't think I didn't notice you at those cheese balls earlier.'

Frank shrugged at Natasha. 'Your mother's put me on a diet again. Trouble is, I just can't resist her cheese balls.'

'Who can? But Mom, surely there's no need for all this? I think Dad looks fantastic.'

'That's not what Dr Blankfein said last week. You want to see his cholesterol levels. *Oy!*'

'Well, anyway,' Natasha interjected. 'That baby is getting seriously cute.'

At this, Rosalind placed the snoozing infant into her elder daughter's unsuspecting arms. 'There you go, Noo-noo,' she cooed, ignoring Natasha's look of mild panic. 'I was about to change her diaper, give Shira a break before we put her down in the cot upstairs.' With a wicked grin, she nodded at her daughter. 'But you can do it if you like, sweetie. Get some practice in.'

Wordlessly Natasha passed the baby directly back to her mother and fled to the living room, where she found Rachel helping Esther, who had just arrived.

Natasha gave her a hug. 'You look so well, Grandma. I love that skirt.'

Esther beamed. 'Thanks, sweetie, I got it on sale at Macy's. Could you fix me a drink, do you think?'

On the sideboard, Natasha uncapped the bottle of Manischewitz that Ros always got in for Esther on festive Friday nights. Filling a small glass with the sweet red wine, with the easy chatter of the family scene at her back, she allowed her mind to wander for a moment. So she'd lost her job. She'd really lost her job. But she'd made a monumental, unprofessional mistake, and in this climate — come on, it could have been worse. She was still one of the world's lucky ones, wasn't she? Evening was slanting through the

51

parlour windows, illuminating the motes of dust that the many, many books in this house always threw up. This particular early-fall light made Natasha's heart ache every year at the imminence of summer's fading. But it was a hopeful light too: streaked luminous with promise, with *beginnings*. And here she was, in this much-loved home that somehow always had the capacity to enclose and magnify happiness, surrounded by her family, giggling children, a disc of something lovely — Mozart? Schubert? — playing quietly on Frank's crappy and unreliable old CD player, a glass of wine. Here was her grandmother, in her long sleeves and her fancy new skirt: Esther, whose very existence was always a reminder to be extravagantly grateful to life. And there, standing beside her, also remarkable in its way, was her sister . . .

Natasha's reverie was interrupted by her cousin Shira, who arrived to give her a timid hug.

'It's so good to see you too!' Natasha agreed, trying as always not to be taken aback by the sight of Shira's mid-calf-length skirt, her dark headscarf, her scrubbed face. This was the girl who, the summer Natasha was seventeen, Rachel sixteen and Shira sixteen, had got them stoned on the beach in Tel Aviv courtesy of a twenty-one-year-old IDF soldier with whom she was sleeping. The girl whose skin had once contained more ink than a Bushwick barista, but who'd either had her tattoos ingeniously removed or now covered them up with her long, modest clothes. The girl who had taught her New York cousins how to apply black liquid eyeliner and stuff padding in their bras, and who had pierced Rachel's ears that same summer using cheap Russian vodka and a needle, an episode that had seen Rosalind whisking both daughters off for tetanus shots. The girl who, aged eighteen, had spent six months in a famous, expensive Ashkelon rehab for her drug problems. And who had come home from her own stint in the army a few years later engaged to a nice Orthodox Israeli boy, a fellow soldier and latterly diamond trader named Dror Moaz. Shira Moaz was now a Masters student at Yeshiva University in New York, a mother of three young children and a congregant at the Yetev Mikvah *shul* in South Williamsburg; the rebel light had all but gone out of her eyes. It was confounding.

Remembering Shira as she once had been — as they had all once been — Natasha instinctively flicked her gaze over to her sister, now chatting to some of their parents' friends on the other side of the room. And to her astonishment, met Rachel's eyes at precisely the same moment. A beat of such unspoken understanding passed between them, Natasha had almost to catch her breath. *I know,* Rachel's eyes seemed to say. *I absolutely know.*

It had once always been like that, Natasha reflected as she listened absently to what Shira was saying about her kids. A year apart, since earliest childhood she and Rach had seemed to possess an uncanny ability to understand each other; to know what the other was thinking; to converse in contented silences or chatter so rapidly they appeared barely to draw breath, and to switch between the two states without being conscious of it. One year they had even started talking to each other in a secret language. The private dialect, cooked up on a sweltering hot summer afternoon on the swings in the playground in Central Park, had seemed an entirely logical linguistic extension of their connection. They must have talked like that for the best part of a year, at school, at home, driving everyone else nuts, especially their parents. And now Rachel was looking up at Natasha with the eyes of those days, and Natasha was answering her in the same language.

I know, I absolutely know.

It had been so long. And that shared glance

54

— intimating as it did that the thing that had once bound them was not completely frayed, despite their recent distancing — moved Natasha suddenly and deeply. Because in the recognition of this moment's wonder was also the shadow of its loss. If the events of the past few days, the events of this morning, had reminded her of anything, it was how fragile happiness could be; on what tender foundations it rested. Natasha missed her sister with such an abrupt and pressing ache that she began uttering excuses for moving away from Shira and crossing the room towards the only person she really wanted to talk to.

And then all of a sudden there was Josh appearing in her path, a look of sympathy and concern etched across his face. He hadn't seen her since she'd broken the news earlier. As her fiancé moved in to kiss her hello, asking in her ear if she was doing okay, the moment shattered. Natasha was aware, from the corner of her eye, of the long frame of her little sister turning away.

*   *   *

'Ach, *motek*, I've seen it a million times at West Street, people like that, the lengths they will go to get a little attention for themselves,' Esther was insisting as she patted her knee.

Natasha, over dinner, had been equally incapable of keeping her news from her grandmother. 'It was obviously a cry for help. And I think it reflects very well on you that you were fired for having a heart and showing a little empathy for that poor woman!'

'Thanks, *Bubbe*.' Natasha took a mouthful of her mother's roast vegetables and jumped at the opportunity to change conversational tack. 'I meant to ask you the other night: how is West Street?'

Many years ago, Esther and her late husband, the playwright Max Goldfaden, had founded a soup kitchen and community centre in a downtown warehouse building opposite the Hudson with the royalties from Max's play *The Beautiful Goodbyes*, which still played on Broadway from time to time. Thirty-odd years on, Esther was still as busy as ever hustling for her clients, who ranged from drug-addled young transvestites to elderly New Yorkers fallen on hard times. She had two full-time staff members, Jorge and Valentina, but everything else was tackled by a team of eager volunteers. Natasha and Rachel had worked at the centre throughout teenaged weekends and summers, but it was ages since she had last been down there.

'Well, it's just wonderful, darling. We've got

such an exciting project going on. Did Rachel tell you?'

'Tell me what?' Natasha stared hard at her sister, seated on Esther's other side. *Come back*, she thought. But Rachel, engaged in conversation with old Mr Henkel from down the street, did not turn.

'About Leo Zimmer?'

'Your composer friend?'

'He passed along a few months ago, which was very sad, but oy, he was always so good to me, so supportive. And he left us one of his Steinways in his will!' Now Esther nudged Rachel. 'And how much do we love that piano, honey?'

'Oh, we love that piano.' Rachel turned around.

'Well, that sure was nice of Leo,' Natasha said. She felt curiously put out. 'Where's it living?'

'We had a little shuffle and got it into the recreation room,' Esther explained, as she cut her food into tiny pieces. 'Jorge put up some more shelves in there a few months ago and we've painted it up real nice, and I've filled the shelves with books, and the piano's in there, and it's now *officially* the West Street Community Music Room and Library! It's transformed the place. You'd be amazed how many of those dear fellows have a tune up their sleeve.'

'Oh, *Bubbe*, come on,' Rachel smirked.

'Come on what?' Natasha wondered.

'Go on, Grandma, just tell her the real news.'

'*What* real news?' Natasha could scarcely bite back her irritation.

'Okay. You will never guess . . . ' Esther paused for effect. 'You know the Korean dry-cleaning emporium next door?'

Natasha pictured the building: the adjacent former warehouse between Christopher and West Tenth that had long been vacant. Esther, she knew, had lately been rallying a local consortium of concerned West Village shop-keepers and residents in a campaign to stop it from being purchased by the property developers who wanted to turn the whole block into swanky residential condos and lofts.

'Seems Leo had also been somewhat busy in that regard,' Esther revealed. 'Before he died, he did a secret deal through his foundation with the owners of next door. And purchased the freehold *in our name*! So long as we always run it as an extension of the community centre, along its existing principles, the building is ours in perpetuity!' She clapped her hands as Natasha digested this remarkable piece of news. 'Now is that not just the greatest thing you ever heard?'

'We get the keys in a couple of weeks,' Rachel added. 'And our structural engineer has come back with the report saying we're good to go. So we've been putting permit applications into City Hall and starting to discuss possible plans with architects. It's pretty exciting.'

City Hall? Structural engineers? Since when do you know anything about any of this stuff? Natasha wondered uncharitably as she cleared the plates between courses. In the kitchen, supposedly in there to help Ros, Adam and her father were in fact leaning against the island, drinking wine and discussing Adam's latest case concerning evictions from Palestinian houses in West Bank towns. Helping them to ferry out the never-ending dishes of her mother's next course: the beef brisket, the roasted chicken, the lentil soup with shank bones, the carrot, sweet potato and prune *tzimmes*, she barely heard what they were saying. She was too preoccupied trying to make sense of her irritation at the discovery that Rachel was so closely involved at West Street.

'We're going to do something *so* beautiful, you wouldn't believe,' Esther carried on when she sat back down. 'We have big dreams, don't we, darling? Another kitchen, some showers, a new recreation room, maybe even some real *beds*. Wouldn't that be something, if we could finally offer to put a proper roof over people's heads at night?'

'Gran, this is all unbelievable,' Natasha said. She glanced over at Josh, to see if he was listening, but he was deep in conversation with Dror.

'I know. Good old Leo. He always was such a sweetie. And sweet on me, of course.' Esther gave a raffish little wink.

Later, towards the end of the main course, after conversation had turned to other topics and Natasha had talked for a while to Barry Rosen on her left, Rachel returned them to West Street. 'You should definitely come and see the new space,' she suggested. She took a sip from her water glass. 'It's pretty amazing. You'll like it.'

'I will,' Natasha replied evenly. She felt like throttling her sister, who was even now wiping her mouth with the back of her hand in the way she had always done after a drink since she was about three years old and gulping thirstily from her purple plastic sippy-cup. 'Of course I will. After all, I've got so much time on my hands these days.'

Rachel inclined her head. 'Wait. What do you mean?'

'Oh. Didn't I tell you? I lost my job today.'

Natasha refilled her wine glass and stood up. She was going to see if she could bum a secret cigarette off her uncle. 'I got *fired*. So no more excuses, eh?' She kissed the top of her grandmother's delicate head. 'I'll come soon, I promise.'

4

After a riotous summer, the wild flowers were dying on the High Line. Natasha and Josh walked slowly along the rusting train tracks, where the hulking meat trucks had once hauled their loads over the Hudson. Two weeks had passed since she'd been fired, and the shock was gradually subsiding: today was the first day she'd woken without a sickened clench in her stomach and chest. After two weeks of filling out online job applications, making calls to every contact she had, and uploading her resumé to endless networking sites, today she had decided not to think about work at all. It helped that New York was on its best behaviour. A few miles downtown on the glinting horizon, Lady Liberty was looking particularly fine, she thought; out west the sun was skipping like a child across the old Hudson piers; eastwards and up, a sudden gap between skyscrapers around 18th Street yielded a resplendent view of the Empire State. A few blocks further north along the elevated pathway, they found themselves at eye level with a girl out on her fire escape playing guitar, a Holly Golightly for the twenty-first century. On the balcony below her, an old gay couple who looked as if they had lived a long life of curiosity and flair had stretched their legs out under a blanket, spread the Sunday *Times* over their laps, and were cradling coffee cups as they took turns to read stories from the paper out loud to each other.

And in a heartbeat, just like that, Natasha felt like herself again.

'Doesn't that just make you so happy?'

Josh considered this. 'Well, I feel as happy as anyone can be with a ball-breaking job who never sees his girlfriend and is about to spend Saturday afternoon at the office. And who's gone for a walk on a disused rail line because it's supposed to be cool.'

She elbowed him. 'Don't be a dick. Surely you must see what I was saying back there? Don't you love New York more than ever on a day like this?'

Over a brunch with a group of friends just now, two of the women of which were pregnant, they'd all gotten into a dumb argument about the best place to raise kids. Such were the times. Natasha, to her incredulity, seemed to have straight-up lost the New York argument.

'Yeah, of course I see what you were saying,' Josh said. 'Manhattan: it's the ideal place to have children. Safe. Green. Welcoming. All that baby-friendly traffic.'

She gave a mock cry. 'Shut up. I was raised here.'

'Exactly. Look how you turned out.'

'But you were raised in Connecticut, look how *you* turned out.'

Josh grinned. 'Well balanced. Reasonable. Quite sexy.' He ducked as she tried to whack him with her bag.

'You're surely not saying *Connecticut?*' Her boyfriend had grown up in an upmarket, WASPy-Jewish enclave in Greenwich, in a house with a front lawn and the sort of white picket fence Natasha thought only existed in old movies; a father who commuted to Wall Street every day; and a mother who'd driven him and his two siblings to soccer games and Little League, served on a number of charitable boards, and, post-kids, had taken to the cheesecake with an almost ideological zeal.

'Connecticut Connecticut Connecticut . . .' He was laughing.

'You're such a *child*. Just so you know: I am not going to turn into your mother after we get married. Okay?'

'Yes, okay. I don't want you to turn into my mother. It would be kinda weird to sleep with my moth — '

'Josh. Seriously! I'm just saying: if we do ever have kids, they are going to be raised in New York City. You may as well get used to it.'

'Tash, I'm just saying: our kids are not going to be raised here. Not if I have anything to do with it.'

'And what makes you think you'll have anything to do with it?'

'Well, I'll be the one paying for it, for a start. Hey, d'you want to get a gelato?'

Before she could protest, he was over on the other side of the tracks, where a gaggle of tourists were clustering around the food stands, posing for over-excited photographs.

'Really? You really want to stand on line for ice cream now?'

'Their mint choc chip is insane.'

'Fine.' She looked at him. 'Josh, how is it possible we're getting married in six months and we've not had this conversation before?'

'About mint choc chip? The pistachio's pretty great, too.'

'You know what I mean.'

'Probably because you've never been open to the idea of living anywhere else — there'd be no point.'

'And what the hell is that supposed to mean?'

'Well, just because you don't want to live anywhere else, you won't even have the conversation about it. And that's just a *leetle* bit selfish, don't you think?'

He ordered his gelato from the Italian girl in the white cap, and turned to her. 'Want to try the pistachio? No? You sure?'

'What did you just say?'

She half-expected him to answer, *I said: Want to try the pistachio?* But even he didn't dare. 'I said that just because you have that New Yorker thing, where you think the universe revolves around these streets, you maybe aren't considering that the best place to raise a kid is somewhere he can run around, get plenty of fresh air, actually live like a *kid*.'

She ignored the 'he'. 'Well shall we go live in Canada?' she suggested, as they kept moving. 'I hear there's plenty of fresh air there.'

'No. Obviously not. We are not going to move to Canada.'

'How about Australia. New Zealand? Isn't New Zealand famous for its fresh air?'

'Come on.' Josh slung his arm easily around her shoulder and passed her the cone for a taste. 'I'm just saying that, you know, an urban landscape with zero consideration for infants may not be the best place to raise . . . infants.'

She took a lick and rolled her eyes. 'Jesus. I

can't believe this. Sometimes I just think you're so *blinkered* — '

'You're the one being blinkered! You're the one saying it's got to be New York or nothing.'

She had another bite of his gelato, which was irritatingly good. 'That's because it's New *York*.'

'But seriously. What's keeping you here?'

'What do you mean by that?'

'If you're not working, it doesn't really matter where you are, does it? We'll never live anywhere that isn't a quick commute away from the city, so what's the big deal? You'll still see your family, your friends.' He removed the cone from her hands before she finished the whole thing off.

She stopped dead. 'Wait. *That's* what this is about? You're saying, seeing as I don't have a job, we might as well go live in Connecticut right now?'

'I'm not saying that. I'm just looking at the facts, I'm just looking at the practical reality. Because someone's got to.' With his non-ice-cream hand, Josh messed with her hair and where ordinarily she would have enjoyed the affection, this afternoon she yanked her head away as he went on. 'You lost your job, baby, which sucks, of course, but think how tough the past couple of weeks have been; you were

67

saying that just the other night. So the chances are, you're not going to get another job before we get married — '

'Are you fucking crazy?' she spluttered. 'We're getting married in *March*. You really think I'm not going to go back to work between now and then?'

His expression was impassive. 'I don't know, Tash. I don't know. I hope so, if that's what you want. But it doesn't matter if you *don't*, is all I'm saying. I'll always make enough for both of us, and if we were going to start trying after the wedding anyway, then — '

'Josh. Listen to yourself!' It was just possible he was kidding, but she had a creeping and disquieting unease that he was serious. 'Are you actually . . . you're actually saying, you don't care if I go back to work, in fact you would quite like me to *not* go back to work if it means we can move to fucking Connecticut right now and have kids and live five minutes away from your mom, and — '

'Obviously that is not what I'm saying.'

'Shit. But it is! And if you can't *see* that's what you're saying, then we have an even bigger problem.' Natasha dropped down onto one of the wooden slatted benches and drew a hand over her face. 'Wow. Well, *this* was a curveball.'

Josh glanced at his watch before he sat down to join her.

'Yeah, you should go,' she said, without bitterness. 'Go to your work. We can talk about this later.'

He took her hand. 'Tash. It's okay. I don't think we need to talk about it. This is a crazy conversation, because we both want the same things. We do.'

'Mmm.'

'I gotta run. I'll see you later, 'kay? I'll try not to be home too late.'

She lifted her head up to his. He kissed her quickly, and was gone.

★ ★ ★

Josh had walked over to 14th Street to try and get a cab across town to his office, and was midway through tapping out a text to his mate Eddie to say he probably would not make it out for beers tonight when some instinct warned him, just a split second too late, that he was about to slam right into someone heading over the crosswalk from the other side.

He froze.

It was the smell. Even before he looked up, it was the smell of her.

After it had happened, over six years ago,

69

there had been this period of time, possibly a year, where Josh saw her everywhere. The rational knowledge that she was living on the other side of the country did not stop his brain from fabricating the possibility that she was still in fact here. A flick of ash-blonde hair on the subway; a shapely calf or slender ankle on the street in front of him; the particular ring of a laugh in a dark bar — he had lost count of the number of times he had felt his heart jump-start at the sense that she was somehow near.

But she never was. In fact, ever since that phone call from California when she'd told him she was *too young to be doing this; too young to be settling down*, he had not laid eyes on her again. She'd only been going to Stanford for a year: she'd won funding for a vascular biology research scholarship during her third year of med school, and Columbia, where she was on a postgrad scholarship, had been happy for her to transfer her credit for a year. But she had never come home. And as he had thrown out all the photographs of them from Yale formals and vacations; as people had stopped asking him about her; as the news about her marriage to that tech hotshot guy in Palo Alto and her baby (so much for not settling down!) had stopped filtering through to him, he had gradually stopped seeing her everywhere; had stopped wondering; had just about reassembled himself and got on with the business of life without her. He hadn't stopped thinking of her, of course: there were days when he seemed to feel her very presence in his bloodstream, circling around and around him. But whole days, even weeks began to go past and it became bearable, he bore it. Especially after he had met Natasha up at Eddie's beach house last Memorial Day weekend. That had helped. Only on the very occasional dark nights of the soul, or when some Spotify shuffle hit upon a particular song, or when he was out with the old Yale crowd, was he revisited by that disconcerting sense of being not quite in one piece, because of her. Because of the absence of her.

Against the clang of the traffic he heard an astonished gasp. His name, in her mouth. And then, 'Oh my God.'

When he finally allowed himself to look harder, to confirm he wasn't hallucinating, Josh became dimly aware of the car horns blaring around them, of the other people on the crosswalk in motion, of the lights being about to change. But something had paralyzed him; both of them. Neither had moved.

'Kris?' he managed, finally, his voice a strange croak that seemed to come from not its normal place.

'Oh my God.'

Somehow they made it to the sidewalk, where they stood and stared at each other.

'You . . . ' he said, stupidly. 'You're here.'

Kristen Polley's pale blue eyes shone with sudden tears. 'Oh my God,' she repeated. 'I'm sorry, I just . . . Oh my God, Josh. I can't believe it.'

He managed to get out a few more stilted words. And somehow registered that she was saying she had moved back to the East Coast with her daughter Riley two months ago, and was now working at NYU Langone as an anaesthesiologist and living over on First Avenue. For the first time, he registered the purple scrubs stitched with the too-familiar white NYU torch, her scraped-back doctorish hair.

In this grand collapse of time and space he dared not look too closely at her face.

'And you?' she asked tentatively. 'How are you, Josh?'

'I'm fine,' he heard himself say. 'I'm good. Thanks. Really good. I'm fine.'

★ ★ ★

72

At his desk in Midtown a short while later, Josh gazed at his computer screen for an unknown amount of time before pulling out his phone again, to confirm that what had just happened had really just happened. To check it was real.

Kristen 646-707-3426

Fuck.

Fuck, fuck. A million things cycled through his mind. He considered deleting the entry instantly, he considered calling it. He thought about scrolling down to N — oh, Christ, *Tash* — and hopping on the first cab he could find to wherever in this city his girlfriend might be. To find her, to hold her, to be reminded that it was about Natasha now.

Instead, he threw the phone across his desk and pulled up the client presentation for the major telecoms deal that he was due to give Monday to the team of Brazilians who were flying in from São Paolo. He tried to force his brain to concentrate on anything, anything but her.

After a minute he clicked open his email and typed rapidly.

From: Joshua.Liebowitz@zenithpartners.com
To: Edward.Strauss@cravath.com
Sent: September 20, 15:06 ET

Re:
I just bumped into Kristen on 14th. She
moved back to NYC.

Within seconds, a reply hit his inbox.

From: Edward.Strauss@cravath.com
To: Joshua.Liebowitz@zenithpartners.com
Sent: September 20, 15:07 ET
Re: Re:

KRISTEN POLLEY??? Oh holy fuck. Give me
20 mins, I'll meet you in that bar on the
corner by your office.

5

When her sister pushed open the door to Pulse a week or so later, the thought that popped into Rachel's head was an old phrase of Esther's: '*oysgemutshet un oysgematert*' — basically, 'exhausted and exhausted'. Overworked, permanently stressed, driven by alpha tendencies that were alien to Rachel, Natasha had spent the past few years looking increasingly tired. But Rachel was sure she'd never seen her looking quite so — well, *grey*. Curious about most everything the world had to offer, there was usually a gleam of engaged interestedness in Natasha's honey-brown eyes; today they looked pretty much empty.

'Hey,' said Rachel, coming around from behind the counter.

'Hey.'

There was an awkward moment. Did they hug now; what did they do? Rachel had been surprised to get the phone call from Tash last night. Weirdly, she'd been thinking about her sister a lot since Rosh Hashana a few weeks ago, and now all of a sudden she was on the phone asking if they might have lunch; something they had not done in years. 'How about tomorrow?' Rachel had suggested before she thought the better of it.

Forgoing the hug, Rachel led her sister to their nicest table, right by the window, and pointed out today's menu, which was chalked up on a board by the bar. 'Order whatever you want, it's on us. I told Oren, the owner, that my sister was coming for the very first time.'

She didn't add: *Oren was amazed. He had no idea I even had a sister.*

'Wow. It all looks great. I don't even . . . ' Tash frowned. 'Jesus, Rach. I haven't even heard of half these foods. Why don't you order for both of us?'

Rachel did.

'So how'd the interview go?' she asked, back at the table. Tash had told her last night she was meeting an editor this morning about a possible job — her fifth interview in the past few weeks, she'd said.

'Total fucking disaster.'

Rachel pulled a face. 'What was it for, again?'

'Some new hi-tech online news and comment aggregator. Conrad Muntz has given this guy, like, ten million bucks to launch this thing. He looked barely legal.'

'Conrad Muntz?'

'You know, the MediaVision mogul? I

understood about seven percent of the words this kid used. Pretty sure I failed to convince him that I was down with, y'know, the wonderful world of contemporary online discourse.'

Rachel exhaled. 'Sounds stressful. Do you need a drink? I think we might have some rye in the back. Or a beer?'

Natasha laughed: a dry, bitter sound that it shocked Rachel to hear. Tash was like their dad: she entirely lacked cynicism. It was one of the things Rachel liked most about her — that naïve vulnerability lurking beneath all those flashy achievements and summa cum laude Ivy degrees.

'I'm okay. But thanks.' There was a pause. Then Natasha said, 'So how are you, Rach?'

'I'm really good.' Rachel didn't know what else to say: she *was* really good. Her life was simple, it was full. It was far away, she'd bet, from Natasha and Josh's.

'How's Skye?'

'She's . . . well, she's kind of magnificent.'

'I'd so like to meet her.'

Rachel felt a prickle of guilt. When Natasha had called last night, they had been lying in bed. 'So it seems I'm going to have lunch with my sister tomorrow,' she'd ventured after hanging up. 'Want to join us?'

Skye, one hand on the inside of Rachel's

thigh, the other tracing abstract patterns on her stomach, had laughed out loud. 'Uh, I don't think so.' Knowing full well what Skye's commitments were the next day, Rachel had removed those strong, electrifying hands from her body and tipped a finger under her chin so they were eye to eye. 'You're busy?' she'd challenged. 'Really?'

Skye, who was, addictively, fully capable of meeting any charm or challenge Rachel threw her way, did not even blink. 'Nope. I'm free all the damn day. I just don't want to meet your sister.'

'Why?'

'Well, I sure as hell ain't interested in talking about finance and I doubt she'll be interested in our Chekhov project!'

'But isn't that a little, I don't know, judgmental?' Rachel had countered, with a sting of shame about the way she might have talked about Natasha in the past. 'I mean, Tash is a *writer*. Not a banker. She's a literature major. And she loves Chekhov, as it happens.'

'She works for the *New York Times*,' Skye had snorted. 'Can't get much more corporate than that. Plus she's *marrying* a banker.'

'Worked,' Rachel corrected, mildly. 'But in any case, she writes — wrote — about things that matter to us, too. You remember she did a whole feature on city charter schools? That made a huge difference to us.'

'Sorry, princess.' With a sass that somehow managed to be uncontrived, Skye had shimmied her Afro from side to side, then deftly, unexpectedly rolled Rachel over, trapping her underneath that powerful body of hers. Putting dark lips to pale breast, she had murmured into Rachel's skin, 'She just ain't my bag.'

Rachel, liquid with desire but forcing herself to push Skye away, had hunched against the wall, wondering how you could know someone wasn't your bag before you'd even met them. And wondering why it suddenly mattered to her that Skye clearly had no interest in meeting a single member of her family. Why had Rachel ever given the impression she was okay with that? Why *had* she ever been okay with it?

'She wants to meet you too,' she lied to Natasha now. 'She was just really busy today. So how are *you*?'

At that moment, though, Oren arrived with their plates, which created a useful diversion. As they ate, they alighted on safe topics, like how nuts it was to see their cousin Shira up close in her new Orthodox incarnation, or how cool Esther's expansion plans at West Street were. But they were circling around

each other; both subject to the old gravita-
tional pull. Rachel, deep down, found she did
want to talk to Natasha: to ask roughly one
million questions about what was going on in
her life. She even wanted to hear, to her
surprise, about the stupid wedding plans. But
Natasha, who had always been adept at
ducking enquiries about herself, in turn kept
coming back to Rachel — Rachel's work,
Rachel's heart, the seismic turn her life had
taken a few months ago after she'd kissed
Skye Jackson in an old whaling dive in Red
Hook. It wasn't that Rachel didn't *want* to
talk to Tash about her girlfriend; she just
didn't know how. Her feelings for Skye,
unexpected and unbidden as they had been,
had sort of tipped everything upside down.
Everything she'd thought she understood
about herself was now different. The answer
to everything she thought she knew about
love had now changed the question. And how
was she to begin explaining any of that to
Tash, with whom she had not had a proper
conversation about anything in so long?

'So is this it now . . . ?' Natasha was asking.
'I mean, you know it doesn't matter in the
slightest to me, right? I'm not Mom. I
couldn't give a shit about your reproductive
schedule or what you do with your ovaries.'

Rachel laughed. 'Thank God. Maybe we do

need that drink.' She eyed her sister, wondering if Natasha was remembering the same thing — all those teenaged nights when they had kept each other's romantic counsel until the sun rose. Those times had ended the moment Natasha's high-school sweetheart Ethan Schlesinger had asked Rachel to their senior prom, and Rachel had gone; the memory of which still made her want to vomit. But, once upon a time, she and her sister had shared so much, and thinking about those times made Rachel sad. She sort of wanted to reach over and say, *Hey, Tash. I'm still here. I haven't gone anywhere. I'm still me. We're still us.*

Instead, she ate some food. 'Truthfully, Tash, I don't know. I don't know if it's a . . . thing. I don't know what it means. I think it's more about a person. About the specificity of this one person, rather than her being a woman. Skye happened to me, we happened to each other. That's all.' *And that's everything.*

Natasha nodded imperceptibly. She reached for the water carafe and busied herself with that for a bit. Dipped a piece of sourdough in olive oil. Ate. Exclaimed at the deliciousness. Avoided Rachel's eye.

Rachel sat back and watched her. She wondered if Natasha even believed in that

81

anymore: that people could just happen to each other. She kind of wanted to slam her hands down on the table and scream: *Come on! Don't you remember what we swore we would always fight for? Don't you remember that time in Jerusalem, after we read Grandma's letter in the museum when we were like, fifteen and sixteen? How we always said it would be a betrayal of everything Esther lost if we didn't fight for that ourselves?*

She recalled the row they'd had after Natasha had returned from a vacation in Rome earlier this year with that gigantic diamond on her finger. Rachel, appalled, had told her she was crazy and making a huge, huge mistake. They'd fought. Natasha had accused her of exhibiting — what had she said? — 'the most tedious kind of lazy, liberal, reflexive prejudice'. But Rachel was not prejudiced. She couldn't give a fuck what Josh did: she truly did not care that he was a banker or a hedge fund person or a management consultant or whatever he was. He could have been an astronaut or a charity worker, an oil driller, an accountant, an opera singer. It was irrelevant: he was not the right person for her sister. And that fact was unanswerable. Tash, Rachel knew better than anyone, had a wildness within her, buried deep perhaps, but inherent — a ferocious curiosity about the world, a love of adventure, a fascination with people and cultures and human interactions in all their messy glory. Josh Liebowitz met absolutely none of that spirit of enquiry. Rachel had liked Natasha's previous boyfriend Simon, a raggedy British literary critic who'd been doing a PhD at Harvard, but they'd broken up horribly after Tash had left the *Boston Globe* and had moved back to New York, shipwrecked of heart but triumphantly holding the job of her dreams.

And then last summer, this Josh character had appeared on the scene after they met at a weekend in the Hamptons, introduced by a mutual friend. And it was as though Tash had finally succumbed to the invisible pressure that their mother had been adminis-tering through osmosis in their officially liberal household ever since the girls had hit puberty. Ros would of course be *outraged* if you accused her of any such thing: she was the cool, open-minded Jewish mom who could be as open-minded and liberal as she liked so long as her girls were marrying nice Jewish bankers with straight white teeth and Yale degrees and good families in Greenwich, Connecticut. Rachel saw through the shtick instantly. And it wasn't even that Josh wasn't smart (he was) or well-read (he seemed to be) or even (which would weirdly have made it less depressing) the wrong side of the political divide; he had supposedly donated a fat cheque to the Obama re-election campaign. On paper he ticked a bunch of boxes and appeared to offer Natasha something that presumably assuaged her deep-seated insecurity about men. An insecurity, to be fair, that Rachel knew she had played her own part in over the years. But underneath the paper, Rachel knew, lay an emotionally attenuated, small-souled person who would make her sister miserable in the long run. That night, she had predicted something along those lines, and Natasha had completely lost it.

'How the fuck would you know? You don't know *anything* about us. You don't know anything about me anymore?! And how fucking dare you, anyway, after *everything*? How dare you tell me who I should love?'

And Rachel had shut up right there. Knowing, after Ethan and after everything, that Natasha had a valid point, and that she had indeed relinquished that right.

That had been pretty much the last time they'd talked.

'You'll meet Skye. You'll see what I mean.'

'Well, I'm just glad you're happy. I really am, Rach.' Her voice was all artless warmth:

Rachel did not doubt it.

'Are *you* happy, Nasha?' she asked. 'How is Josh?'

To Rachel's alarm, Natasha's eyes beaded quickly with tears, although she blinked them away. Rachel didn't know why she'd employed the name she'd called her sister from the moment she could speak — the first word she had ever spoken, in fact. It had just slipped out. Perhaps because she knew they were now dancing on an ancient sisterly fault line and she must disarm where she could.

'He is great.' Natasha recovered and took a mouthful of quinoa scramble. 'Or at least, he was. Right after I was fired, he was amazing, but — '

'But now?'

Natasha hesitated. 'It doesn't matter, forget about it.'

'Come on, Tash. Please. You can still talk to me.'

Natasha looked up, slowly. Everything in her expression seemed to ask: *can I?* 'Well, it's been a strange couple of weeks. He's hardly been home, he's working on this massive deal. He's gotten kind of distant and weird around me.'

Rachel noticed Billy, the tattoo artist from the parlour across the street who came here every day for his broccoli-bread sandwich.

She waved. 'Well, you're probably the first person he's ever met in his life who's lost their job,' she suggested, turning back to her sister.

And there was that broken little laugh again. 'Right. I may be an alien species to him: someone who's actually *failed* at something.'

'Oh, Nash, come on; you've never failed at anything. You'll get another job in a hot minute.'

'I don't think so.' Natasha was shaking her head. 'It's a war zone out there, Rach, and it's getting uglier by the day. All the papers are screwed. And if my only hope is people like Mr Teenaged Media Mogul this morning, forget it. Josh keeps saying he doesn't mind, that he's happy to pay our rent until I find something. But I hate not paying my way, I can't stand it. All this just feels so wrong. It wasn't meant to be like this.'

'And there's really nothing opening up anywhere else?'

'I've signed on with a freelance copy-editing agency, which kind of makes me want to jump off the nearest bridge. But it doesn't guarantee anything. So I have to do something else, even if just to earn enough cash to buy a MetroCard and eat.' She wiped her plate clean with another piece of bread, arranged her cutlery, leaned back. 'Speaking of which, that was *so* good. Thank you. You don't need an extra pair of hands here, by any chance?'

Rachel snorted. 'You're kidding.'

'Half kidding. Right now I'm pretty much up for anything. I told Esther I'd be around a lot more to help her over at West Street, maybe a day or two a week, but I have to figure out something for the rest of the time.'

A thought occurred to Rachel as she cleared their plates, out of habit, and went to make them coffees at the bar. 'Well, listen,' she said as she sat back down, handing her sister a pretty little cortado. 'If you're really stuck, you should maybe go meet my friend Nathan, who runs this great bookstore in Brooklyn. We had dinner with him the other night and his assistant just left. I know he's looking for someone.'

Natasha was staring at her as if uncomprehending. 'A bookstore?'

'I mean, maybe it's a bit beneath you now, sure, but it's a beautiful store,' Rachel shot back. Natasha had worked vacation jobs at the Strand throughout their teens and in the library at Harvard; it surely wasn't *that* outrageous a suggestion. 'And Nathan has such gorgeous things — first editions, rare bindings, association copies, you know, like,

T. S. Eliot's copy of *Ulysses* with his own notes and scribbles in it?' She pulled out a pen from her shirt pocket and jotted down the Lorimer Street address on a paper napkin. 'I mean, it's not going to cover Nolita rent cheques or anything. But it's a charming place, and Nathan is a wonder. One of the most intellectually . . . ' Rachel searched for the right word, 'intellectually elegant people I've ever met. He's cool. He's just your type.'

Natasha inclined her head. 'Seriously?'

'Seriously. Just go meet him. I think you'll love him.'

6

He'd suggested a generic, anonymous Starbucks on the East Side. It was in that
monotonous no-man's-land stretch of First,
close to the apartment she'd told him she was
renting in Stuyvesant Town, not far from her
NYU Langone building. As a place in which
to meet the former love of your life, the girl
who had completely fucked with your heart,
the girl you thought was safely married with
kids way over on the other coast and not
somebody you were going to slam right into
on 14th Street, you surely could not get more
sterile, more neutral than this.

But now that innocuous Starbucks on 17th
Street was rocking with the words she had
just uttered, and Josh found he was struggling
to breathe right.

*There hasn't been a single day. Not a
single day.*

Christ. Christ, Christ. He had rehearsed
this scene in his mind for so many years; so
many years, and now he found he could
barely speak. Kristen was staring very hard at
the white and green mug in her hands. Her
nails were bare and bitten and there were

traces of glittery pink and purple paint on her fingers. Make-up-free, her ash-blonde hair in a scrappy ponytail, she looked exhausted and strained, but the same old Kristen radiance somehow managed to escape anyway. Once again he forced himself not to stare too closely at her face; every detail of which he found he could remember with heartbreaking precision.

The silence between them was a presence. Josh waited. He watched as Kristen closed her pale eyelids, put a hand to her forehead, squeezed her brow.

'I never thought I wouldn't come back to New York,' she finally offered. 'I never thought I wouldn't come back to you after I finished at Stanford. I never imagined that we wouldn't be together. Not for a single day.'

Over her cup, she forced him to meet her eyes.

'You broke up with me out of the blue, over the phone,' he swallowed. 'After everything. Then got pregnant with some other guy. And married him six months later.'

Rage curdled anew in his gut. A rage six years old, a rage that had passed through so many other shapes and colours in that time but today, here, this afternoon, seemed ultimately reducible to this. *After everything. You got pregnant with some other guy. And married him six months later*. At last he thought he understood. If Kristen, now divorced and a single mom at thirty-two, was taking an indulgent, regret-laced look back at the past and wondering if, hey, her old boyfriend might still be around to pick up the pieces, he had a clear and unassailable answer for her. He sure as fuck was not.

'I understand why you see it like that,' she said, evenly, as if this was a scene she too had rehearsed. 'I understand why you hate me; I'd probably hate me too.'

I don't hate you, he corrected, silently. *Even now, even after everything, I do not hate you.*

He cleared his throat. If only he could just corral his voice, his breathing, make everything behave normally. 'Do you want to tell me how I could have possibly seen it another way?'

She stared back down at her clenched hands. Her whole body broadcast tension.

'Oh, God. Josh . . . When I got out there I was stupid and selfish, I know that. We'd been together so long, and everything we'd gone through . . . and I was, what, twenty-five? I went a little nuts. That whole line about needing time and space was true. But I knew even then that we'd end *up* together, that I'd never love anyone — '

'Kris! Listen to yourself. What the hell are you doing? What are you *saying?*'

'You're right. I'm sorry.' She took a sip of the coffee that must have cooled long ago and grimaced. 'So anyway.' There was that forced, bright smile. 'I heard you're engaged. That you're happy and that your girlfriend is lovely. I'm happy for you, J, I really am.'

'She is lovely.' Josh forced himself to say her name. It seemed suddenly important to physically place her in the space between them. 'Natasha.' The second syllable snagged distressingly in his throat. He wondered who had told Kristen about them. 'She's . . . she's incredible.'

'I'm sure she is. And you deserve someone incredible. Look, I promise I didn't ask you to meet today because I wanted to interfere in your life or in any way make things difficult for you . . . '

He managed not to snort.

'But after we bumped into each other like that, I just . . . well, there is something . . . ' Kristen had a wretched expression on her face; she seemed to be steeling herself for something. His heart began to race. What could this girl possibly be about to tell him now that could still have power over him?

'I have wondered for so long, literally for so many *years,* whether it would be worse to ever tell you, or to never tell you. But now that we're here . . . now that you're getting married, I don't know, it seems only fair somehow. I just think you deserve to know.'

From its temporary lodging somewhere in his throat, Josh felt his racing heart constrict. 'Know . . . what?'

Kristen exhaled. When she spoke, the words came out clotted, and slow. 'When I found out I was pregnant, I wrote to your mother.'

'My *mother?*'

'Yeah. You remember the row we had that time, in Greenwich? When she called me a *shiksa* slut to my face and threw the plant at the wall?'

He did. So clearly. And how Kristen had wept outside in his car afterwards, inconsolable; and how he had made up his mind then and there that he was going to marry this brilliant, beautiful girl, his family and their tribal concerns be damned. Just as soon as she returned home from her year at Stanford.

That had been less than a fortnight before Kris had boarded the plane for San Francisco.

'Well, that whole delightful little scene was also part of the reason why when I got out West I sort of cut loose. I felt like I could *breathe* again for the first time in so long. I

93

don't think I even realized how oppressive that had all been, the weight of your family and their expectations and their disappointment about us all that time. Please understand, J, I know that had *nothing* to do with you. But I got out to Cali and I was like, okay, well fuck that. And then disaster struck. I mean, not *disaster*, Riley is pretty much the greatest thing that ever happened to me. But it *was* a disaster in its way, because there I was, alone and pregnant and shit-scared, and the only person in the universe I wanted to be with was three thousand miles away on the other side of the country and probably never wanting to speak to me ever again. So, one very dark night, I wrote to your mother. I explained what had happened. I admitted to her that I'd . . . *egregiously* screwed up, that I'd made the most unbelievably stupid mistake, and that I desperately regretted breaking up with you.' Kristen bit her lip and looked at him. When he did not respond, she carried on. 'Josh, I told her I was prepared to have a termination.'

'*What?*'

'Yeah. And you can imagine how that would have gone down with Seamus and Brianna Polley . . . '

He was wrecked by a sudden memory:

Kristen's parents in their condo in New Jersey; their kindnesses; their laughter; the raucous mealtimes and the whisky-soaked Christmases with all the Boston cousins, so very different from holidays in his own house.

'I told her I'd give up the Stanford scholarship, come straight back to New York on the next plane,' Kristen was saying. 'And . . . I told her I would convert.'

He stared at her.

'If you'd still have me, that is. But I also told her that I needed her blessing.'

Josh felt his stomach flip over.

'And?' he said, very quietly.

'She wrote me back.'

'What did she say?'

'She said that it would be very difficult for the family if you were to marry me. She talked a little about what had happened to her family. The upshot was basically, 'if my son marries you, Dachau was for nothing'. And I guess . . . Well, I guess I finally understood.'

After a moment Kristen added, 'She also told me that she'd passed on my letter, but that you told her to tell me you'd moved on and wanted nothing to do with me.'

'Why didn't you call *me* and ask me if I'd moved on?' he croaked.

'Josh, you have to remember that I was

totally all over the place. I was pregnant and sick and so ashamed and working insanely hard and I was just a mess. You *had* told me you never wanted anything to do with me ever again. It seemed entirely possible she was telling the truth about that.'

She wasn't, he did not need to say.

'But mostly I didn't call you because I knew your mother, I'd seen how she reacted to me, I'd watched her throw a *plant* at your head, for fuck's sake. I'd seen her hurt and her fear, and now it was there again, all laid out in front of me in this terrible letter. And I understood then that it really would break up your family if you were to be with me again, and I couldn't do that.'

'That should have been my decision,' he swallowed. 'Not yours. Not hers.'

Kristen gave a sigh, ancient and deep. 'I see that now. Which is why, when you agreed to meet me today, I . . . well, I brought the letter. I've kept it all these years and after we bumped into each other I thought you should probably have it.'

She dug into her pocketbook and pulled out a dog-eared envelope. Passed it across the table. Josh recognized his mother's handwriting instantly, the monogrammed blue DDL stationery. As if in a trance, he pulled out the letter, read a few lines, caught the weight and the heft of the words. Put it straight back in the envelope.

Grief rammed his chest; grief at the mess and the exhaustion and the waste of it all. And to his horror, right there in that Starbucks, right there in front of Kristen, holding this letter that his mother had written to his beloved six years ago, he began to cry.

Kristen watched him in silence. Then she said, 'I love you very much, Joshua. I have never not loved you. And I am telling you this as somebody who loves you and who cares about you. Not as somebody who wants to ruin your life or your fiancée's life. I promise you that.' She reached over, and with the tiniest tip of her finger, she stroked his hand.

And at her touch, all in him was instantly rewired.

'I am presuming nothing,' she went on 'But just in case there is even a *single* part of you that still, in any way, thinks about us or about me, or still wonders what might have been or *should* have been, well . . . I just need to tell you that being married to someone while you are thinking about someone else is like being buried alive. I know, Josh, because I did it for five years.'

With the greatest tenderness then, Kristen

brought his fingers to her lips and kissed them briefly, as if he were a child. Her child. And then she rose, and gathered her things. 'That's all, Josh. That is all. You don't need to say anything. I'll see you around.'

7

Frank had placed a disc of Chopin on the CD player, had put his feet up and was mid-way through a long article about judicial reform in the *New Yorker* when Ros appeared in the doorway with his evening glass of scotch. He thanked her with extravagant appreciation, and patted the couch next to him.

'So I just got off the phone with Tash,' Ros was saying, and now he could hear how his wife was *plotzing* with whatever it was she wanted to tell him.

'Oh yeah? How's she doing?'

'She has a job, apparently.'

Frank put his tumbler down in amazement. 'She does? Already? What is it?' In his mind, he was thinking: *Wall Street Journal, Washington Post,* maybe even the very publication on his lap . . .

'She's working in a bookstore.'

'*What?*'

'Yeah. A bookstore. Not, like, a Barnes and Noble or anything. A little independent one in Brooklyn.'

Frank frowned. '*Really?*'

'She said that something about it 'just felt right'.'

'Why didn't you put me on? I'd have liked to talk to her.'

'She had to jump off. She'd been trying to reach Josh all evening. She promised she'd ring back later.'

'So how did she sound?'

'That's the crazy thing. She sounded *fine*. Happy, even.'

Frank considered this. His immediate sense of surprise — my brilliant little girl stacking shelves in a *bookstore?* — subsided as he reflected that maybe it wasn't so bad, as an interim measure at least. There was no getting away from the fact that, in this climate, and given the incident at the *Times*, Natasha might struggle to get another good reporting position. And like her history-teacher mother, she had always been obsessed with books. He recalled one memorable night spent in the Beth Israel E.R. years ago after a twelve — or thirteen-year-old Tash, hurrying down Amsterdam Avenue with her nose in a particularly engrossing novel, had slammed right into a lamp-post and conked herself out. She still had the scar, just above her eyebrow. Or, long before that, all those nights when he and Ros would peek into her bedroom after spotting the reading lamp still on, and would have to gently remove another plastic-coated library book from underneath their sleeping daughter's flushed cheek.

'Well, maybe she is happy.'

Ros collapsed on the shabby old couch and put her socked feet over his. Then she crossed her arms and said: 'Well, I personally think she's nuts.'

'Why, because she's way overqualified and should be holding out for a proper job?'

Ros gave him a sideways look. 'I of all people obviously have no problem with her selling books. But I do think it's another classic case of Tash jumping into something without giving it a moment's thought.'

Natasha's impetuousness had been a pet theme of Rosalind's lately; especially since the engagement, which they had both thought might be a little soon. Tasha and Josh had been together for less than a year when he asked.

'Well, I guess she wants to keep herself occupied. No harm in it.'

'Maybe not. But she could just give herself a break. She's so highly-strung these days, don't you think?'

Frank didn't know if he would quite call it that. Maybe more like, an inability to rest on her laurels. Tash had always been industrious: since childhood she had been incapable of

101

sitting still, of wasting a moment of precious time. Rachel had a degree of that in her too; the two of them had always been racketing around, busy little city kids, no lounging about on the couch watching TV all day or emerging cross and crotchety as teenagers from their bedrooms at lunchtime. But Tash had taken this aversion to doing nothing to extremes.

'Did we make her that?' his wife wondered aloud. 'Did we put too much pressure on her to achieve things? I feel like we'd chilled out on the parenting thing by the time Rach came along. But maybe Tasha's, I don't know, *mania* is partly our fault. Remember how crazy ambitious she became at college? Maybe we should have encouraged her to do *less*, not more.'

'Maybe,' Frank conceded. 'Maybe we did put too much of an emphasis on education being the most important thing, and how she should strive to be the best she could possibly be. But I don't think we did it in a negative way. I think it's in her character to strive. And trust me, she was by no means the only person going crazy at Harvard.' Proudly, he reminded his wife: 'And she did graduate *summa*.'

It still made him prouder than he would ever be able to say. Even to Ros, Frank did not often talk about his early childhood in that tenement downtown, nor of the trauma that had preceded it, but he had never taken a day of his life, or a moment of the modest success he enjoyed in his own work, for granted. Natasha, of all of them, seemed to understand and enact that in her life too, and he loved her all the more for it.

Ros stroked his knee with a fond expression on her face. 'Seventy-one, my darling Frankie, and still so much to prove to the world.' She stole a sip of his whisky. 'You're right, of course. But it's like she's so *stubborn*.'

'I can't think where she gets that from.'

She poked him with her toe. 'All right, smart ass. By the way, this is heavenly, what is it?'

'I don't know, honey, you poured. Shall I go fill us up?'

'No, no, the music. What is it?'

'Uh . . . it is Maurizio Pollini playing Chopin concertos, I think.'

They listened in silence for a while, Ros humming gently under her breath. 'I think my father used to play this,' she murmured. 'Terribly. But he always did have a thing for E-minor.'

Frank smiled. Knowing little about music

except that he loved it, he enjoyed it when his wife let slip these occasional pearls of knowledge. His mother Adela had been a keen amateur singer, but Otto had been, by his own admission, 'tone deaf' and never seen it fit to send Frank — or later, Adam — to music classes in New York, much to Frank's regret.

'E-minor, huh?' he echoed, having no idea what that really even meant, simply recognizing that the wrenching beauty of the music was speaking to him on some profound level. He leaned across and retrieved the CD box from the sideboard. She was right, of course.

'E-minor it is. Clever girl.' Shaking his head, Frank pulled his wife into his arms, and wondered for the millionth time how he got to be such a lucky son-of-a-bitch.

8

October

Nestled in the triangular junction of Eighth Avenue, Abingdon Square and West 12th Street, the grand old apartment block where Esther lived was almost as familiar to Natasha as the brownstone on West 83rd. The Goldfadens had moved here from Brownsville, Brooklyn with their baby Rosa following Max's first success on Broadway in the 1950s. Natasha and Rachel had spent countless days here over the course of their lives. And even after Max died, when the girls were little, Esther would not hear of moving out. Rosalind was often trying to move her mother uptown to be closer to them, and had even started dropping hints about some nice retirement communities she'd been reading about in the Berkshires, but Esther was adamant that New York was the city that had saved her life, and that she fully intended to die here.

'Also: why would I schlep all the way uptown when I live in the greatest neighbourhood in the city for *bubkes?*' she would ask, with irrefutable Estherish logic. And, rent-control being what it was, nobody, not even Rosalind Bernstein, could really argue with that one.

'So what does my future grandson think of this?' Esther was enquiring now as they locked up her front door.

'He thinks I'm insane,' Natasha admitted, as she took her grandmother's arm and they stepped out onto the street. After much irritation, Esther was finally reconciled to the walker she had been forced to use since her hip operation, but today, in the surprisingly warm sunlight of an early October morning, she had decided she wanted to go without it. They were headed over to West Street, where Esther was due to meet the new architect who'd been assigned to the extension. Rachel was supposed to be there but had been held up teaching in the Bronx, and Natasha had been glad to step in at the last minute. 'He can't believe it.'

'A *bookstore*?' Josh had echoed, baffled, during the tense phone conversation they'd had after she'd accepted Nathan Temple's part-time job offer at Uppercase Books. She'd spent the afternoon doing a trial at the store, and in doing so had experienced a quiet surge of joy, or at least consolation; as if a place like that, existing for no other reason than to serve people words and beauty and intellectual space and contemplation, was proof, somehow, that the world and all the humans within it would probably be okay. Suspecting it would be wiser not to mention this — nor that the bookstore had been Rachel's idea and Nathan Rachel's friend — she'd had to remind Josh that she'd worked the cash registers at the Strand throughout high school; that she'd earned extra cash re-shelving books in the Widener during college; that she probably spent more of her disposable income on literature than anything else. That although it was not the *Times* masthead, selling books was not only no great psychological departure for her, but was something she might actually enjoy while she trawled the miserable wasteland of print publishing for any elusive journalism openings. 'Not only has Josh not entered a physical bookshop since he got his Kindle a few years ago,' she added, disconsolately, 'but he said he thinks they're now 'pointless'. He said it was a meaningless distraction.'

'Well, I have to say that doesn't surprise me,' Esther shrugged. 'I would have thought that underneath it all, Josh actually quite liked the idea of you turning into a nice little *baleboste*.'

Natasha glanced at her grandmother as they crossed Hudson Street. Out of nowhere, she'd been reminded of something Esther had asked of that journalist at the event a few weeks ago. *Have you ever done anything truly mad for love?*

She doubted her little performance earlier in the week counted.

★ ★ ★

It had been a long shot, but after the way Josh had been behaving recently, she'd been willing to give anything a go. The belief that every woe the universe might throw at a person could be solved with a home-cooked meal was not one she shared with her mother. But Josh was always teasing her about her skills in the kitchen and idly wondering why she'd never learned to cook like her mom. And he liked lasagna, which she remembered learning in a middle school Home Ec class, years ago. And so, having extracted a promise that he'd be home in time for dinner, Natasha — who, as the old Manhattan cliché went, was more likely to store her shoes in her oven than cook food in it — had swallowed her pride and sense of irony and called her mother. On the phone from the staff-room at the high school where she taught history, Ros had patiently talked her through the recipe, step-by-step. It hadn't even turned out too bad. But as the evening minutes, and then hours, had steadily ticked past, with no word from her boyfriend other than a text to apologise for being held up in the office, she'd finally collapsed on the couch and called her best friend Gretchen with a creeping sense of panic. 'So I feel like I'm in a corny fifties movie,' she'd admitted, 'where little wifey prepares herself all day for her husband to get home and meanwhile on a split screen we see husband drinking Scotch in a bar with his buddies and it gets later and later and all the while she is sitting at home and the food is going cold and she is getting slowly more and more wasted and hysterical and eventually she throws the dinner in the trash. Or against the wall. Or something.'

Natasha had just about restrained herself from chucking the lasagna at the wall that night, even after polishing off the best part of a bottle of red on her own. But she had felt the knot of anxiety that was already firmly lodged in her gut tighten. And the realization, when it came, was bleak: that what was bothering her was not that they weren't discussing the wedding tasks that were stacking up, or even that they weren't discussing *anything* much at the moment. The fear was far more elemental: a fear that perhaps Josh might be having second thoughts about this marriage. And about what that might *mean*. For him, for her, for them both.

'So anyway,' she said now, conscious she was yet again shoving that particular dread to the back of her mind as she steered her grandmother down West 10th Street. 'Mom mentioned you'd had some more interview requests recently. She said something about a neuroscientist?'

'Mmm.' Esther nodded vaguely. 'A scientist from Sweden, maybe, or Switzerland, I forget. She's examining 'neural networks' and something to do with how the brain generates hope to overcome traumatic events. I think that's what she said. It all sounds fascinating, but I told her I wasn't sure I would be very useful to her.'

Natasha rolled her eyes. 'Oh, *Bubbe*. You'd be perfect for that kind of thing. And what about the others?'

'There was an academic based somewhere in the UK. Nottingham? At the Shoah centre there. And a screenwriter from Iowa who wanted to talk about doing a screenplay.'

'And . . . ?'

'I told him I didn't think I'd be able to help.'

'But why?'

They had just arrived at the centre. Natasha could see her grandmother reaching

110

for the usual line she employed whenever this subject came up.

'There are so many people whose stories deserve to be told more than mine. And I've talked to enough strangers about what happened in my life, I don't need to do it on a formal basis.'

Natasha opened her mouth to protest, then closed it again; she knew it was not worth arguing with her. On this, as on anything.

But as she followed her grandmother through the door, the first shape of an idea was declaring itself to her. Now was not the moment, but she resolved to give it some more thought.

★ ★ ★

The man at the door was holding out his hand, and for one fleeting, crazy instant Natasha had the sensation that she already knew him.

'Hello,' he said.

'Hello.' She shook it.

'I'm Rafi.'

He smiled at her, and she thought perhaps she'd never seen a face like it. Which was strange, because she also felt she somehow recognized it. 'I'm the architect.'

She'd been expecting, she didn't know

111

why, some old guy with white hair and professorial spectacles. This lovely-looking man looked about thirty, her own age. He was, in fact, wearing spectacles, with thick black rims, but also sneakers and a plaid shirt. His face was open and inquisitive, like a child's.

'I'm Natasha.'

Rafi still had her hand in his. The fingers, she noticed, were peculiarly long; those of a concert pianist, she might have said. Glancing back up, she found him looking directly at her, a curious expression on his face.

'Oh *good*, you've met Tash already.' Esther had arrived behind them. 'You must be Rafi?' Beaming at him, she held out her own hand and, after what felt like an infinitesimal beat, he released Natasha's and shook Esther's. As she heard them greet each other, Natasha found herself doing something very odd: helplessly looking down at the hand he had just been holding.

'So please come into my office,' Esther was saying. 'Our delightful intern Emily will make us some tea and we can talk. Then we'll give you the grand tour.'

As Rafi followed Esther, Natasha hung back momentarily, weirdly shaken. She told Esther she'd make the tea, not to bother Emily, and fled to the kitchen.

When she returned a short while later, bearing a tray, three mugs and a plate of cookies, she discovered Esther and Rafi already deep in conversation about the projects he'd recently been working on. He'd pulled out a portfolio from the brown leather bag at his feet and was showing Esther some drawings, photographs, renderings. Esther meanwhile was busy doing her Esther thing: asking questions and efficiently extracting biographical details. Where had he studied? What was he interested in? What drove him? Rafi was telling her that, having studied architecture here in New York at Cooper Union, he'd been back in the city for about a year. Between qualifying and now, he'd been working on post-Katrina reconstruction in New Orleans, and had also lived in Portland, Oregon for a couple of years building some kind of environmentally sustainable housing project.

'Is that this one?' Esther enquired, pointing at a photograph. 'Oh no, silly me. That doesn't look like Oregon.'

'No . . . Uh, that one's sort of . . . Well, that's sort of my passion project,' Rafi admitted, as if suddenly shy.

'What is it?'

'A social housing development. In the Middle East.'

Esther peered more closely at the page. 'How interesting. Whereabouts in the Middle East?'

'Jerusalem.'

'Really?' Natasha was struck by the coincidence. 'Our uncle lives in Jerusalem. We go there all the time.'

'Are you *from* Jerusalem, Rafi?'

He ran a hand through his curly black hair and laughed. 'Me? Oh. No. I'm from Michigan.'

Esther inclined her head. *'Michigan?'*

'Yeah . . . Sorry about that. I was born in Dearborn. Near Detroit.'

'And where do you live now?'

'Greenpoint.'

Esther nodded, her eyes narrowing ever so slightly, and Natasha, surprised that her usually ultra-diplomatic grandmother was allowing her natural curiosity to make it sound as if he was failing some geography test, jumped in stupidly. 'I *love* Greenpoint. There's that fantastic Polish piano bar . . . ?'

Rafi looked up at her. He had the most remarkable-coloured eyes, she noticed. A pale, pale blue-green, iridescent against that olive skin. And again, here was that overwhelming sensation that she recognized him from somewhere.

'Finest establishment in town,' he cracked,

before turning back to Esther. 'So what about you, Esther? I know you're not from New York.'

She shook her head. 'Originally, way back in the mists of time, I'm from a little town in Galicia. Zholkva. Do you know where that is?'

'Poland, right?'

'Well, my town actually became part of the Ukraine. But I very much consider New York my city. It was my greatest fate that I washed up here after the war. I do truly believe this city saved my life.'

Rafi was now leaning forward. His look was one of mild enchantment, Natasha thought. So far, so Esther.

'You know, my father once said something similar to me,' he said. 'Admittedly, it was about America in general; nobody ever thought *Dearborn* saved their life. But it made me think. About how much I was taking it for granted, being born in a particular place at a particular time. When it's so much about chance, or fate, like you say.'

'Well, indeed.' Esther nodded. 'In my life, at least, geography has always been destiny.'

Rafi smiled. 'I remember hearing you say something like that a long time ago.' At Esther's surprised look, he held up his hands. 'Okay. In the interests of full disclosure here, a little disclaimer from me. When this pitch came to us at the co-op, I really pushed for it. I felt so strongly we should do it.'

Esther seemed intrigued. 'Why did you feel that, Rafi?'

'I think I first heard you speak, I don't know, maybe eight years ago, while I was at Cooper. You were talking at the 92nd Street Y on a panel with Edward Said? And then I started reading about what happened to you and . . . Well, I've always been fascinated. I just thought I should mention that before we get started, you know, get the fan-boy stuff out the way.'

Esther, clearly delighted, gave him an outrageously flirtatious smile. '*Well*, that's very kind of you indeed.' She patted the portfolio. 'You certainly seem like the ideal man for the job. And we are thrilled to have you on board. We would love for you to start as soon as you can. Did you get the plans from the structural engineer, everything you need?'

'I think so.' He nodded. 'Now I'm just itching to see the space.'

'Well, I'm afraid I exerted myself a little too much with our walk over here, so you'll have to excuse me. Natasha will give you the tour. Did I mention she's my granddaughter? She's been helping me out here for almost her entire life. We couldn't do *any* of this without her. So you're in very good hands.'

Rafi glanced up. 'I have no doubt,' he said, after a beat.

★ ★ ★

Outside Esther's office, Natasha found herself standing next to this tall beautiful person in a sort of dazed trance.

'This has been bugging me since I arrived,' he was saying. 'But I *finally* got it. We've met before.'

'We have?'

'In the elevator, in the *New York Times* building. A month ago or so. The one that got stuck?'

Of *course*! Jewfro guy. He'd had a haircut, although the curls were still pretty mad. And the glasses . . . He had not been wearing glasses before, she was pretty certain.

'How crazy is that?' He was grinning. 'Don't you love it when life does stuff like this?'

'That *is* pretty crazy,' she agreed. 'Of all the architects in New York City . . . '

'Of all the elevators! So you work here every day?' he wondered as she led him through the centre to the recreation room, or rather, the new 'West Street Community Music Room and Library', which now

117

contained Leo Zimmer's grand if battered old
Steinway. The soup kitchen hours were over
and there weren't too many people around:
just a handful aged between what seemed like
fifteen and one hundred and fifteen. Reading;
talking — to themselves or to each other;
playing card games and Scrabble; using the
computers; hanging out. 'Seems like a pretty
cool place.'

'It is. But no, Esther was wildly exaggerat-
ing before. She has a tendency to do that, as
you'll discover.'

'So what do you do, Natasha?' he asked, as
they carried on past the counselling room, the
LBGT youth clinic, the kitchens.

'I — uh. I work at a bookstore. Or rather,
I'm about to start working at a bookstore.'

He looked mildly surprised. 'Oh. Nice.
Which bookst — '

'Until a few weeks ago, I used to work at
the *Times*,' she blurted.

He paused. 'Ah. Okay.'

'That morning, in the elevator, I had just
been fired.'

His eyes widened. 'Jesus. No wonder you
were having a bad day. You know, if it doesn't
sound too creepy, I was actually a little worried about you. I was *this* close to asking if
you wanted to go for coffee, just to try and
cheer you up.'

'That does sound a little creepy.' She couldn't help but smile. 'Well, I would have been spectacular company.'

'Yeah. Or I might have decided you were such a loser that I didn't want to work on your grandmother's awesome project.'

At that moment they were interrupted by two eager-looking interns, who had bounded over to introduce themselves. Emily and Ned had been assigned, they said, by the NYC Coalition against Hunger to assist with the West Street computing, financial systems and day-to-day administration. 'We help out with things like deliveries, grants and application filing, food stamp advisory, volunteer co-ordination, liaising with the NYC Department of Homeless Services, things like that,' Ned informed them earnestly. 'We also oversee things like the Tumblr, Twitter, fund-raising stuff.'

'And really anything Esther needs,' Emily added. 'She is such an inspiration.'

'Yikes,' Rafi said, when they had disappeared back to their work. 'I thought *I* was a do-gooder.'

'Trust me,' Natasha shook her head. 'You will never, ever compete with the shiny-eyed paragons of virtue that flow through these doors. May as well just get over that now. Do you want to see next door?'

They headed out onto the street. With the honking bustle of the West Side Highway at their back, Rafi pulled a camera from his satchel and began snapping the exterior of the adjoining building. 'So Esther wants to integrate the two buildings, create more rooms, a sleeping area, another kitchen, a new shower block. That right?'

'Yeah.'

'And this is about more than just doing something straightforward and functional?' he said as they entered the building: an enormous open shell with the dead plumbing of what had once been numerous industrial washing machines and dryers sprouting out of the walls.

'What do you mean?'

He ran a hand through his curls. 'Well, to be perfectly straight with you, Natasha, most contractors could probably figure out how to put up the walls in the right places and create the internal spaces she's after without too much difficulty. But what really fascinated me about the pitch was the bigger vision behind the centre . . . ' He turned to her. 'This is the one place that some of these people can rely upon, right? The place in the city they might come to shower, get a meal, get some help?'

'Yeah. Read a book, if they can read. Get

online. Eat. Or just, you know, talk to other people. A lot of the folk who come here are just perilously lonely. They come for the company and the camaraderie.'

'In which case, all the more responsibility to make the space as beautiful as we can.'

She stared at him. 'Right . . . I guess there's a fine line between what makes something a building and what makes it architecture.'

Rafi raised an eyebrow. 'No kidding.'

Natasha leaned against the door as Rafi headed into the space, trying and failing not to watch him too closely. Soon he was reaching into the back pocket of his jeans for a notebook and pencil: sketching here, photographing there; his eye seemingly caught by things she would never have seen. Rafi was left-handed, she noticed, and humming lightly to himself. He was crazy tall and expressive and animated, and he seemed to be paying attention to everything. In Esther's office earlier he had mentioned that, as the youngest partner at the Jay Street architecture co-op, this was the first project he would be leading himself. But his grasp of what Esther envisaged for her beloved West Street community seemed intuitive.

She couldn't help it: she was charmed.

After a while, Rafi bounded back over to her, chattering about something to do with the details of the cast-iron frame, and about the amazing flexibility of these reclaimed spaces. 'That's why they've attracted such imaginative re-use across the city,' he said, and she nodded enthusiastically, conscious that she was already anxious for his approval. Even though most of what Rafi had just said had gone way over her head. Even though she'd known this person but a single hour.

A *single hour*, she reminded herself as they walked back into the main building to find Esther. *Get a grip*.

9

'It's all right for *you*, ring girl,' her best friend Gretchen was muttering as she dabbed under her eyes with a tissue. 'But remember: some of us are trying to get laid tonight.'

'Oh, we *are*?' Natasha smirked. 'Who's the lucky guy?'

They'd headed directly to the ladies' room after the wedding speeches. Steve, one of their great friends from college, and his new husband Mike had just made a wonderful double speech that somehow managed to be passionate but political, personal but universal, hilarious but poignant; even Gretchen — who generally refused to succumb to the public histrionics they'd become accustomed to at these weddings — had shed a tear and was now attempting to fix her smudged eye make-up in front of the restroom mirror.

'Duh! It's a Harvard wedding! Who d'you think?'

Natasha snorted. 'Silly me. Well, it's fair to say I don't think Master Patrick Nathaniel Cornelius Vanderbilt Junior the Third or whatever he is gives a shit about your eyeliner, G.'

Gretchen and their friend Patrick had had some sort of unfeasibly efficient friends-with-benefits deal going on since they'd left college, almost a decade ago. An unspoken contract whose terms they'd both agreed upon: namely that whenever they were both single, both at a wedding, say, or both in the same Hamptons house over the Fourth of July weekend, the deal was on. If they felt like it. And there was zero pressure or awkwardness when it wasn't. Natasha was amazed they could make this unlikely arrangement work. This year, the ultimate when it came to peer weddings, Gretch and Patrick had probably hooked up more weekends than they hadn't. On the Jitney home from a celebration in Montauk at some point over the summer, Natasha had asked her why they didn't just, heck, do something radical like go on a proper date. Gretchen had looked horrified. 'Are you fucking *crazy*? Me go out with that prepster hedge-funder? No way, José. What the hell would we have to talk about?' And, sure enough, back in the city, Gretchen and Patrick would kiss each other sweetly goodbye like the fond old friends they were, then assiduously avoid each other's tribes until the next wedding rolled around.

'Still, one has standards to uphold.' Finished with her eyes and looking flawless once again, Gretchen pulled out a red lipstick, applied it expertly and gave a pout.

Natasha sighed at her own reflection, which was all puffy eyes and blotchy skin. The tears for her had started even before the speeches. It had been easy enough to pass off her heightened state as too much champagne downed too quickly and too much emotion. This, after all, was the first Big Gay Wedding amongst their crowd, and hundreds of their old college friends had descended upon Mike's parents' place in East Rock, New Haven, adding the specific tang of university nostalgia and vintage friendship to the general high pitch of the occasion.

But the truth was that Natasha had had a wretched morning. Last week, in what she'd thought was a stroke of logistical genius, she had arranged with Deborah Liebowitz — who'd been kvetching to her endlessly via email and voicemail that she and David hadn't seen them for *so long* — that they'd stop for brunch with Josh's parents in Greenwich en route to East Rock. Josh had looked exasperated when she'd told him, saying he'd already arranged to have brunch in New Haven with his boys; Mike being a friend of Josh's from Yale. He'd relented, but had been in a tense, phone-checking and generally uncompromising mood throughout brunch at his parents', during which conversation had revolved almost entirely around Josh and Tash's wedding. With David Liebowitz caring as little as his son did about table-linen choices, flower arrangements and guest lists, that had left Natasha mostly fending off Deb's formidable barrage of questions and suggestions. And then, when Josh had been in the kitchen with his mother, helping to bring out dessert, something shocking had happened. Natasha and David, seated opposite each other and making small talk, had fallen mute when they heard Josh yelling at Deborah to 'stop fucking interfering' and to 'leave me the fuck alone, just for once in your life'. Deb had burst into tears and run upstairs, which had provoked a furious rebuke from David and led to Josh walking out and slamming the front door. Walking out!

In the car as they continued east, Natasha had challenged him about his irrational and uncharacteristic behaviour. And Josh had thumped the steering wheel with his fist, saying he'd just had it up to here with his mother's meddling in his life. At one point he'd looked so upset she thought he might be about to cry, which was unthinkable — Josh never cried. And he had not. But eventually, after a long, tense silence, he'd apologized for being so difficult lately, and blamed the stress of this Brazilian telecoms deal, for which he'd been working absolutely insane hours, even for him. For one mad moment Natasha wondered if perhaps Josh was about to lose his job too — she could not think of anything else that would make him so anxious. At the Yale Club, where they were staying, Josh had remained in such a gloomy and impenetrable state that Natasha had abandoned trying to get him to talk to her, and had opted for a different tack. Wrapped in her towel after her shower, she had tried to kiss him and lead him over to the bed, hoping that might help. A disturbing thought had flashed through her mind: *how has it got to this, that I am trying and failing to lure my fiancé into bed?* They might have other issues to wrinkle out before the wedding, but they'd never had problems when it came to *that*; at least, not until the past few weeks. But Josh had given her a sexless little kiss on her forehead and murmured: 'Not now, baby. Sorry.' As he had pulled on his tux and dashed out to join the boys, who were kicking things off with beers and shots over at Mory's, she had felt an equally disquieting relief that he was gone — that she hadn't had to go through with it.

★ ★ ★

127

In the ladies' room now, there was the sound of a toilet flushing. A woman of around their age emerged from one of the stalls, looking a little unbalanced. Taking a free spot next to Natasha before the mirrors, she pulled some tipsy faces at herself, mussed up her hair, peered a little more closely at her reflection, then wrinkled her nose. Eventually she opened her purse and fished around for something that was clearly eluding her; then, catching Natasha's eye, asked if she had a hairbrush. Natasha handed her the comb she'd just borrowed from Gretchen's clutch.

The woman, focusing her slightly blurred eyes on her, said, '*Waaaaait*. You're Josh's fiancée, right?'

'Yes, that's right.' Natasha didn't recognize her. 'Sorry, I don't think we've . . . '

'We were all just talking at our table about how *amazingly* cool you're being about the fact Kristen's here. And that she's back living in New York. I would be fuh-*lipping* out! Still, I guess you're the one with the ring on your finger — *ohmigod*, it's so pretty, by the way! Can I see?'

Natasha stared uncomprehendingly at her. 'Sorry, uh, have we met?'

'Oh, hi! I'm Heather.' She held out her hand. 'I went to Yale with Josh and Kristen.'

'Josh and Kristen?'

128

'Kristen Polley?' The woman began to look confused. Then a hand flew up to her mouth. 'Oh. Shit. Shitshitshit. Sorry, ignore me, I'm like, wasted. It's *none* of my business.'

Abruptly handing back the comb, she turned and fled.

Gretchen raised an eyebrow. 'What was that all about?'

Natasha frowned, clueless. 'I have no idea.'

'Who the fuck is Kristen Policy?'

The realization, when it came, floored her. *Kristen?*

Josh had only told her once about his long-term college girlfriend. Just once, years ago, right at the beginning. Natasha had been in that new-boyfriend phase where she wanted to know *everything* about him, and one afternoon in his old apartment in Murray Hill, long before they'd moved in to Kenmare Street together, she'd discovered, to her glee, his Yale yearbook. There had been a picture inside of Josh and a blonde girl, arms wrapped around each other, looking irritatingly radiant and not unlike something out of an Abercrombie ad — him so tall and dark, her so petite and fair — under the banner 'Most Likely to Get Hitched'. When she'd teasingly questioned him about it, he'd been snappish. 'Well, they clearly got it wrong, didn't they?' When she'd pressed further, he'd

129

told her they'd split up more than three years ago, that she lived in California and was married with a kid. That there was nothing else to say, really nothing else to say, about Kristen Polley. That she should just drop it.

Which she had. And neither of them had ever mentioned her again. That name had not been heard since.

Racing breathlessly upstairs now, Gretchen a source of calming reason at her heels — 'it's probably just a coincidence, it may not mean anything' — she rushed over to the elaborate table plan that was set up on easels outside the dining area. There was no Kristen Polley listed, which sent a jolt of relief through Natasha until she saw that there were, however, two *other* Kristens placed elsewhere on the vast guest list. Had she taken her husband's name? Natasha tried to recall what the girl hanging off Josh in the photo had looked like. Had Heather been mistaken? Was this all just a coincidence? Where even *was* Josh?

She located his best friend Eddie Strauss doing his trademark crazy dance to 'Jump Around'. Ditching Gretchen, she strode across the ballroom and snatched Eddie's arm, throwing a brisk apology over her shoulder to the girl he'd been twirling. Then she hauled him off the glitterballed parquet.

'Hey, gorgeous!' Eddie exclaimed, grinning in a way that to Natasha in this state looked suspiciously like over-compensation. Come to think about it, Eddie, one of *her* friends too — the mutual friend who'd introduced her and Josh — had been unusually distant today; he'd barely said hello at the champagne reception earlier, and she'd thought something about his manner was a little off. Now he tried drunkenly to spin her around in one of his moves. 'What's up? Super wedding, huh?'

'Ed, where's Josh?'

Eddie looked around with exaggerated focus. 'Uh . . . I don't know. Haven't seen the J-man for a while. Maybe he's in the other room?'

There was a 'chill-out' room next door, with soft furnishings, tables of cupcakes and a string quartet playing Mozart.

Unlikely.

Natasha, with a strength she truly did not feel, took her old friend by his shoulders and forced him to meet her eye. 'Eddie. Tell me something. Is Josh's old girlfriend Kristen here?'

Something darted across Eddie's boyish face, Natasha was sure of it. He flushed, his bright blue eyes fluid and unfocused. 'Uh, what?'

Natasha swallowed, forced herself to try and stay calm.

'Kristen Polley, is it? Josh's girlfriend from Yale? The one that broke his heart when she went to California?'

Eddie attempted to look surprised. He was pretty guileless at the best of times, Ed. And having been drinking solidly since lunchtime, this was not the best of times. 'Uh . . . look, I don't know, Tash. Maybe. I guess she was a good friend of Mike's back in the day, when we were all at college, so . . . '

'Is she *here*?'

'Uh . . . '

Tash closed her eyes. 'Eddie, Eddie, Eddie, please don't do this to me. I know Josh is your best friend, but how long have you and I known each other? *Please*. I just need to know if she's here.'

Eddie shrugged imperceptibly, almost a nod. Natasha felt a swoosh of nausea. As the DJ dropped 'Don't Stop Believing' and the crowd on the dance floor burst into ironic cheers, she struggled on. 'Did you know she was back living in New York? Did *Josh* know she was back in New York?'

Eddie's face was turning a deeper pink by the moment. He looked even sicker than she felt. 'Tash, I really don't know what you're trying to — '

132

'Jesus, Ed, do you ever sound slippery right now!' she cried. '*Did* he know?'

'Tash, sweetheart, this is not a conversation you should be having with me. I — '

'He did!' she gasped. 'He knew she was back in New York. Why didn't he tell me?'

Eddie's face fell. 'I don't know. I guess he didn't feel it was . . . necessary. Or appropriate, or relevant, or something.'

'Has he *seen* her?' she choked. 'Has he seen her before today?'

'I honestly don't know.'

Natasha paused, drew as deep a breath as she could manage. 'Ed, I love you, okay, but you *can't* lie to me. Not about this. Because Josh has been behaving *really* fucking strangely the past few weeks and I just need to know. *Had he seen Kristen Polley before tonight?*'

Eddie bowed his head. He hesitated, and then half whispered: 'Yes.'

She gave a keening little cry.

'But not intentionally!' Eddie clarified. 'I swear, Tash, he literally just walked into her one day on the street.'

'When?' Her bottom lip was trembling.

'I dunno, I think about — a month ago? Three weeks?'

The quick calculation in her head flayed her. 'And . . . since?' she croaked.

'I don't know.'

'I mean, has he been *seeing* her, Ed?' The room appeared to be deliquescing in front of her eyes. They dropped silently onto two decorated white chairs at a nearby table strewn with wedding detritus: favours and flowers and half-eaten desserts; abandoned lipstick-stained wine glasses, glittered clutch bags, cashmere shawls.

Eddie looked dismal and deflated. 'I think maybe they went for a drink a couple of weeks ago. But please, Tash, you have to try and talk about this with Josh.' He cast his eyes around desperately.

'They went for a drink.' She said the words slowly, as if testing them out. Artifacts from a foreign or ancient language, she understood them both too well and not at all. Josh and Kristen went for a drink. When, when, when? And why hadn't he mentioned it?

'Yes.'

'And he didn't think to tell me?'

'I think he thought . . . I think he thought maybe you wouldn't understand.'

'Understand?'

'Why he needed to see her.'

'Needed?'

'Well, exactly.'

'Wait, this is *my* fault now? He had to lie to me about seeing his ex-girlfriend because of what *my* reaction would be?'

'No, of course not! Listen, I don't know, Tash. It was a private thing that Josh just felt he had to do. There was a lot of history there, and . . . ' Eddie was taking her hands. 'Oh, Tash, honey, this really sucks. I'm so sorry. Do you want me to come find him with you?'

But right at that moment, Gretch appeared at the table. It briefly occurred to Natasha, in a different part of her brain, that she had never seen her friend look so grave. 'Tasha, sweetheart. You need to come with me.' She held out a hand. 'Now . . . '

10

November

A wand of dazzling winter sunlight was slicing through the studio windows as she awoke to an unlikely sensation.

'Ohhhh. *Jackson*,' she groaned, quickly squeezing her eyes back shut. Groping blindly for the overaffectionate pug that was industriously licking her face, she shoved him unceremoniously away. 'Come *on*, dude.'

Jackson, hurt and unimpressed, jumped off the makeshift futon with a grudging snuffle and went to join his sister Zelda, who was snoring noisily and contentedly in the studio kitty-corner.

'Gretch?' Natasha yelled groggily, her eyes still closed. 'You awake?'

After a moment there came a low, slow bellow from behind the decorative screen that marked off Gretchen's sleeping area.

'You *alive?*' Natasha struggled to her elbows and half opened her eyes again. 'What *happened?*'

They'd been at a perfectly civilized dinner last night with some friends in the East

Village when at some point, triggered by yet more talk of marriages and babies and the cost of two-bed condos in Cobble Hill, she had turned to Gretchen, raised her glass and said: '*Fuck this*. I've had enough. Let us boldly and wholeheartedly lay waste to probity.' They'd ended up throwing down dollar bills and lame excuses and skipping out of the restaurant before dessert; and, in a throwback to the years they'd lived together when Natasha had first moved back to New York, had tripped downtown to the Canal Rooms '80s dance party. After which they had taxied back to Brooklyn and ended up drinking rye and talking shit to two old Polish codgers at a Greenpoint dive before finally rolling into Gretchen's Wythe Avenue studio at an unholy hour that Natasha did not particularly want to think about.

'*Man*.' Gretchen appeared from behind the screen. 'Guess we really needed to let our hair down, huh?'

She wandered over to kiss Natasha good morning, and then, ignoring the frantically overexcited pugs, headed to the kitchen area, where she pulled a brown paper package from the freezer, tipped coffee beans into the grinder and switched on the machine.

'Agg! You're *grinding* coffee? Now? Really?'

Gretchen raised an eyebrow. 'Welcome

back to Williamsburg, my friend,' she proclaimed over the racket. 'You and I may be the most ancient people in the neighbourhood by at least a decade, but old clichés die hard. Besides, this coffee might just be your salvation.'

Shutting her eyes again, a second later Natasha shot upright in panic. 'Wait . . . what time is it?'

Gretchen checked the clock on the stove. 'Uh . . . quarter of eleven?'

'Oh fuck. *Fuck!* I promised Esther I'd be at West Street by ten thirty! Raf's doing his model showing for everyone. I gotta run. Can I borrow some clean underwear?' Natasha had been sleeping in her old bedroom in 83rd Street since Mike and Steve's wedding; she had not been intending to end up in Williamsburg last night. She threw on the underwear Gretchen offered her, and last night's clothes, then splashed some water on her face from the faucet before taking a quick scalding slurp of the coffee that Gretchen was now holding out with a curious expression on her face.

'I'll call you later!' she yelled as she raced down the stairs, two at a time.

* * *

It was pouring outside. The driver took Williamsburg Bridge, logically enough. Beyond the greasy glass of the cab window, Manhattan wavered in the rain. And as they wove through the Sunday-morning-empty streets of the Lower East Side and then Nolita, the streets of her and Josh's neighbourhood, Natasha was assailed by a small grey sorrow. Last night with Gretch had been fun. And the past few weeks had been better: despite the wretchedness of sleeping in her childhood bed and the nightly 3am regrets, she was keeping busy at the bookstore and busy at West Street; she was surviving. After the tumult of the past couple of months, she even felt like she might just about be getting her life back together.

But now as they turned off Delancey onto the Bowery, they were held at traffic lights right outside the café where she and Josh had last seen each other. And the sight of the place where she had said goodbye to the man she had thought she was going to marry, the life she thought she was going to live, undid her all over again.

And she thought: *who are you kidding?*

It had been one of the hardest conversations she'd ever had. For a week, after busting him and Kristen at the wedding, she had flat-out refused to talk to him. And then, after days of soul-searching, of walking around New York replaying the kiss on a loop in her mind, she had finally called him and said she was ready to talk.

Josh, when they met, was all contrition and sadness: he'd looked wrecked, as though he too had not slept all week.

'I saw what was happening between you,' she'd said, right off the bat. Being here was painful enough; there hadn't seemed any point in ducking what had become so devastatingly obvious to her: that Josh's emotional reticence, so long known and worried about, was not in fact a deficiency in his personality but proof of a raging conflict in his heart. He was in love with somebody else.

But he'd chosen to take the statement at face value; as though he had believed she was talking about the kiss. 'Tash. I don't know what to say. I'm so sorry. It was just a kiss, we never slept together, it had never happened bef — '

'It's not about the kiss, Josh. It's what I saw *between* you.'

'What do you mean?'

'You know what I mean.'

He'd hesitated. 'I don't know what you mean.'

Natasha had sat, silently, and waited.

'I don't know what anything means,' he'd admitted. 'Listen. I used to be with Kris a long, long time ago. And there she was, at Mike's wedding, and she was crying, and we meant a lot to each other, and I guess maybe, maybe she hadn't got over it, and — '

'And you hadn't got over it.'

'Tash, I'm so sorry. I don't know what was going on in my mind that night. I just lost it.'

'It's not the kiss, Josh, like I said. It's not the kiss, or even that you thought it was a reasonable thing to do, to make out with your ex-girlfriend when your fiancée was downstairs — '

'Of course I didn't think that was a reasonable thing to do!'

'It's *none of those things*. It's the way you were with her, just simply in that moment. It was so clear to me. As soon as I walked into that room. Because I knew that you've never been like that with me. That we have never been like that.'

Natasha had started to cry. Josh had run his hands through his hair, more grim-faced than she had ever seen him. She'd blown her nose with a Kleenex and tried to regain her composure, but the tears had kept coming and finally she had just talked through them, not even caring about making a scene.

141

'I'm not even angry,' she'd told him. 'I don't know why, but it's true, I'm not even angry. I am just trying to understand what it means. I have thought about nothing else all week, and I think I'm seeing things a bit more clearly now. I saw how you feel about *her*, and I know that it's not the same as how you feel about me. It's not. And maybe that's all that matters.'

'But what does that even mean?' Josh had shaken his head. 'How do we *know* what really matters, what matters most?' He'd taken her hand across the table, and held it, and she had let him. 'Please, Tash. Kristen broke my heart, I admit it. And it took me a long time to get over it. But you were the first woman who made me feel okay again after all that. You woke me up, Tash, you did, and I fell in love with you. I did. I wanted to be with you. I wanted to be with you all the time. You made my life so much better, and you're so lovely, and I thought I knew. I thought I could live like this, with you, always, and that we could be happy.'

'But then Kristen came back.'

'She did.' He'd closed his eyes, and when he spoke, his voice had been so small and sad. 'You know, the thing I most hated Kris for was shattering our world, our future, for ruining what might have been. And if I've done that to you, I will never forgive myself for it. Because I do love you, Tash. And I never wanted to hurt you, I swear, and I am so fucking sorry. I love you. You have to know that.'

'I do know,' she'd whispered. 'And I love you too. We wouldn't have got this far if we didn't love each other.' She'd drawn a deep breath, and they'd sat in silence for a while. 'Josh. It's just that I think this is the moment when our eighty-year-old selves would look back in our lives and say: there, *there it was. That was it.* That was when we knew. And that was when we should have been honest with ourselves.' Unthinkingly, Natasha had removed the diamond from her finger. She hadn't meant it to be a moment of great theatre, but it had seemed impossible to keep wearing it. This was over. She knew. Josh had looked appalled; the ring had sat gleaming on the dull wooden table between them. 'So we must be honest with ourselves. Deep down, you know this. We have never loved each other like *that*. That's a different kind of love. A different kind of love.'

★ ★ ★

In the cab in the rain now, Natasha wiped condensation from the inside of the window

143

with the edge of her sleeve and watched her city, strewn with remembered kisses, go past. For the past few weeks a memory had been nibbling at her consciousness without ever quite coming into focus. Out of nowhere she now recalled the scene clearly, and with it came the understanding that it was the thing that had given her the strength to say those things to Josh. The memory was of her and her sister, maybe fifteen years ago, holding on to each other at Yad Vashem, tear-streaked and in pieces after reading — and properly understanding — their grandmother's love letter for the first time. *Let's promise each other this, always,* they had vowed urgently to each other in Jerusalem that afternoon. *That we will fight for that kind of love in our own lives. It would be a betrayal of everything Grandma lost if we don't. So we must. We must.*

You must, she reminded her thirty-year-old self. *You must. You are.*

★ ★ ★

When Natasha arrived at the centre, hung-over and inexcusably late, she still felt a little hollowed and haunted by the cab journey. Her head continued to hammer with last night's excesses and she had the thought that if she didn't eat something right now, she might throw up. Through the window, she could see Esther, Jorge, Valentina, Rafi and Rachel seated around a makeshift table in the new part of the building. Raf's laptop was open, surrounded by renderings, and the large 3-D model. Some momentary impulse made Natasha stop and hang back in the rain for a moment. It looked like Raf had just cracked a joke, as everyone was laughing. Rachel leaned over to strike him playfully on the arm and Natasha recoiled instinctively, as if she herself had been struck. On top of this morning's layered melancholy she felt an old, old ache settle. Her sister and her easy interactions with beautiful men. And, no shit: from the expression on his face, Rafi Haroun seemed to be just the latest in a long, long line of males to be smitten by Rachel. *Well, good luck to you*, she thought, uncharitably.

As soon as she joined everybody at the table, though, Natasha's mood shifted. What Raf had dreamed up for the extension was magical. His model was a miniature universe of wit and caprice; even at this scale, you could see the imagination at work behind his approach to space and form — the restrained romance, the poetry. Nothing was uniform, nothing monotonous. The other day, she'd bumped into Raf here at lunchtime and they'd gone to grab a sandwich across the street. She'd asked him why he'd wanted to become an architect and he'd talked about his belief that buildings, and the space they enclose, should try and help us be alive. 'It's a hard thing to put into words,' he'd admitted. 'But I have this crazy sense that a building should enable . . . I don't know . . . the heeding of things. Does that even make sense? I had this professor at Cooper who used to say that a building could create behaviour, like it's complicit somehow. He used to quote Winston Churchill, who supposedly told the British parliament this one time that 'we shape our buildings, and afterwards our buildings shape us'. I had that speech tacked up on my studio wall for the longest time. I just loved that you had this fat old British Prime Minister expressing this profound truth about the nature of architecture to a bunch of politicians who probably couldn't give a shit. I loved that!'

This morning, she was not alone in her admiration; everyone seemed transfixed by Raf today. Even Esther claimed to be speechless. 'I don't know what to say!' she cried, after he had finished showing them his plans. 'It is too beautiful, Rafi, too beautiful. I just do not know what I could possibly say!'

Rachel laughed. 'Jesus.' She turned to Raf.

'It takes something to overwhelm this one. In case you hadn't noticed.'

'That's kind.' Raf was all professionalism as he addressed Rachel, Natasha noticed, eyeing them closely. 'But Esther, you must treat all this as a work-in-progress. Anything you're not happy with, just say the word. I won't be on site once construction begins, and I'm due to head back to the West Coast in a few weeks. But you can call me any time and we can talk things through.'

Esther shook her head. 'I just *love* it,' she said, her voice almost a whisper. 'It's more than I could have dreamed. And trust me, I was already dreaming. *Thank* you, Rafi.'

They wrapped up not long after. Jorge and Valentina had to prepare for the afternoon lunch rush, Rachel had to dash off somewhere and Esther was due at her Sunday-afternoon song club: a group of folks in their seventies, eighties and nineties who met every week in someone's apartment to sit around a piano and sing Sondheim and other Broadway numbers. Esther often swore it was what kept her alive, especially when the many old Yiddish-speakers among them would later start singing the old *shtetl* folk songs of their youth.

Natasha said her goodbyes and walked out onto the street, intending to head directly to a

147

burrito stand and then back up to West 83rd to crash out. It was still raining. Momentarily, Raf joined her at the crosswalk, carrying his satchel.

'Nice weather. Want to get a coffee?'

She hesitated. 'Um, sure.' What she needed was to get out of last night's clothes, take a shower, eat food, and sleep. What she wanted was harder to know. But it was impossible to say no to this boy. And coffee might help.

They wound up in a little place round the corner on West 11th, where a few late-brunching couples were drinking Bloody Mary, eating eggs, reading the paper and looking like every other happily-ever-after couple in this newly cold and heartless city.

'So you were pretty quiet in there,' Raf observed, his face all seriousness as they sat down at a little wooden table by the window and ordered coffee. 'You could have at least *faked* that you liked my plans. Even just a little bit.'

'Shit. Was it that obvious?'

'Or you know, just come right out and say it: Raf, your ideas suck. They're horrible.'

He winked at her. She smiled.

'Your ideas are amazing, Raf, and you know it.'

He waved a hand. 'You don't have to say that, either. I was only kidding. Just wanted to see if you were cool?'

'I'm cool. I had a really late night.'

After a moment it dawned on her, what he was actually getting at. She swallowed. 'Oh . . . right. Did someone tell you what's been going on?'

He looked a little sheepish. 'Well, Rachel may have mentioned something . . . '

She glanced out the window, where her eye was caught by a hot West Village couple, two super-groomed men walking with their designer dog, their designer stroller, their designer umbrellas. Rachel, Rachel, Rachel. She didn't really know what to say.

'Well, hey. Turns out my boyfriend is still in love with his ex. It's not the world's most original tragedy. I expect I'll survive.'

'What a guy.' He played with the menu on the table between them. 'Do you want to talk about it?'

'Not really. It's painful, but it's pretty straightforward. Turns out they should never have broken up. They never stopped loving each other.'

Raf leaned back in his chair. 'But you . . . ' he said. 'That was your life right there. You got caught in the cross-hairs of *their* drama. That doesn't really seem fair.'

As their coffees arrived, she studied him from behind her cup; this curly-haired, turquoise-eyed giant. And caught herself thinking a terrible, terrible thought: *this is a relief*.

Jesus. Yes. That was what she felt: *relief*, that for the first time sitting opposite Rafi Haroun, she no longer needed to worry about the fact she was engaged to someone else. *Are you fucking crazy?* she asked herself. *You have a broken heart and he's clearly in love with your sister. Are you actually insane?*

She drank some coffee. Forced herself to give a parodic shrug. 'So when is life fair?'

He smiled. 'As my mother never tired of telling us when we were kids.'

Natasha heard herself talking. 'I don't think when he told me he loved me that he was lying. I don't even think he *didn't* want to get married to me when he asked. But he didn't love me like he loved her. And she came back. So it's a mess. A wretched, wasteful, all-too-human mess.' She stopped herself. 'Ack. Enough. I'm sorry. Oversharing.'

'Not at all . . . ' Raf exhaled. He took off his glasses and rubbed his eyes. 'Sounds rough. I'm really sorry you've had to go through all this, Tash.'

Without his glasses, the sight up close of Raf's super-naturally blue-green eyes was startling. Natasha often turned her mind back to that afternoon a few months ago, when she'd opened the door to him at West Street and thought: *you! it's you.* Raf's presence continued to have such a weird effect on her. He made her want to come across as more smart and more curious and more interesting and more interested than perhaps she really was, because he seemed so much that way himself. More than that, he made her want to *be* all those things. In a quite profound way — a way that she did not quite trust, because she could not explain it. But looking at him now, it also occurred to her that, in terms of hard facts, she actually knew very little about him. The times they had eaten lunch or got a drink together near the centre they had usually talked about the progress of West Street, or about Esther, or about neutral topics like baseball or politics or the weather or what was on TV or just stuff that was happening in the city. Almost by an unspoken agreement, they had never touched upon anything more personal. She'd never talked to him about Josh until now.

She tried to recover a studied breeziness.

'Thanks, Raf. So what about you? How many girlfriends have you got?'

'In New York?'

She snorted.

'You know I'm gay, right?'

She stared at him. 'Oh — right. No,

actually, I didn't realize. So — '

'I'm kidding, Tash. You should see your face.'

She drew a deep breath and ignored his teasing tone; she did want to know. 'So *are* you in a relationship?'

'Nope. Not right now. My family set the bar pretty high; I look at what my mom and dad have and it feels pretty unachievable.'

She grimaced. 'Boy, do I ever know *that* feeling.'

'How about Rachel?' he asked, a propros, she thought, of nothing. Her heart seemed to slam to the ground. So that *was* what this little coffee was all about. A wave of exhaustion came over her. Exhaustion that yet again she was having to deal with some pretty boy who'd clearly gone gaga over Rach and was now trying to enlist the ugly-duckling older sister as his ally and accomplice. This exact scenario had been visited regularly on her since Rachel hit thirteen and grew breasts. The ancient agonies of Ethan Schlesinger and their high-school prom aside, Natasha had lost count of the number of boys she'd liked at school or even college, only to find they were only using her to get to her hot little sister. *Enough already!* she wanted to scream. *Anyway, she's into girls this year.*

152

So man up and get over it!

'Oh, if I had a buck every time some guy asked me that question . . . ' She cradled her coffee, hoping that had come across as ironic rather than bitter. 'But she's taken. Sorry to report.'

Raf looked mystified. 'No, I was going to ask if you thought she was really happy with Skye. She's quite a character, right?'

Natasha gaped. 'Who, Rach?'

'No, Skye! Well, Rachel too, but no, I meant — '

'Wait. You've met Skye?'

'Yeah, we've all been out in Brooklyn a few times. She's kind of insane, right?'

Natasha felt heat spring to her cheeks. 'Oh, right. Of course.'

You fool, she thought, concentrating furiously on the coffee dregs in her cup and hoping her trembling voice would not betray her astonishment and her hurt that Rachel should have introduced her new girlfriend — her first girlfriend! — to a complete *stranger* before her own sister!

'Uh — I don't really know Skye,' she mumbled. 'But I do know that nobody on this earth knows her own mind like my little sister, so my guess is, if she weren't happy, she'd be out of there quick as a flash.'

'Yeah.' He put down his cup. 'I figured.

Anyway, I did not ask you for coffee to talk about Rachel's love life. Or even yours.'

'So why did you, then?'

'Just wanted to hang out.'

'Well, that's noble of you,' Natasha muttered.

'Don't sweat it.' Draining his coffee, Raf threw down some bills from his wallet and jumped up, grabbing his blue parka and satchel.

Natasha was expecting him to make his excuses and leave, but he seemed to be holding out his hand towards her. 'Come on. I got a plan.'

'What?'

'You ever been to Fat Cat?'

She pulled a face. 'That divey-looking games joint on Christopher?'

'The exact same. There's no heartache that place can't fix, trust me.'

Natasha tried to protest, but allowed herself to be led, five minutes later, down some inauspicious-looking stairs into a sepulchral basement.

And Raf was as good as his word. Over the course of the next few hours, they ended up playing two games of pool, both of which he won easily, despite his best efforts to help her be less disastrous at it; three epic rounds of Scrabble, which Natasha won 2-1; and giant

154

Connect 4, which they decided to leave at a respectable 1-1 tie. Fat Cat was murky and sticky-floored, the pints were cheap and the cracked leather couches had their coils and stuffing seeping out, but by the time she and Raf emerged back into the glowering light of a wintry late-afternoon, Natasha had decided it was her new favourite place in all of New York. Her mood had improved so dramatically, in fact, that she found she didn't even want to go home yet.

'Do you want to catch a movie?' she asked. Then hurriedly said, 'I mean, it's no problem if you have something to get back to. I realize you may have better things to do.'

'Yeah, because it's true: there *are* better things to do than go to the movies on a freezing cold Sunday evening,' Raf nodded, solemnly. 'Taking out the garbage. Doing my laundry. Unsubscribing from email lists. Watching re-runs of *American Idol* Series Seventeen on TV. Do you mind if we take a rain check?'

He went to hug her goodbye, then dummied away at the last minute. 'Of course I want to go see a movie, you crazy girl.' Grinning, he rubbed his hands together. The temperature had dropped whilst they'd been downstairs in the warm, gloomy lair of the Fat Cat and it was cold. He took hers in his, and blew on them, and as he did so it struck Natasha that Raf must be a person for whom any gloom was surmountable. He had an enigmatic intensity to him, certainly, but it was all leavened by wit and laughter. The overall effect, she had to admit, was pretty contagious. 'The question is, though — cheesy blockbuster? Or you want to walk over to the Angelika or Film Forum, see what's on there?'

In the end, they did the former, a quick consultation with Google having thrown up a choice between the latest Apatow or a festival of Arab cinema at the Film Forum, opening this weekend with a documentary about the 2006 Israeli-Lebanon war.

'Hmm, Apatow or Arabs,' Raf said. 'Tough call.'

'I would definitely *like* to see the documentary,' Natasha said; Raf seemed like the kind of person who would also be into that sort of thing, and she didn't want him to think she was totally vapid. 'But maybe just not tonight. I'm not sure I could face the guilt, you know?'

They were still on Christopher, crossing Bleecker.

'The guilt?' he echoed curiously, after a beat.

'Don't you ever get that? How *clearly* Israel

is being disproportionately aggressive and it's so depressing how the reporting is usually so incredibly one-sided, and yet you can never say that because . . . '

She broke off. He was looking at her a little strangely. The lights changed at the crosswalk, but he didn't move.

'Don't you ever feel guilty about that?' she repeated.

'Um, Natasha, I'm not sure if you . . . ' Raf rubbed his hands together again. The tip of his nose was turning pink in the cold. 'Okay, so this is weird . . . You do know I'm not Jewish, right?'

'You're *not*?' she gaped. 'I just always assumed . . . Oh, Christ, that's embarrassing.'

'No, it's not. This is New York City, there are more Jews here than in Tel Aviv.' He smiled. 'Even my *falafel* guy's Jewish.'

'That's because falafel's an Israeli food, duh.'

He let out a squawk of indignation and disbelief as they headed across the intersection towards the movie theatre. 'Oh, Natasha!' He shook his head. 'Natasha, Natasha, Natasha. She looks so smart, and yet: such tragic holes in her knowledge.'

She tried to check the thrill of hearing her name in his mouth. This might be getting dangerous, whatever it was. 'So what *are* you then, genius?' she wondered as they entered the cinema. 'Where are your family from?'

'Oh, here and there,' he said breezily. 'I'm a bit of a hybrid.' They'd joined the popcorn line. 'Much more importantly: sweet or salty?'

'Salty, obviously. I'll go get candy.'

She headed over to the candy section and called over to him, 'Mike and Ike, or Swedish Fish?'

He rolled his eyes. 'Is that even a question? The Fish, Natasha. The Fish. Every time.'

The movie was pretty funny, although at times she'd barely been able to concentrate for the nearness of him. And for wondering what it meant that she could feel so completely comfortable in this person's company; so relaxed; so much herself. She realized she had not thought about Josh and Kristen again all afternoon, ever since they'd arrived at the Fat Cat. That had to be a record.

And now, outside the cinema, Raf was asking how she felt about getting pizza.

'But you just ate seven thousand Swedish Fish! How can you possibly be hungry?'

'Don't you know the rules? You *always* chase high-fructose-corn-syrup fish with pizza, it's like a Jewish thing,' he told her, his eyes laughing. 'I know this great place around the corner on Bleecker.' He took her hand and started walking.

'But we pretty much just ate our body weight in popcorn,' she tried to protest, hurrying to catch up with his long legs.

'Yeah, but it's Jewish pizza. You have to taste it. Come on.'

By the time Raf deposited her on an Uptown 1 train much later, stuffed, her ears ringing with laughter, Natasha felt transformed. How could this be? How could he be? Happiness, she realized as she took an orange plastic seat, had caught her entirely unawares.

At 14th Street, an old woman, dread-headed and in layers of tattered garments of nondescript grey, staggered onto the train hauling three plastic garbage sacks behind her. The carriage filled with the bouquet of special scents she brought with her. And then, to everyone's dismay, she decided to talk to them.

'Ima gonna sing a song,' she announced, at which point little white ear buds or giant black-and-red headphones were quickly found, magazines were pulled from bags, devices attended to. Natasha, curious, sat back and watched the lady as she arranged her bags around her in what seemed to be some kind of careful pattern, stood firm as the train lurched forward, and opened her mouth.

'*I was born by the river* . . . ' she began.

Natasha's skin prickled instantly to goose-bumps. And all around the carriage, eyes were slowly raised, books were abandoned in laps, Kindle and iPad screens were ignored. In the woman's astonishing voice, everything was there. It was all there. Everything.

A current of electric recognition seemed to pass between Natasha and her fellow passengers as strangers caught each other's eyes across the carriage; each seeking confirmation from another: *yes, this jaw-dropping, unexpected thing is actually happening, from nowhere, and we are here. And yes, we are witnessing something uncommon, something extraordinary. And finally: yes, that this is in some way what it means to be human — that we are alive and have fleeting access to beauty like this.*

At the end of the song, people did something that Natasha, in thirty years of riding the New York subway, had never seen. They applauded. The woman's cracked plastic cup was passed enthusiastically between them. Natasha pulled a twenty from her purse, which was all she had, and also quickly ripped a page from her notebook on which she scribbled down the West Street community centre address and phone number.

'We can help you,' she said. 'Please come and sing for us.'

The woman glared at her, possibly uncomprehending, possibly simply unable to read. Then, with a grunt, she shuffled away, dragging the plastic sacks that contained her worldly goods off that particular carriage, and on to wherever and whatever life held next.

★   ★   ★

Back at West 83rd, Natasha had finally taken a shower, and was brushing her teeth in the upstairs bathroom. She spat, rinsed, and met her reflection evenly in the mirror. *What a day*, she thought. *What a gift of a day.* And climbing the stairs of the narrow brownstone to her old childhood room, it came to her: a small gleaming kernel of knowledge that, despite the recent derailing of both her professional and her personal life, she was going to be okay. In her pyjamas and socks, cross-legged on her bed with her laptop, she knew what she had to do. She sent an email to Esther outlining the secret idea she'd been thinking about for weeks: that perhaps she might talk to *her* about her story. Then she sent an email to Nathan, agreeing to more shifts at Uppercase Books. She was enjoying the work, she was good at it, and although the salary was minuscule, if she worked there as much as possible plus took on more freelance copy-editing gigs, she'd surely be able to afford a little studio of her own. Much as she loved her parents, she could not camp out at West 83rd for much longer or she would likely go insane. And then, finally, she Googled a bunch of Brooklyn realtors after a quick scan of Manhattan real-estate prices made her eyes bleed, and scribbled down a list of numbers to call in the morning.

A change gonna come.

11

December

'Double zero!' Rafi whooped in triumph. He pulled a pencil from behind his ear to make a quick adjustment to the plans on his clipboard, then held up a hand to give Tommy, his genius contractor, a high-five. Raf's hoodie and jeans were already covered in construction dust and his ears were filled with the sounds of drilling, banging, and the generic pop that blared from the ghetto blaster in the corner. It was Day One of construction on West Street: the boys had come back from City Hall earlier with the requisite permits signed off, and he and Tommy — after a bloodcurdling moment when one of Tommy's team had started removing the plasterboard from the wall they'd been planning to use as their common grid line only to discover that it wasn't actually straight — had now established a new geometric point, zero on the x, zero on the y, to which the whole project would now relate. Double zero. They were officially under way.

Watching Tommy and his guys at work, Raf felt totally wired — even more so than usual. Most of the projects he worked on were built from scratch, and although there was always something thrilling about breaking new ground, there was an altogether different satisfaction to converting a space that had already lived its way through former lives. The sight of plasterboard falling and dust billowing and old floorboards being torn up sent a ripple of deep fulfilment through him. He was proud of this: proud of the people it was for; proud of everything it stood for; everything it might go on to be.

'Hello,' he suddenly heard a familiar voice say, breaking the spell.

Except the spell was her. He spun around. And breathed again.

'Hello.'

He hadn't heard from her since last week, when she'd called out of the blue one afternoon to ask for his advice about a studio she was considering renting. 'Esther actually suggested I ring you,' she'd apologized. 'If you don't have time, please don't worry, but I'm looking at a place pretty near to your neighbourhood, I think, and I could really use your expert opinion . . . '

He'd been at work in the office in Dumbo but not too stretched, so he'd jumped on his bike and met her at the address on Meserole Avenue. The price they were asking was totally outrageous, as ever, but she told him she'd looked at more than ten places over the past two weeks and this one seemed like the least outrageous of all. It was a walk-up with high ceilings and wooden floors. With a lick of paint and nice furniture, it could be great. 'But is it even, like, *structurally* sound?' she'd grimaced, looking up suspiciously at the elevated platform hovering above the kitchen, where her bed would allegedly have to go.

'Well, I surely hope you're not claustrophobic,' Raf had joked as he sized the place up using the measure and spirit level that he'd picked up from his desk before he left. As the broker had excused himself to take a call outside on the stairwell, he'd quickly assured her that so long as she didn't mind climbing a ladder to go to sleep and didn't sit up too quickly once she was up there, it would be totally fine. And then he had given her an inventory of things she could use to negotiate on the price.

'So this is it. You're really moving out?' he'd asked afterwards, over a coffee next door at Cafe Grumpy. 'I mean, obviously I approve of your choice of neighbourhood, but this must be a pretty big deal.'

Natasha had pulled a face, but said nothing.

'It's totally over, you're really leaving Josh?'

'I am. Or he's leaving me. I don't really know. It's been a mutual implosion, I guess. We saw each other again last week when I went to start getting my stuff out of our apartment. It was horrible and sad and strange. He cried. I cried. But it's done. And maybe I'm just in denial, but I think I feel better about it now than I have done in weeks. It's almost a relief.'

'Must have been a pretty fucking awful choice to have to make.'

Natasha's goldenish-brown eyes had been splintered with resignation. 'It wasn't a choice. I mean, not one that was mine to make. How could I possibly have married him, knowing he was in love with someone else?'

He'd managed to not say what he'd thought, which was, *how could he be in love with someone else?* And had swiftly changed the subject. 'So. You going to make an offer on that place?'

'Do you think I should?'

'Well, if you can beat him down a bit, it's a great location. We'll be pretty much neighbours.'

'Well, in *that* case . . . ' She'd laughed, her

166

excellent infectious laugh. 'I don't know. It's expensive, but it's better than anywhere else I've seen. I gave myself a deadline that I'd be out of my parents' house by Hanukkah at the absolute latest, so I'm kind of running out of time. The lease starts on December first. I might call you if I need further advice, so long as you don't mind?'

'Please. Any time.'

She had not called since. And now she seemed to be telling him she couldn't stay long. 'I have to run back to work. We have an author event at the bookstore tonight and I'm hosting it. I just wanted to pop over and see how it was going.'

'Did Esther tell you we're having a breaking-ground ceremony just as soon as Rach arrives?'

'She did. It's all very exciting.'

Raf smiled. 'It is. Hey, so I was wondering, did you — '

'Hey, buddy? Sorry to interrupt.' Tommy had appeared, scratching his head. 'Mind if I borrow you for a moment?' Turning to Natasha, he explained, 'Sorry, just need the genius for something. We won't be long.'

'I'll be right back,' Raf told her. And thought, *please don't go anywhere.*

★ ★ ★

After they'd gone ceremoniously through the ritual of 'breaking ground' — which in this case, there being no actual ground to break, involved Raf and Tommy helping Esther take a blow at the wall with a sledgehammer and then the rest of them having a go while Ned and Emily snapped photos on their iPhones to post to the Tumblr and the Twitter feed — Natasha disappeared back to work. As most of the other volunteers and clients began filtering out for the evening, Rachel appeared brandishing a couple of beers from the staff fridge, and the two of them dropped onto one of the couches in the recreation area. Raf was too buzzed to sit still for long, though; almost immediately he jumped back up to seize the battered old guitar that had not been put back in its case by whoever had been playing it earlier. Perched on the edge of the pool table, strumming random chords, he asked Rachel about her day. Reclining on the couch, her blue-black hair streaming out behind her, she resembled some insanely beautiful odalisque tonight, even in her biker boots, ripped jeans and oversized woolly jumper. She started to tell him a funny anecdote about one of the kids she'd been teaching this afternoon, but paused mid flow to listen.

'Wo-ow,' she said, after a moment. 'So you

can really play, huh?'

He stopped immediately. 'Not really. I just kind of like to muck about on it. When I was a kid, my dad taught me to play this instrument called an *oud*. It's like a sort of — '

'Lute,' she said. 'I know.'

'You do? How come?'

She shrugged. 'I secretly dated this Syrian dude once. *Shh.* Don't tell my mother. He used to play the *oud*. And the *nay*, too. That's the flute thingy, right?'

'Seriously? My cousin Leila plays the *nay* professionally.'

'Okay, so you're a *musical* person.' Rachel looked amused. 'Don't mention it to Esther, or next thing you know she'll be roping you into one of her big Broadway extravaganzas and you'll be trapped for ever. How's your Sondheim?'

He gave a strum. 'Nonexistent. But Esther could probably rope me into anyth — '

'I know,' she laughed, a little cruelly, he thought. 'You'll do anything for her. You're a groupie, we all can see.'

He blushed.

'No, don't be embarrassed. It's a good thing. Trust me, we wouldn't even let you *be* here if you didn't have the Esther bug.'

'You mean some people don't?'

Rachel shrugged again. 'Well, nobody *I've* ever come across. But I'm sure there are some losers out there who don't get it.'

'Losers out there who don't get what?' enquired Esther as she emerged from her office bundled up in her winter coat and scarf.

Rachel jumped up and extended her arms to her grandmother. 'Nothing, *Bubbe*. We can't tell you or your head would get so big it would fall off this tiny little body of yours.' She squeezed her grandmother's frail shoulders. 'Speaking of which, we should feed you. I'm starving.' She turned to Raf. 'Care to join us, Mr Haroun? We're just going next door.'

'Thanks, but I have a bunch of things I need to run through here before I go.'

'You'll come to our official celebration dinner next Saturday night, though?' Esther insisted. 'Ned emailed everyone the details, I hope. We're going to my favourite restaurant in the whole city.'

Raf smiled. His firm had wanted him to fly to San Francisco that day, but he'd told them he couldn't go anywhere until Sunday night. 'I got it, Esther, thanks. Obviously I wouldn't be anywhere else in the world.'

★ ★ ★

Raf ended up staying late that night, long after everybody else had left; he told Jorge he'd lock up. Now that construction was officially under way, he would not be coming back on site too much — only when Tommy needed him, or to check in from time to time. There was still a long way to go; the extension would take at least six months to build. But from the architect's point of view, the start of construction also meant an ending of sorts. Raf's main work here was pretty much done. His co-op had a huge new project about to start on the West Coast, a public auditorium they were building in Oakland, and although he would revert to being very much the junior partner on that project, having led this one, it would swallow up a lot of his time. He'd likely be in San Francisco until Christmas, and having promised his parents he'd spend a proper amount of time at home in Dearborn over the vacation, he actually wouldn't be in New York much at all over the next month or so. He'd miss this place, he realized as he wandered back through the original community centre building with an unlikely pang of nostalgia. It had sure been an intense and exhilarating couple of months.

After straightening a pile of books on the table in the recreation room, he retrieved his parka and bag from the hooks in the staff offices, and was about to switch off the lights, lock up and head home when his eye was caught by a ribbon of light escaping from underneath Esther's office door. She must have left it on by mistake when she left with Rachel.

Approaching the door, however, he heard a muffled noise, and the strains of what sounded like music. Had she left the radio on? He paused. From the other side of the door now came the sound of a human voice singing, a simple and poignant melody, unmistakably live; unmistakably Esther. She must have come back here after dinner and not realized he was still working next door. Raf, torn, and strangely moved, did not want to disturb her, but nor did he quite want to leave. Not yet. She was singing what sounded like a folk song, Yiddish presumably, although there was something in the tune that struck him, in some deep, atavistic way, as familiar. After a moment, he realized with a start that the music was so like the melodies his mother would sometimes sing around the radio in their Dearborn kitchen; or, decades ago, when he and his siblings were all little, the lullabies she used to croon to them as they fell asleep. Songs of grief and love, of a homeland that could never be returned to, of longing, of loss. Of what it meant to be a people that would persist, or perish.

After a few moments Esther fell silent. Waiting a beat, he knocked gently. He did not want to alarm her. 'Esther? It's me, Rafi.'

'Oh!' she shrieked from the other side. 'Dear God! I thought I was the last one left! Do come in, come in.'

He opened the door and was charmed to see her blushing slightly. 'I was just finishing up some paperwork. Carmen, my blessed help, is coming to fetch me once I'm done. But won't you sit, Rafi darling, and have something to drink?'

He demurred, but she insisted he run to the staff kitchen and fetch a bottle of champagne. He'd never seen her drink anything stronger than tea before. But noticing the dubious expression on his face, she cried, 'Of *course* we must have champagne!' with the implacable Esther Goldfaden logic he had seen employed often over the past couple of months. 'I meant us all to drink it earlier, but what with Tash running off back to work, and this application I'm dealing with, I was a little distracted and I clean forgot I'd put it in there.'

'I keep meaning to ask Tash, which bookst — '

'So will you just pop that damn thing, and let's toast your magnificent new extension, shall we?' Esther's eyes lit up. 'In fact, shouldn't we go and spray it over the wall or something for good luck? Yes, let's do that!' She held out her hand. 'Come on!'

★ ★ ★

Esther only drank the tiniest sips of champagne, and at some point back in her office, noticing that the bottle was two-thirds empty, Raf realized he should slow down. He was more of a beer guy than a champagne guy, and between the bubbles, the fact that he hadn't yet eaten dinner, and Esther's disarming manner, he was talking far too much. They'd been chatting about this and that — about particular clients from the shelter; about his work; about her late husband Max, whose collected plays Raf had on his bookshelf; about New York architecture and which buildings he most admired — and then out of nowhere Esther was saying, 'I've been meaning to ask you for ages. Haroun is such an *interesting* name, isn't it? I used to know a lovely man called Haroun, a wonderful old Iranian Jew, who ran a Holocaust oral history project in Chicago I once did some work with . . . ' She tailed off, and inclined her head, as if expecting him to pick up the thread of her blithe non-sequitur.

174

He wondered if Esther might, in fact, be a little tipsy.

'Well yeah, I hear there are a lot of Iranians called Haroun,' he said, after a moment. 'I think it's even the name of a place there. It means Aaron; the prophet, I guess. Which is why there are Jewish Harouns, Arabic Harouns, Christian Harouns. He was one of those rare unifying figures of the Abrahamic faiths.'

Esther smiled. '*Yes.* That's it. I'm a little hazy on my Old Testament, but he was the brother of Moses, if I'm not mistaken. And mentioned in the Qu'r'an, of course.' She pushed the bottle of champagne towards him.

He resisted. 'Esther Goldfaden, are you trying to get me drunk?'

'As if I would do any such thing!' she scolded him. 'You can top me up too. You see, I was just interested, because I'm nosy, and you said you were from Dearborn, Michigan, and the only other person I ever knew about from Dearborn, Michigan was Henry Ford! Haroun doesn't sound like a very Michiganite name, whatever that might be. Where are your parents from?'

Raf ran a hand through his hair and topped up their glasses. He was playing for time, wondering how to answer. On some level he knew that Esther, one of the most perceptive people he had ever encountered, had been trying to ask him this question ever since he'd first sat in her office on that sunlit September afternoon. He wondered what she thought the answer would be; what she thought she knew; why she wanted to know. What she would think of him if she did. What any of them would think of him.

'Jerusalem,' he said evenly, handing her the glass. He'd made sure to only top it up a little.

She was looking at him very intently. 'Go on . . . ' she implored. 'Where in Jerusalem? Who were they? What happened to them? Nobody from your parents' generation in Jerusalem doesn't have quite a story to tell, I'd bet.'

And perhaps because of the champagne, perhaps because Esther could elicit whatever she wanted from people, Raf finally took her questions at face value. 'Well. My father was from a neighbourhood in Jerusalem called Qatamon,' he started, then stopped. 'Wait. You *really* want to know all this?'

'All of it, please,' she replied. 'I told you, I'm very nosy. And I'm fascinated.'

Well, then. 'He was born in Qatamon, like I said. In April 1948, when he was five, his family left . . . '

'Their house?'

176

He nodded. 'Yeah. In the middle of the night. Him, his mom and dad, and his baby brother. Things had been getting bad for a while, it was Operation Maccabi, everyone in the village was getting out. But my grandfather had been resisting for weeks. The way my dad tells it, he kept saying ' 'no, no, no, this is *my* house, these are *my* books, this is our life, this is our town, we live here, this is insane, nobody can kick us out of our houses, we're not going *anywhere*!' Then Deir Yassin happened and some people they knew were killed. My grandmother had given birth not so long before, and as things got worse they became really worried about the kids, my dad and his baby brother, so they wanted to get out of there during what they thought would just be this bad period. A finite time, you know? A couple weeks. My grandfather had this neighbour, a taxi-driver friend who was going to help them out. They were just going to drive over the border to Damascus to stay with some family until everything calmed down. My grandfather collected books, he had this beautiful, beautiful library, thousands of volumes, and my dad says he remembers so clearly the night they left, his father praying in front of his bookshelves, touching his fingers to his lips and then to their spines.' He paused. 'Then he remembers his mother coming into the library to hurry her husband along. He left every single one of those books behind, except for a single bible.'

Esther was silent for a moment. Raf heard the clock ticking, the murmuring buzz of traffic outside on the West Side Highway, a lone car horn, the perpetual chatter of the city.

'Your family are Christian?'

'My father's family.'

'And they never went back.'

It did not appear to be a question.

Rafi drained his champagne glass. 'They never even got over the border into Syria. They ended up being sent to a refugee camp. My grandfather and grandmother both died in that camp. A lot of my family still live there.'

'And what became of the house in Qatamon?'

'My father still has the key. He was five years old the night they left, and my grandfather gave it to him after they locked up and told him to look after it always. He said that he was the keeper of the key, and it was very important he looked after it, as they were going on an adventure and he was now the big man in the family. Years later, my dad went back. He met the family who were living there. They were kind: they let him walk around the house, see his old room, even take a cutting from the ancient olive trees in the grove behind the house where he'd played as a boy.'

Esther held his gaze for what felt like a very long time, as if registering everything, all the unsayable things. 'And your mother?'

Raf closed his eyes. He had no idea why he was telling Esther all this. 'My mother's family was pretty wealthy, not that that made much difference,' he said. 'They lived in the Old City, in this beautiful house in what's now the Jewish Quarter. They were also evicted in 1948 and also ended up in refugee camps. Some of my mother's family went to Jordan, some to Lebanon and Syria, and some, unbelievably, actually made it back to Jerusalem before 1967, including my grand-mother and grandfather. But my mother never went back.'

'Why not?'

Raf cleared his throat. He wished he had a glass of water, but Esther had also cast her spell on him and he didn't want to move. So he began to talk about his mother. 'When she was fifteen, she was sent to Gaza to live with a distant cousin of my grandfather's.'

Esther was leaning forward, her eyes trained on him. '*Gaza?* Why on earth?'

'She'd fallen in love with my father.'

'And that was a problem for your family?'

'It was against the law! It's still against the law. If you're a good Muslim girl you can't just run off and marry your Christian sweetheart. My grandfather, Walid, would have practically had my dad killed if he could. The only other options were for her to immediately get married to someone her dad approved of, or be sent to Gaza.'

Esther's eyes widened. 'And they managed to stay together, your parents, even after she was exiled?'

'Well, sort of. That's a whole other story. It took them twelve years to find each other again. In Damascus. For twelve years they never saw each other for a single day. It's kind of miraculous how they eventually tracked each other down, but it's also pretty devastating, what they had to sacrifice for it.'

They sat in silence for a moment. 'Sometimes the tragedy is not the love that doesn't last,' Esther murmured. 'But the one that does.'

The clock ticked on.

'Emanuel?' he ventured. The champagne was making him bold.

She looked at him.

'Sorry. That's none of my — '

'You know, people often ask me,' she waved

away his apology, "*do you think you survived Buchenwald because of him?*' And I suppose if I was being really romantic I could say 'yes! *Yes! I kept myself alive just through the possibility of seeing him again!*' Because of course, of *course*, if he was still alive, still in this world, it was too awful to imagine that I wouldn't survive it to ever see him again.' She took a sip of her champagne. '*Schmontses*, you know. Utter nonsense. The fact that I survived, like everyone who lived or died, was entirely random.' She inclined her head, ever so slightly, and in the slant of the light Raf saw tears gleaming in her shrewd and intelligent eyes. They did not fall. 'I *have* to believe it's nonsense, otherwise why didn't he survive for me?' She smiled bravely at him, then patted her desk impatiently. 'Anyway, back to your parents. Did their families ever forgive them their love for each other?'

'Not at first,' he answered. 'They were both estranged from their parents for years. They'd left Palestine, they'd disobeyed their families, their societies, their homeland; nobody forgave them that. Once my eldest sister was born, though, things got a little easier. Then two years after that, they finally managed to get visas to come to the US. And the rest, as they say . . . ' He took another sip from his glass, studied the little old Jewish woman before him who had lived such an unimaginable life.

'I have told very few people that story,' he said, bewildered, after a pause.

'Thank you, Rafi, for entrusting me with it. What a tale.'

'Well, it's just one family. Everybody has these griefs, don't they?'

'Oh yes. They do.'

'You know, the reason I first came to see you talk,' he heard himself confessing, 'was because I'd read somewhere in an article or a book this description you'd written about the night you left your house in Galicia with your family . . . ' He broke off; his heart was so full, now he was really going too far. 'Forget about it, it doesn't matter, I'm being way too indulgent.' He glanced at the clock and was genuinely shocked at the time. They'd been in here talking far longer than he'd realized. 'Jesus, Esther, it's getting late. Can't I help get you home?'

'No, no, go on,' she insisted, laying a fragile hand on his arm. 'I want to know what happened when you read about that night in Zholkva.'

Raf hesitated. 'Well, it just — I don't know. It resonated, I guess. It changed something in the way I was thinking about stuff. My parents are not particularly political, or rather, *politicized;* in a way they had to consciously abandon all that. For them, they made a choice: it was about love. It wasn't about their homeland because it couldn't be. If it was about that, then they couldn't be together. So that was their choice. It was wrenching, but in its way it was simple. And my brothers and sisters and I pretty much grew up as apple-pie-American as Rachel and Tash. While my cousins were fighting in the *intifadas,* I was hitting Little League baseballs and dreaming of playing B-ball for the Detroit Pistons. But of course, you do grow up with a certain feeling about things in your background; it's inevitable. And I read that passage of yours and it just capsized me, I guess. Because nothing I'd ever read about the Holocaust felt relatable before — not to me, living my little American life in Dearborn. So sometimes it was less intellectually . . . exercising to simply absorb what some people in my wider family, like if I went out there to visit, were saying.'

'Which was?'

'Well, I guess, to put it really bluntly: why were the Palestinians the ones being made to suffer for the Holocaust? Why were they all being forced out of their homes and losing their livelihoods as well?'

He tailed off. He had definitely gone too far: Esther was looking lost in thought. Christ, why had he said that?

'I'm sorry, Esther, it's not my place to talk about any of that. My point was, I had never been able to relate it to anything I knew. And then here was this description of you leaving your house with your family in the middle of the night, carrying your little sister, and getting to a border, and being turned away, and never going back . . . ' He looked up. 'Please don't get me wrong, Esther, I am not in *any* way comparing what happened to you and your family to what happened to my father and his. But — '

She raised a hand. 'Please, Rafi. You don't have to explain anything to me. I understand. I really understand. Everything. Thank you for trusting me with that.'

Esther smiled at him then, and it seemed to Raf in that instant that this wasn't just Esther Goldfaden's usual beguiling expression; it was something deeper and more tender, more generous, something that felt private and powerful between them. He didn't understand, quite, what she was communicating to

184

him in that smile. But he felt the effect of it, and was grateful.

'Okay. Enough of this. We should get you home,' he said.

But neither of them moved. And after a moment she stood and opened her arms, and for a long time, a long time, they embraced.

12

Zipping up her suitcase, Natasha felt a jangling clash of emotions, uppermost of which was something like relief. She officially got the keys to her new place today, although her new landlady had kindly let her go in and repaint it before her lease began so it would be habitable by today. Rosalind, meanwhile, was leaning on the door frame with a wounded expression on her face, watching her daughter pack.

'You really don't have to do this, honey, you know.'

Natasha turned. 'Yes I do, Mom.' She moved across the room and, wrapping her arms around her mother, repeated: 'I do.'

'But *why?*' Ros exclaimed. 'You can stay here as long as you like. You know we love having you. Save your hard-earned cash. And then . . . then, maybe, when you guys have figured things out — '

'Mom!' Natasha reprimanded. 'Please. There is no more 'us guys', okay? It's done. Josh got the confirmation back last week. They've refunded everything but the deposit. It's not going to happen.'

'It's ready, girls!' Frank appeared just then at the top of the staircase. He was in his weekend clothes: a sloppy Mets sweatshirt of 1980s vintage, shapeless slacks. While Ros ruled the kitchen the rest of the time, weekend breakfasts were Frank's domain; ever since they were kids, he'd always spent them in the kitchen listening to NPR, juicing oranges, rustling up his 'magic' pancakes and waffles and his egg bialys. Natasha felt a crumple of affection at the sight of the two of them, standing there together.

'Oh honey,' Frank said, opening his arms. 'This is such a sad day.'

'No it's not, Dad,' Natasha countered as she hugged him. 'It's a pretty happy one. And Brooklyn's not another country, remember? I'll come visit all the time, I promise. Now can we please go eat those bialys? The smell's driving me insane.'

⋆ ⋆ ⋆

Later, on Meserole Avenue, she parked the rented Zipcar outside her new building and unloaded the cases she'd brought with her from West 83rd. The rest of her stuff was still in the apartment on Kenmare; Gretchen was meeting her here shortly to accompany her downtown to help her pack up. She'd arranged it with Josh when they'd spoken last week; he promised he'd be out all day today and she'd had no desire to ask where. She might have been the one, finally, to decide they clearly had no choice but to say goodbye — but the thought of him with Kristen still felled her. As did the general untethering tumult of the past few months: the fact that, in the blink of an eye, after a few wholly unexpected turns, she seemed to have gone from being a reporter at an iconic national newspaper, engaged, and resident of a covetable apartment on Kenmare Street, to this — a single thirty-year-old woman, basically skint, working shifts in a tiny independent bookstore and living in a shoebox studio.

But the shoebox was hers, at least on a twelve-month lease, and it had its own charm, she reflected as she climbed the stairs to the top floor. She'd got a great deal in the end, thanks in part to Rafi's inventory of negotiable details, and she and Gretch had redecorated it last weekend. As she unlocked the door, the smell of fresh paint struck her as not altogether unpleasant; an almost palpable reminder, in fact, of the things all spurned lovers must eventually repeat to themselves: that she was free, that this marked not only the turning of a new page but the possible writing of a whole new chapter.

She closed the door behind her, leaned back against it and took a deep breath.

★   ★   ★

The world had turned, in a way he could not put his finger on. But it had turned. He seemed to be balancing all too precariously on an edge of something. Raf was considering this as they gathered around the long wooden communal table at Esther's chosen restaurant, Frank and Vera's, on the corner of Second Avenue and Fifth. Esther had determinedly sat him next to her, and like some pathetic schoolboy he'd been furtively saving the seat on the other side of him for Natasha. But she'd been deep in conversation with Jorge at the bar before they all sat down, and suddenly there was the intern, Emily, taking the seat and smiling up at him, and Tash was somehow all the way down the other end of the table.

Emily turned out to be super-intense: every time he tried to disengage, to talk to Esther or even to Rachel — who was, he could see, dazzling Tommy, opposite him — Emily would touch his arm and laugh, or ask another question about architecture, or look at him in a way that, who knows, in other circumstances, another life, he might even have found cute. Tonight, he barely saw her. He ordered another beer, hoping it was not outwardly obvious that he was unable to focus on a single word she was saying.

Afterwards, having put Esther in a taxi for the short trip back to her apartment, the 'youngsters', as she called them, decided to stay out for another drink. Ned directed them to a tiny unmarked bar around the corner on Sixth and B that brewed its own bitters and mixed allegedly the finest Old Fashioned in town. It was rammed. Raf moved to the bar to get a round of drinks. And then, at some point, as he waited for the bartender's attention, he became aware that in all the hustle and jostle she had somehow ended up right next to him. How, he wondered, when and why had this girl come to be the thing he most wished for? Leaning her back against the bar, she was facing outwards and chatting to Rachel, her body ever so slightly inclined towards her sister's, as he had noticed the two of them unconsciously did whenever they were together. And pressed close in the throng, the outside of her left hand was grazing the outside of his left hand.

And that was all.

Handing the bartender his credit card with his right hand, Raf, electrified, did not move, and neither did she. Once the cocktails were mixed, he inched his hand away; his skin no longer quite touching hers, divided but still connected by the air that seemed now to vibrate between them. He gave a drink each to Natasha and her sister, as if the world was still in its place.

'Cheers.' His voice to him came out strange. He almost dared not look, but was compelled. And then his eyes found hers, where his own wonder and apprehension appeared to have been met. In her expression was something hiding; something declaring itself. Somehow excessive; somehow not enough.

'Cheers!' Rachel held up the heavy cut-glass tumbler. 'This looks like a very fine cocktail.'

'Oh, you *hero*, you made it!' Having been caught up in conversation with Tommy, Emily had once again appeared by Raf's side. He slowly handed her one glass, and then another. 'Do you want to take that one over to Tom?' he asked.

'Sure! But why don't you join us? There's a little more space over in our corner. It's crazy in here!'

★　★　★

The rest of the evening passed in something of a blur, and not because of the rye. Outside on the sidewalk, as the group went through the rigmarole of parting and sharing up the rare illuminated cabs according to the logics of New York geography, he heard himself saying good night to her with studied casualness. Whatever was going on, whatever current had passed between them back there, it could not, surely, be real: this was not what happened to him, not how he rolled.

He leaned over to kiss her goodbye, but she seemed to be saying to him, mystifyingly, 'Do you want to maybe share a cab?'

At his momentary confusion, she reminded him, 'I moved into my new place today . . . I'm pretty much down the road from you.'

'Right! Of course . . . Yeah, that makes sense.' And all of a sudden they were the last ones left, standing on this corner of Sixth Street in the bitter, bitter cold. Natasha was rubbing her hands together and hopping up and down as the longed-for taxi proved elusive. Ordinarily, he would of course have put an arm around her, given her shoulders a friendly rub to try and keep her warm. Now he dared go no closer.

'Shall we walk for a bit?' she wondered, her nose turning red and her lips already taking on a bluish tinge. 'Do you think it's going to snow?'

'Yeah, we might have more luck closer to the bridge.' Fuck it: he held out a hand. 'Come on.'

★ ★ ★

For an instant, at this nondescript juncture of Sixth Street and Avenue B, Natasha's mind filled with the many thousands of times her feet must have pounded these sidewalks; a different girl in a different life. The other snow-dusted or sun-soaked or wind-lashed or leaf-filled strolls she must have taken around here with her family, her friends, with Josh, with other boyfriends; alone. Almost every street corner in Manhattan, she realized, was littered with the individual instances that together made up her whole life. She didn't know what she and Raf were chattering about as they moved through streets upon which she had perhaps partied as a teenager, reported from as a twenty-something, met people, lost others, but she understood very clearly all over again that this city was her closest ally, offering solace: a reminder both physical and spiritual that, whilst some things in life might shift beyond comprehension, others would remain unerringly constant.

And as she walked alongside this curious, beautiful person who seemed to have retuned something so deep within her, she knew that such an alliance was one of the great gifts of growing up your whole life in a single place. This place.

They walked past a little garden, familiar, which she had not seen or thought about in many years. Natasha remembered sunny afternoons spent playing there with her sister on visits with their grandmother, who would afterwards chat for hours with the hobos and wastrels who congregated in Tompkins Square and around these Alphabet City streets, all considered off-limits to sane denizens of Manhattan at the time.

At Clinton and Rivington she finally dared inch her glance towards Raf, somehow knowing that an irrevocable change had taken place within her. With every familiar turn around these streets now seeming new and strange and brimful of possibility, she could almost feel the city willing her on, saying: *everything changes; sure, so you aren't the person today that you were yesterday, and you'll be many others in the future too, but I'll always be here, kiddo, we'll always have New York . . .*

And also: *you go, girl.*

By the time they hit Delancey, he had no idea whether they had even seen any empty cabs go past: at some point he seemed to have stopped noticing everything but her.

'I mean, shall we just *walk* over the bridge?' she wondered, in a slightly deranged tone, as they hovered on the corner.

'Do you think we'll make it?'

'Well, I guess there are worse places to go than the Billyburg Bridge. One foot in Manhattan, one in Brooklyn, straddling the river: it feels like quite an appropriate metaphor for my life right now.'

'It would be a bit of a shame, though.' Regaining a modicum of sense, Raf properly took in Natasha's chattering teeth, her streaming eyes and frozen purplish lips. 'You do actually look like you might be about to perish. Come here, you.'

Before he knew it, he had slipped his arms inside her coat and they were embracing each other. He rubbed her back, to keep her warm. Just to keep her warm. They stayed like that for a long time, too long for sense; he had no idea how long, but definitely hypothermia-risk-long; their hearts beating close, so close, with the snow beginning to fall in earnest around them now. She was quite little, Tash, and he was very tall, and at some point he found himself touching his lips very gently to her cold forehead, to the long, narrow scar that ran above her eyebrow and which he'd always wondered about. She tightened her grip around his waist. She was shivering.

He suddenly wanted to kiss her more than any boy had ever wanted to kiss a girl in all of history.

And he was a bit troubled by it. Normally, Raf was one of the lucky people who made his way through life pretty much untroubled by conscience. He did what he believed in and he loved to do it. But it did bother him, at some level, that he should be standing here with Natasha Bernstein dying to kiss her and wondering if she felt the same and plotting how he might. However you looked at it, it was not cool. Her break-up with Josh was still so recent. He was the professional architect employed by her grandmother, relaxed as that relationship was. His firm would be furious with him if they knew he was kissing their client's granddaughter. And then — then there was the fact he hadn't told her anything about his background; cravenly, he realized now, in simple fear of her turning away.

And yet this desire to kiss her was stronger than anything he had ever felt. What was the alternative? To *not* kiss her?

A cab pulled over on the other corner of the sidewalk and disgorged a couple. Raf quickly extricated himself from her just enough to whistle for it, and as it glided up next to them, they moved apart and got in.

'Where to?' the driver asked.

Raf cleared his throat. 'Meserole Avenue, right? What's your cross-street again?'

'Um . . . ' Her eyes looked wild; the cold. 'Unless . . . I maybe need more Scotch. How about one nightcap at that mad Polish piano bar? Seeing as it's my first night in the neighbourhood and all?'

He raised an eyebrow. 'Seriously? Okay, crazy girl. Your call.'

Giving the driver the directions to the Manhattan Avenue dive, Raf sat back against the leather of the cab. *I want to kiss you*, he thought. *I want to kiss you I want to kiss you I want to kiss you.*

When they arrived in Brooklyn there was a minor tussle over who paid, and Raf ended up grabbing Natasha's wrist, laughing, as he managed to shove his twenty into the driver's hands first. And then it was the most impossible thing in the world, with her wrist already in his hands, not to bring it to his lips.

'Don't know how that happened,' he whispered, after a moment, gently placing her arm back down by her side. 'Sorry.'

Natasha rose on her tiptoes. 'You *actually* have snowflakes on your eyelashes.' He bent towards her as she kissed the snow away in a gesture that was as tender as it was erotic, and which nearly killed him.

'Oh God,' he murmured, his eyes closed. 'Tash . . . '

They were very, very close now, their lips touching. Was this okay? Was she okay with this? He didn't quite kiss her, but his lips moved on hers as he spoke. 'I seem to be . . . I'm sorry. I seem to be . . . '

I seem to be completely infatuated.

'I don't know how this happened.' He made himself inch backwards, away from her. 'I do know this is the last thing you need in your life right now. I'm sorry.'

Natasha looked up at him again with a sort of crazed inquiry in her eyes, still not saying anything. *Talk to me*, he begged silently. *Tell me what you want. If this is okay. Or just kiss me. That would also be fine.* Amid the clamour in his brain he registered something usefully clear: *nobody else in the world has ever made you feel like this, ever.*

Tash didn't make another move. So he played it safe; what else could he do? He wrapped his arms around her until he was hugging her very tightly, then kissed her forehead again. 'I adore you, Tash,' he told her. 'You are the prettiest possible thing to me, and I think you're amazing, and I adore you. But I don't want to complicate your life. I can be your best friend, your brother, whatever you need me to be in all this. Whatever this is, we don't have to do it.'

In his arms, he could feel her breathing, and they held each other like that, for the longest time.

'You're right,' she said finally, looking up at him with a crooked little smile. 'This is crazy. We don't have to do this.'

Neither of them moved.

'Okay!' She jumped away and held out her hand. 'The piano bar and the Polish crazies await. Let's go drink some whisky.'

★ ★ ★

Natasha didn't even like whisky that much.

'Uh . . . I probably should have told you before we went to the bar that Scotch always makes me a bit sick.' She was teetering a little on Raf's arm as they approached her front door. He'd walked her home after she'd decided she'd had enough. She drew a deep breath. 'And please don't take this the wrong way, but now I'm really feeling sick. Which is, like, the worst reason ever to ask a boy to come in. *But* I'd really like you to come in

199

. . . because I actually think I might be. Am I making any sense?'

'Kind of,' Raf inclined his head. 'Although, that's definitely the weirdest reason I've ever been asked back to a girl's apartment.'

'I'm serious, that's the real reason.'

'Then I am definitely coming in.'

'I'm drunk, I think. Or maybe I'm not. I don't know what I am.' She was rootling around in her bag. 'Oh, man, I can't find my new key.'

'What's that in your hand?'

She looked down. 'That is my new key.'

★   ★   ★

Her little studio was as cool as he remembered it, although stacked with suitcases and unpacked boxes. As she let them in, she turned, a little unsteady on her feet. 'Raf, just so you know — I'm really glad you're here, and I'd really love you to stay, if you want to, but I don't think we should . . . This isn't . . . I don't want you to think — '

'Relax, Tash. I'm celibate. It's a religious thing.'

'Really?'

'Kidding. Shall I get you some water?'

'Thanks.'

Raf went to the sink and Tash moved

200

towards one of the suitcases, which she unzipped and started rifling through. He became aware of her removing her scarf, her coat, her sweater. There was nothing on earth he wanted to do more than turn around.

'Don't turn around, okay?' she said, 'I'm getting ready for bed.'

He smiled. 'Okay, tell me when. I'll just stand here and think about urban planning.'

In a crate on the sideboard he found a glass, and eased the faucet on so it wouldn't spray too much. He glanced up and realized Natasha's image was reflected in the kitchen window. He had to force himself to stare down into the sink. He gulped down the water himself, and poured her another one. He was the good guy here; he would not be a creep. But still, it was pretty hard to think about anything other than the woman he most wanted to see getting undressed undressing behind him.

'Okay, I'm ready,' she said.

He took the water towards her. Shit. She was now unimaginably cute in her pyjamas and mussed-up hair.

'So I guess I'll sleep on the couch,' he coughed.

'I found you a spare comforter.'

'Thanks.'

'Okay. Goodnight.' She gave him a brief hug, and made her way gingerly up the ladder to her bed. Raf went to the bathroom, peed, and brushed his teeth using his forefinger and a blob of Natasha's toothpaste.

Back in the living room, he turned out the light, got out of his jeans and shirt, and climbed onto the couch, pulling the comforter over him. His legs were dangling far over the edge, but he didn't really care.

'Raf?' he heard her call softly, after a while.

'Yeah?'

'I'm glad you're here.'

'Me too. Shout if you're going to throw up, okay. I'll come up and rescue you.'

There was a prolonged beat.

'I think I'm going to throw up.'

He opened his eyes. 'Really?'

'Not really. Just wanted to see if you'd come up.'

Raf hesitated. 'Shall I come up?'

'Maybe.'

'Maybe?'

'Yeah.'

Raf slid off the couch. He was wearing his T-shirt and boxers. He climbed up the ladder. It was ridiculously cramped up there, but he manoeuvred his way awkwardly into the bed, remaining a chaste distance away from her body. Every single fibre of his being was keyed to the moment, wondering what this all meant.

You just got into bed with Natasha Bernstein.

'Hello.'

'Hello.'

'So I'm going to sleep here.'

'Yeah.' She was lying on her side, with her back to him.

After a moment, Raf said: 'I think I'm going to throw up.'

She giggled.

'Kidding. Goodnight, you.'

She reached her arm behind her and found his hand, which she held. 'Goodnight, Rafi.'

13

At 7:06, Natasha opened her eyes, confused and nauseous, wondering where the hell she was. Her head was pounding with the mother of all whisky hangovers and her mouth was a thick carpet; it took her a moment to wrestle her brain back into action. She was in her new apartment. And Rafi Haroun was in bed next to her. *Rafi Haroun.* Jesus Christ! She dared herself to glance over at him. He was fast asleep, a faint smile on his face, breathing quietly next to her. She tried not to look at him too hard. She slithered out of the bed, past his feet, which were hanging over the edge, and all the way down the ladder. Then she locked herself in the bathroom, avoided her eyes in the mirror and took a long, scalding shower. She tried to unpick the tangle of emotions in her head. They ranged from guilt to shame to excitement to desire and back again to guilt. What the fuck was she doing? She'd only just broken off her engagement with Josh. Raf was her grandmother's architect. What must he think of her, dragging him into her bed?

She'd only just broken off her engagement with Josh.

Out of the bathroom, she walked quietly back into the living room, wrapped in her towel. She saw Raf's shirt lying on the couch and for a fleeting, insane moment contemplating putting it on. When she heard his voice from up above, she jumped as if busted.

'Jesus, Tash,' he was muttering, 'your next boyfriend's going to have to be a midget.'

She couldn't help but smile.

'Guess that rules me out. I'm going to try and prise myself out of here. If I make it down, would it be okay if I had a shower?'

'Of course.'

'What size is your shower, just so I know?'

'Wait a minute. *You* chose this fucking apartment,' she reminded him, laughing, as a stooping Rafi struggled to get his long legs down the ladder.

'Yeah, but I didn't think I was going to be sleeping here when I did.'

Natasha blushed. He'd made it down, and was facing her now. He was in a white T-shirt and boxer shorts, and his face was all wrinkled with sleep, and his hair was crazed, and she thought she'd never seen a lovelier sight in her life.

'But I am pleased to be sleeping here,' he said. 'Just so you know.'

She made them coffee while he was in the shower, and when he emerged from the steamy bathroom in his towel, she was still in hers. She walked towards him with a cup, holding it in both hands, and handed it to him. Suddenly they were very close.

'Thanks,' he said, then put the mug down. He swallowed. 'Come here, Tash.'

She put her arms around his waist and then he touched his lips to her brow, chaste but intimate. She waited a moment. He didn't move. All she had to do was tip her head back a little and then he was kissing her nose. All she had to do was tip her head back a little further and then he was kissing her lips. And then he was kissing her, and they were kissing, and Natasha felt her entire being liquefy as, in a fumble of limbs and towels, they tumbled down onto the couch.

★　★　★

Three hours later, a little dazed with sex and wonder, they were eating breakfast in a cafe on Meserole.

'So you're going to San Francisco *tonight*?' she teased. 'Wow. That is great timing.'

He toyed with his cup. 'Yep. American Airlines.'

'Really? I'm so glad you told me: I *had*

been wondering which carrier you were on . . . '

'Mmm. I bet you were.' He smiled a little goofily. 'I just didn't know what to say. I didn't really expect . . . '

'No.' She met his smile with her own. 'Me neither.'

'But here we are.'

'Here we are.'

'Eating grilled cheese.'

'And pickles.'

He affected concern. 'I was actually thinking you should probably lay off the pickles a little now, Tash.'

After a moment she said, 'Rafi, remind me: why are you going to San Francisco?'

'I just feel I need to reconnect with my gay side after the events of the past few hours.'

'Uh huh.' She crunched down on another pickle, affecting cool while her heart jumped about her chest like a crazy insane thing.

'Jesus, you're so Jewish,' he said.

'Jesus wasn't Jewish — that's the whole point.'

'Yes, he was — *that's* the whole point.'

'Not by the end.'

'No. Maybe not. Maybe he was Christian by then.'

'Guess we have to hope so.'

'Otherwise the whole Middle East is like a

really bad three-way misunderstanding.' He grinned.

'Anyway, try one,' she said, pushing her plate in his direction. 'These things are not just pickles, they're like, *Brooklyn* pickles. They're artisanal, man.'

'I'm going to San Francisco for work. We're building that big auditorium in Oakland. I'm number eighteen on the project. I'm essential. The entire thing will probably collapse unless I get there and support the number seventeen. I did tell Esther.'

'Yeah, I remember now. I just didn't know how long you were going for.'

'Three months. Officially.'

She gulped. Passed her reaction off as too-hot coffee. 'Officially?'

'Yeah. Well, obviously, I'm hoping to be flying back every weekend now.'

Another gulp. 'And why would that be?'

'Well, I met this really cool girl.' He met her eyes. 'And I want to see as much of her as possible.'

She looked away, momentarily flustered. 'Um . . . so listen, obviously I want to see you too, Raf, but — '

'But you've just come out of an engagement and you need some time to get your head around everything and get your shit together and the last thing you need is some other guy all up in your grill.'

'That obvious, huh?'

He sat back. His eyes were all warmth and understanding, but still looked madly sexy as hell to her. She had a sudden flashback of his body, his naked body, their limbs entwined, things he had done to her on that couch, and her stomach flipped over all over again.

'I can still call you though, right?' he was saying. 'And maybe SMS you, like a hundred times a day?'

She toyed with her cup. *What was she doing, what was she doing, what was she doing?* 'You know, I hope this doesn't sound weird, but I think maybe we shouldn't do anything until you get back.'

'Anything?'

She shrugged.

'You mean, like proper *radio silence*?' He exhaled. 'No texts no calls no nothing? That feels pretty medieval. But if it's what you want, Tash, of course. I get it. Of course I do.'

'It's not what I actually want,' she swallowed. 'It's just what I think we should do. Maybe.'

He eyed her, his turquoise eyes glittering. 'Okay. Cool. Let's maybe do that, then. But — just so you know . . . I really like you, Tash. And I'm gonna come hunt you down the moment I'm back.'

You'd better, she thought.

'I really like you, too.' She drained her cup and gave him her brightest smile. 'Now, Mr Haroun. Don't you have a plane to catch?'

'I do.' He frowned. 'I'm pretty sure I maybe left something at your apartment though. On your couch? Maybe we should swing back there first?'

'I think that's probably a good idea.'

Part Two

14

May

It was a remarkable thing, she often felt, that a place defined by death could in any way affirm life. But as they drove into the cemetery, the splendour of Green-Wood struck her as it always did. On this very fine spring morning, sunlight was licking the Belleville brownstone of the magnificent gates. Birds wheeled overhead and flocked in the many trees, whose leaves shone greenly in the morning light. There were few visitors at this hour, and it was possible, despite the views of Manhattan across the water, to remember that this spot had once been entirely rural. Rosalind retrieved the walker from the trunk of the maroon Ford and unfolded it; together they moved slowly along the winding paths to the simple granite tombstone that marked the place where Max Goldfaden lay.

After twenty-five years, their Yahrzeit traditions were long-practised. With her left hand Rosalind placed a stone on her father's grave; while Esther bowed her head and quietly recited not the Kaddish or any other traditional lamentation, but some beautiful lines of Rilke that her dear late husband, poet and wordsmith that he was, had loved.

This fleeting world, which
Strangely keeps calling us. Us, most
  fleeting of all.
Once, for everything, only once. Once
  and not more.
And we too once. Never more.
But this just one being, even if only
  once:
To have been consonant with the earth,
  seems immutable.

They stood in silence awhile. Then Ros said, 'I wonder what Dad would make of all this.'

And Esther knew she was not talking of their commemorative rituals.

'He would be glad to see her so happy,' she ventured, watching her daughter's face closely.

Rosalind glanced skyward, and blinked.

Max, darling Max, open-hearted as he was, would have adored Rafik Haroun, Esther thought but did not say. 'He would also understand, of course, why you have felt concerned.'

Just as Ros seemed about to interject, Esther laid a hand on her daughter's arm. 'I know,' she said. 'I understand.'

Ever since March, when Raf had returned from San Francisco and walked back into their lives and into Natasha's heart, Rosalind had been despairing. On the outside, her argument was about what she saw as yet more impetuous and even reckless behaviour from Natasha — hastily calling off a wedding, leaping almost immediately into another relationship, moving to Brooklyn, with no care for the fallout around her. But Esther had a suspicion that Rosa's disquiet at the unexpected turn Natasha's life had taken was about something other than Tash's impulsiveness. Ros did not like the fact Rafi's family was Palestinian: it was clear. She also probably didn't much like the fact she didn't like it, which is why she would not admit it to anyone including herself. But her unease leaked out, regardless.

'I just don't *get* it,' she'd been kvetching even now, in the car on the way over to the cemetery. 'How this stranger has managed to inveigle himself into our family. Even Rachel seems smitten with him. He's building your extension. He got Tash to call off the wedding. Now he's whisking her off to the West Bank? Am I the only one who finds this

215

all a little sudden? I mean, I can see that he's charming and pretty. But really, what's the big deal with this guy? Am I missing something?'

Esther did not rise to any of this. She was privately disturbed that any child of hers might exhibit such confounding narrow-mindedness — she hoped it wasn't, in fact, prejudice — over what seemed to her to be a fundamentally straightforward matter: they have found each other, they love each other, they should be together. But at some level she understood, too, that Rosa's tribal response was a manifestation of something complex at the heart of their own lives, Esther and her daughter's. Life could be tough on the children of survivors, it was often said, and there was in her child a scrupulously concealed but acute anxiety about faith and family. Even as a little girl, Rosa had seemed instinctively to feel the need to compensate for what had happened to her mother.

At her husband's graveside now, Esther recalled the excuses she had made to a weeping, teenaged Rosa for not attending *shul* even on Yom Kippur, although she later relented. She remembered Rosa's dismay at her mother's unwillingness to accompany her and Max to Israel even once; and the row between Rosa and her father when he castigated her for daring to question Esther's reasoning for doing or not doing *anything*. And then that evening in the bathroom in the old Howard Avenue apartment: a memory that was probably scored as deeply on both their minds as the numbers themselves, although neither had ever spoken specifically of it again.

So Esther saw the pathos in her daughter's stance, and knew her own part in it; in the truth that Rosalind's deepest fears had much to do with Esther's own complicated and closely guarded emotional defenses.

'I think, my darling, that perhaps you just have to let her be.'

Ros looked irritated. She crossed her arms over her chest. 'That is unfair, Mom. You know, I am actually *sick* of being cast as this nightmare interfering mother — by you, by her, by Rach. It's not true. Everybody thinks that just because I do all the dinners and I round everyone up all the time and I pick up all the pieces when things fall apart that I somehow care about the superficial stuff, the performance. I don't. I couldn't give a shit. I don't care if she marries Josh, who she marries. I only want her to be happy. You know that.'

'Of course — '

'And *she* knows that, deep down. But *all*

these decisions she makes, every single one, they're always so improvisational, so on the fly. She accepted Josh's proposal in a heartbeat, then dropped it just as quickly. Now she's with this *boychik*, and it seems equally rash. Remember all that drama with the British guy in Boston? Tash is just not a girl to know her own heart, and she keeps muddling her way into these disasters. You don't think I got married to Frank without a long, hard look? You don't think I thought it would always be a bowl of cherries?'

Esther thought: *but that's different.*

'And now she's rushing off to Jerusalem and she won't know what she's doing there any more than she did here.' She threw her arms up. 'I mean, why do they need to go on this trip? Why now?'

'Because they both deserve a break!'

'So what's wrong with Mexico? Or, heck, Paris? Why can't they be like every other couple in the first flush of love and go to goddam Paris? Why does it have to be a war zone?'

Esther had decided not to mention that part of the reason Natasha was taking this trip to Israel and the West Bank with Rafi was her doing: she had written to the director of Yad Vashem and he'd agreed to let her granddaughter spend a few days in the

218

private archives, doing some research, even offering to find her a student intern who could help with the Yiddish and Polish translations. Their secret memoir project was coming along well. Perhaps prompted by today's anniversary and by her looming ninetieth birthday this summer, when Natasha had first suggested the idea to Esther it had struck her as perfect. They were taking it slowly: just a couple of afternoons a week, for a few hours. At times it was difficult and painful. But Esther had started talking, and Natasha had started asking, and who knew where it would end? With publication, not necessarily, not yet. But it was becoming something important to both of them. The process also seemed to have given Tash some of her confidence back: she'd had two magazine features and a literary review published recently; nothing huge, not the *New York Times*, but Esther had seen how happy it had made her granddaughter to be in print again — how reaffirmed, somehow. And was glad to be a small part of that.

'If it's a war zone, it also happens to be where most of Rafi's family live,' she pointed out. 'So spare a thought for them. Besides, you must not worry. Adam is there, Rafi knows it well, Tash is very familiar with Jerusalem — '

'Not *East* Jerusalem.'

'Besides, as a reporter she has been to far more dangerous places in the world than Israel.'

'How would you know how dangerous it is? You've never even been.'

Esther calmly ignored this. 'And tell me, have you ever seen her so happy? Isn't that enough?'

Ros looked thoughtful as she led them over to a nearby bench. They sat down. 'Last week she told me she feels like she has been — what was it she said? — an 'explorer in her own city' since he came along. And when I asked what that even meant, or why she needed to explore New York City of all places, she got all furious and told me 'it is not about exploring in any sense of the word you understand!'' Ros looked uncharacteristically tired, Esther noticed. It was nearing the end of the semester, the school year. She always had such a lot on. 'All I am trying to say to her, and maybe I am not saying it very well, is, you know, Tash, sweetheart, just *stop*. Stop and take a moment to think about the rest of your life.' Ros looked at her mother, as if for reassurance. 'It's not about controlling everyone or fulfilling some nightmare Jewish mom cliché. It's about loving my daughter and wishing only that she could see her best self more clearly.'

Esther was flooded with pity and love for her own daughter all of a sudden. She linked her arm through hers. 'Rosa. I'm sorry. You're right. It's not easy being a mother.'

'It's not easy being a daughter.'

Esther looked at her strong fierce beautiful girl. Saw Rosalind through all the decades; all the triumphs; all the tears; all the little and big things she had worried about over the years; the things she had thought mattered; the things she learned did. And she contemplated the great secret at the heart of their relationship: a secret Ros guarded more ferociously than anything else. The truth, they both knew, was that Esther had not been a good mother. She had been so many other things, but not that. And Ros had protected the world from knowing this, always. Protected her, always.

So you do want to control everyone, Esther knew. *And I know why. I know what that's about. And you shouldn't be ashamed of it. But you cannot control your daughter's heart.*

She spoke very softly. 'Darling, the thing is . . . Whether you approve or not, those two were drawn together from the first moment they met. It was obvious to me that very first afternoon at West Street, how they looked at each other, how they saw each other. You

221

might think they rushed into it; I'm amazed they waited as long as they did. Three months they were apart, they never even saw each other or spoke! And still it was there, more powerful than ever, when he came back. So you must . . . I think you must stop worrying about her and try to be happy for them. *Nu?*'

Ros sighed. 'Okay. Fine. I will. I will try to be happy for them. And when it all falls apart again, I will be there and I will love her.'

'Feh!' Esther cried. 'Nothing is going to fall apart. Not this time. Not with him.' She rose to her feet. 'Now we should stay a little while longer here with Max, and then you can please take me back to my apartment. I am loath to admit defeat, but I think I will need a little rest before tonight.'

★ ★ ★

There had been a heatwave in Brooklyn that summer, she remembered, as she navigated them towards the Brooklyn-Queens-Expressway.

They had been at the beach. She must only have been about five or six years old. It was a sweltering morning, and her father had announced that he'd had enough, he was taking them all to the beach. They'd packed a picnic. And there, for the first time, she had seen women in polka-dot bikinis, colourful sunglasses, pretty patterned scarves over their hair — just like the pictures she and her friend Janet sometimes saw in the fashion magazines Janet's mother left lying around her house. Those women had splashed delicately in the shallows while their husbands and children jumped and played in the waves. Then they had scampered back to the sand, laughing, rubbing scented suntan oil on each other's backs and elegantly lighting cigarettes. Had it really been like that, or was she remembering something from the movies?

She did remember her father taking three folding deckchairs from the back of the station wagon and setting them up on the sand. And her mother standing stock still, staring out to sea, a look on her face that her daughter had not understood. Usually her mother's face was one that gleamed: even the smallest things could make her laugh or weep for joy. She was the sort of mother who might take half an hour over the peeling of an orange: sniffing the rind, licking the juice off her fingers with little exclamations of delight, biting and sucking each segment as if it were the most extravagantly delicious thing she had tasted in all the world. The sort of mother who would sit watching the new washing machine turn around and around in astonishment. Or stand outside on the street on a sunny day and simply hold her face up to the sky for a few moments, a smile dancing across her face as if this were some kind of miracle rather than just the regular, everyday blue of a New York summer morning.

Sometimes Rosa found her mother's behaviour a little embarrassing; none of her friend's moms seemed to go crazy over an orange rind or a load of laundry or a blue sky. But then she would feel bad, for she loved her mother more than anything in the world. And today, at the beach, with the sun bouncing off the sea, she wanted nothing more than for her mom just to be her normal joyful self; to laugh or smile or sing with her usual glee. Instead, Esther had just stood there, as if she and her father and all the pretty women frolicking in the waves did not even exist — as if *nothing* existed. That terrifying emptiness in her mother's eyes had made Rosa feel cold, even in the searing heat.

Her dad had opened a striped umbrella over their three chairs and positioned the blue icebox containing their Cokes and sand-wiches just in front, grinding its base into the sand. Then, pulling out a brown paper package from Loehmann's from behind his back like a magician, he'd told her he had a present for his little princess. And she had unwrapped the package with breathless excitement — to discover, folded in tissue paper tied with a yellow ribbon, her first ever bathing suit. Red, with white spots, it had a picture of Minnie Mouse on the front and a white frill along the top. She had been immediately, headily in love with it. She'd slipped out of her dress and wriggled the bathing suit on right there in front of everyone. And it had fitted her *perfectly*. 'Mommy, Mommy, look, look!' she'd exclaimed, leaping over the sand to tug at her mother's hand. But her mother had kept staring out to sea, had not even looked down to see her child in her new bathing suit; it had almost been as if she could not even feel Rosa tugging at her hand, her skirt. After a prolonged and frustrated moment of being ignored, Rosa had burst into tears, only to be instantly scolded by her father, who told her not to be so spoiled, so damned selfish, and to *leave her mother in peace for just one moment*.

Her mother had eventually sat, rearranging her face into its usual loveliness, exclaiming at the bathing suit. But her eyes had not come back. And she hadn't removed her stockings, her hat, her summer dress or her long-sleeved blue cardigan that afternoon. She hadn't even removed her shoes. She had remained there in silence, not even noticing that people were pointing at her, until eventually the sun, dropping lazily into the sea, had disappeared altogether and in the warm grey-blue light it had been time to pack up and drive home.

Back in the apartment on Howard Avenue that evening, a still-furious Rosa, wearing her Minnie Mouse bathing suit under her shorts and T-shirt, had deliberately barged in on her mother in the bathroom, even though it was expressly forbidden. And there, with the glistening, translucent bubbles of her mother's bath unable to hide them, she had seen the five numbers, as black as night, inked indelibly on Esther's forearm.

'I'm sorry we never talked about it,' Esther said now, just as Ros was clicking her indicator to change lanes on the expressway. Astonished, Ros drew a sharp intake of breath. Esther had been silent ever since they'd left the cemetery; she assumed she had been asleep. Had her mother in fact been reading her mind?

Her voice, when she spoke, had gone rusty.

'I wish you had been able to talk to me about it.'

She glanced towards the passenger side. Her mother's eyes were still closed. After a moment, a single tear leaked from one closed eye and trickled down that ancient, lined cheek. Ros, battling the onslaught of many emotions, swallowed her shock. She had not seen her mother cry in so long.

'But I couldn't.'

'I know,' Ros whispered, as the cars in front began to swim in her own blearing vision. She gripped the steering wheel a little tighter. 'I know.'

'I hope you understand.'

'I do.'

Esther still did not open her eyes. 'Then do something for me, will you? Let the girls live their own lives. Let them be who they need to be. Let them be who they are.'

15

'Are we nearly there yet?' Raf half opened one eye and cracked his lazy morning smile, totally busting Natasha, who, never one to sleep on flights, had been dozily watching him sleep. Even with his mouth slightly open, his mad hair even more unruly than usual and his neck cricked at an awkward angle against the window, the sight of him was a wonder. She was fascinated by the precise details: the line of his jawbone; his nose, broken in a soccer game when he was thirteen; his mouth, whose lopsided smile felt sometimes like her undoing . . .

It was two months since he had walked into Uppercase Books that drizzling Sunday afternoon. St Patrick's Day, as it happened, the very afternoon that in a former life she had been due to marry Josh Liebowitz. The skies outside had been a damp, gunmetal grey; inside, though, a benediction. Natasha had been in the back stocking shelves as the bell had tinkled and she'd heard a too-familiar voice tell Nathan that he'd seen on the website that the store had acquired an annotated copy of Mahmoud Darwish's poetry collection *Unfortunately It Was Paradise*, which he was interested in purchasing for his parents' upcoming wedding anniversary.

You. It's you.

She hadn't seen him since he'd left her apartment that other Sunday, back in December. And now she had wondered if the world might cease turning at the fact of him.

She'd turned around slowly, and there he was. Rafi Haroun. After all this time. She wondered if she had ever been gladder to see a human face.

Raf had looked staggered, too. He had collected himself, and then smiled slowly at her. *Well, well.*

'Natasha Bernstein. Mine eyes dazzle.'

'I love you,' she managed not to say. She cleared her throat, somehow gathered words. 'I was thinking about you just the other day.'

Now, on the airplane, she said: 'We're about to land. Wake up, sleepy-head.'

They'd transited in London last night and caught the red-eye along with dozens of Jewish families, many in yarmulkes and tzitzis, tichels and shpitzels that Natasha had seemed to notice for the first time as they'd boarded at Heathrow. A weighty sense of homecoming hung in the recycled cabin air and she wondered if it was always like this; if every time she had flown to Israel with her family on vacation it had been the same, and she simply had not picked up on the atmosphere before. While they were planning this trip, she had been shocked when Raf told her that even as an American citizen born on American soil who had never held a Palestinian ID, he would still need to get prior permission from the Israeli consulate in New York to enter Israel via Ben-Gurion. She'd been confounded. 'How is that even *legal*, if you're an American citizen? I mean, technically, what is the difference between you and me, in this case?' It was just how it was, he'd explained, levelly. Most people of Palestinian descent, including his parents, who had been US citizens for over thirty years, had to enter through the Allenby Bridge in Jordan. They didn't visit very often. He was lucky he was able to come through Tel Aviv at all.

As they landed, Natasha wondered if she would discern, behind Raf's easy and unaffected demeanour, some trace of all that; something that reflected the sense of injustice that he must, surely, feel? This trip had been solely her idea, after she had taken on the daunting task of trying to write Esther's story. She needed to visit Yad Vashem; Raf had some time off coming up; maybe, she ventured, they could go there together? And then the idea had only intensified after they'd visited Dearborn last month.

'Take me there,' she'd demanded, as they'd lain entwined in the single bed in his old boyhood room at his parents' house. They were visiting for Zaki and Amina's anniversary: either their fifty-fifth, if you asked Zaki, the self-professed 'hopeless romantic', who liked to date it from the day they'd met as kids in the Al-Amari refugee camp in 1958; or their forty-third, if you asked the clearer-eyed Amina, who felt it didn't count until the day they were finally reunited in Damascus many years later. 'I want to see where you come from.'

'Mmm . . . I was born in a hospital seven miles away,' he'd murmured sleepily into the groove between her shoulder blades, his hands on her body.

She'd wriggled around to face him, purposefully. His old bed was so narrow, their noses were touching. Placing a hand on his cheek, she'd said, smiling, 'You know what I mean.'

He'd looked at her for a while, and she'd tried in vain to read his face, aware that he was holding something back. 'Okay, *habibti*.' He'd tenderly kissed her eyelids. 'We'll talk about it in the morning.' And then he'd kissed her collarbone, her neck, her lips, her belly; and then all thoughts of travel, of anything, had been submerged in him.

But this morning, other than the slightly red rims of a night on an airplane, Raf's luminous eyes betrayed nothing but his usual barely contained hunger for adventure. He steered them expertly through the Ben-Gurion terminal, which was gleaming in the sunlight that streamed through the wall-to-ceiling glass windows. As they neared the immigration lines, Natasha noticed a succession of retro posters on the other side of the walkway. *Welcome home!* one proclaimed. *We are part of you, you are part of us!* Another read: *One million in Israel! On to the next million!* Internally recoiling, she scrutinized his face again. But he was whistling and looking straight ahead, untroubled.

Having always been welcomed into Israel with a hassle-free *Shalom!* Natasha was braced for a different experience this morning, and she wondered aloud if they were likely to be held up. 'Depends. It helps that a lot of Jews have the surname Haroun or Harouni.' He shrugged. 'Then again, Rafik — not so helpful. I have of course often considered changing my name to Rafa'el.' He winked at her, a cheeky reference to that

232

unthinking comment she had made all those months ago near the cinema, blithely assuming he was Jewish. 'Anyway,' he pulled out their identical American passports from his rucksack, 'even if they don't like me much, there's nothing they can actually do about it.'

They could, however, bombard him with questions. The IDF official whose booth they'd ended up at wanted Raf's father's name, and his grandfather's; the names and addresses of his aunts, uncles and cousins; details of other Arab countries he'd visited; his planned itinerary on this trip, including the names of Palestinians he was going to meet in the West Bank and why. When Raf asked, in his surprisingly decent Hebrew, if the official would mind not stamping his passport because he had family in Lebanon and Jordan he might like to visit, the guy just smirked. At some point he took Raf's passport away and vanished, and when he finally returned, over thirty minutes later, he began to question Natasha. About their relationship, about how and where they had met; about whether Raf had asked her to carry anything or meet anyone while they were on vacation. He took down the names of the Israeli family she assured him she had, looking up with interest when she mentioned her uncle, Adam Bernstein. When they were eventually allowed through to collect their suitcases, she crossly wondered why it was any of their business who they were seeing or why they were here. It took Raf gently pointing out that Israeli concerns at seeing a Jewish woman with a Palestinian boyfriend were to be expected, and on some level reasonable, to calm her down.

They were basing themselves in East Jerusalem for the trip, but their plan was to spend a few hours in Tel Aviv this morning so that Raf could catch up with an old colleague and indulge in a little architecture geekery — there were some new buildings that had gone up since he was last here that he was keen to see. In the arrivals hall, Natasha would have automatically joined the line for a cab, but Raf led her to the train, buying tickets and cracking jokes with the vendor in Hebrew about whether the breakfast was better at Benedict's, the legendary twenty-four-hour place on Ben Yehoda, or Café Masada over on Hayarkon Street, right by the sea.

'She says she swears by Benedict's, but I got this craving for the shakshuka at Café Masada,' he said as they settled on the train that would speed them towards the city. 'Did you ever eat there?'

She hadn't. Café Masada turned out to be a classic Raf joint: unassuming, unpretentious, the sort of place she would have walked past without seeing before he began taking her on his magical mystery tours around inauspicious corners of New York that revealed endless hidden treasures. Raf's attention to things made them radiant — a grimy downtown dive, suddenly beautiful; the wrought iron of a dilapidated balcony in Brooklyn, oxide-blighted but so elegant; a nondescript cornice on the corner of a building on Bleecker, under which was tucked an angel with butterfly wings: he saw it all, he noticed everything, there was nothing he was not interested in.

And being with him was like coming home. The first time Natasha had walked into his apartment on India Street, she had known it. Raf's place was entirely him and therefore already loved; this tiny, light-flooded apartment filled with the spoils of an interesting life well lived. She knew it all, already. The guitar propped up in the corner, the monochrome photographs on the walls, the old Mason jars on the windows overflowing with plants. The wooden cabinet containing stacks of vinyl. And his excellent book collection, which she'd automatically begun to peruse, spotting so many friendly and familiar spines.

His old gramophone co-existed with a sleek black iPod dock; his coffee table, stained with the Olympic rings of former mugs, turned out to be a battered luggage trunk from 1920s Cairo that had belonged to a member of his family. And on a wooden shelf: a black Anglepoise and two blocky vintage cameras, a Leica and Rolleiflex that, she later discovered, he'd restored himself. 'Yeah, fuck Instagram, I like things that are old and beautiful and tell stories,' he'd shrugged. *Me too*, she'd agreed, imagining how perfect her 1922 Corona typewriter would look next to his Rolleiflex. She loved how he noticed things, and the things he noticed.

As they took a table on the terrace, facing the Mediterranean, Natasha was grateful for the shakshuka, a sizzling skillet of baked eggs, tomatoes, onions, garlic and local spices. She realised she was starving. As she ate, she half listened, half daydreamed, a little fuzzy-headed with exhaustion as Raf and his Israeli buddy Gilad chattered in American-inflected English and Hebrew about architects she'd never heard of, people she'd never met, the Shu'fat housing project they'd worked on together. Calm, watching the sea, she found herself wondering all over again how any of this was possible. How they were here. She'd had to consciously try to force herself not to fall too far too fast. But had failed. Falling was the word, too: loving Raf was like losing consciousness. Everything had come at once, her heart was dangerously full.

But New York had been one thing. This would be different. Being here was a test she had set for them, whether consciously or not. And now the possible folly or the wisdom of her decision tussled unanswerably in her mind, and her excitement about the trip was fractured with apprehension. At the heart of it, she knew, she was seeking the answer to a question. She just had not quite articulated what it was yet.

After a moment, Natasha left the boys and went down to put her feet in the sea.

★   ★   ★

Gilad had to go to work soon, but he stowed their cases in his car and told them he'd meet them at the central station later, from where they would take a bus to Jerusalem. The new building Raf wanted to look at was in the Neve Tzedek neighbourhood, not far along the beach from here, so after Gilad left, they strolled by the sea for a while before he took her hand and led her into a rabbit warren of narrow streets. The look on his face as he finally located the building and took in the bold white asymmetric structure made Natasha so happy, and she surreptitiously whipped out her phone to snap a picture. She loved to look at him looking at things: he took such an uncomplicated pleasure in architecture, and was so generous with his passion. In Dearborn, Zaki had shown her photos in an old album of Raf as a little boy, beaming proudly over his impressively complex Lego structures. He had dug out old childhood sketchbooks in which his son's talents as a draughtsman were already evident. Raf still drew, every day, all the time; could hardly be separated from his notebooks and freshly sharpened pencils and was obsessed by what he saw as the virtue of connecting brain and soul and hand via paper and ink, even though the bulk of his professional designs were finished on futuristic CAD technology. Raf believed so uncomplicatedly in what he did, and in the power of the built environment to shape how people thought, felt and acted. How they lived. His heroes, she had learned, were the architects who enshrined in their practice a belief that rational and beautiful architecture could not only make people's lives better but make them behave better too. He liked grand, brave, imaginative architectural gestures that still paid close attention to the detail of being human. 'Think about it,' he'd sometimes enthuse, perhaps after a pint of Guinness too many, or as they hung out in his apartment talking excitedly and rapidly; unhindered, unhinged, like children learning each other. 'Building a space for people to co-exist in, any space, it's pretty much the most powerful physical symbol of the idea of community and civilization we've ever come up with! And all of this, every line, every brick, every roof tile can change people's lives!' In less lofty moments he would catch himself and laugh, and say: 'Whatever — I just like to build stuff.'

But as they carried on south to Jaffa now, chattering about nothing and everything, Natasha again felt like they were circling the elephant in the room, warding off the one thing they should be talking about. Silently she wondered how she might begin to broach the competing anxieties that had been nagging at her since they'd landed at Ben-Gurion this morning. Why were they here? They had a relentless itinerary over the next few days: his uncle Fadi and family in Beit Jala; his grandmother Maha and her uncle Adam in Jerusalem; her research slots at Yad Vashem; seeing friends on both sides. And they were due to spend their final days in Ramallah with Amina's sister, his auntie Shafiqa, and her family, including Leila, Raf's closest cousin. How would Raf's 'real' Palestinian relations, as he dubbed them, react to her presence in their towns, their houses, their lives? What was she trying to prove? To herself, to him, to her family, to his?

'So this is . . . this is sort of weird, right?' she attempted with a cheeriness she didn't quite feel, as Rafi stopped to take more photos — a bench, a window frame, a rooftop, her. 'Us just strolling around Jaffa like we're, I dunno, *tourists*? I wasn't expecting any of this to hit me so hard. Do you think . . . maybe we should be talking about it?'

He stopped. 'Talking about what?'

Having grown up in the let-it-all-out environs of West 83rd Street, Natasha was still struggling to adjust to the private kernel of inner mystery Raf retained. 'Well, Toto, we're not in Brooklyn anymore. So I guess I just want to know how this actually makes you feel. Being here.'

'In Israel, you mean?'

'Yes. Or at least here in Jaffa.'

Raf fell silent and put his arm round her as they walked on.

'I'm not *not* telling you anything,' he claimed, after a few minutes. 'I don't really know how to explain how any of this makes me feel. I never have. There's so much to say and no way to say it.'

'Please just try,' she begged, as they approached the clock tower square in the Old City. 'Talk to me. Tell me things. What about your grandfather's farm, that was somewhere near here, wasn't it? How does it make you *feel* that in 1948 they were all just turfed out, and that was the end of the farm?'

'Tasha . . . '

'And still, even today, the Israelis would kick the Arabs out of Jaffa in a heartbeat if they could, wouldn't they?'

'Listen to you, *habibti*!' he exclaimed, stopping her with a squeeze of her shoulder. 'I'm serious. Don't think for a *second* the Arabs wouldn't kick out the Jews if they possibly could!' He rubbed her arms. 'It's complicated, okay? Understatement of the century. When we go to Uncle Fadi's, you should ask *him* about the farm. He'll be able to tell you much more about it than I can, probably show you pictures, everything.'

'I will,' she said, exasperated. There was something about Raf's apparent bloodless-ness on this that she couldn't quite — what, trust? 'But I love you and I want to hear about this from *you*. I mean, what are you even thinking about right now?'

He gave her his crooked and maddeningly

disarming smile. 'I'm thinking you look especially irresistible when you're a little bit angry. And that I want to kiss you. And that I could really do with another coffee.'

She rolled her eyes as he led her to a café and ordered in Arabic two cups of the sweet, muddy cardamom-scented drink that was served in tiny porcelain cups alongside mini pistachio pastries. Across the little round table, she kept her arms firmly folded.

'Okay,' he finally relented. 'Don't laugh. Here in Jaffa, I feel hopeful.'

'*Hopeful?*'

'If I were to tell you my grand philosophy about hopefulness, on the other hand, you'd think I was naïve and romantic and crazy.' He picked up a sweet and popped the whole thing in his mouth.

'I already think you're naïve and romantic and crazy. We're here, aren't we?'

He grinned at her through his mouthful. '*Alhamdulillah*. Yes, we are.'

'So what makes you hopeful?'

He took a sip of coffee. 'So once upon a time,' he said, motioning out to the square with its crazy maze of streets extending in all directions, 'you had everyone here in Jaffa — families called Chelouche and Hammami and Abulafia and Haroun; my family were here, and it was all mixed up, everyone living side by side, Christians, Muslims, Jews, the whole crazy patchwork. And Jaffa *worked*. Once upon a time, it was possible to be here, and to live together, no matter who you were, or who *they* were, and that — '

'But that was a hundred years ago,' she protested. 'Don't you think we've gone way too far beyond that now?'

'But you asked what made me hopeful,' he shot back. 'And I'm one of those crazy fools who thinks that if you hold on to what's good in the world, what's *been* good and what may still be good, you can change how the world spins — in however small a way.'

'You should meet my grandmother,' Natasha said. 'I have a feeling you two would really get along.'

Raf laughed. He drank some more coffee and for a moment his eyes disappeared behind the cup. Then he said, 'Don't get me wrong. Of course I'm sad for my family when I think about what they lost. But I'm sad for *everyone's* family when I think about what they lost. I'm sad for yours. I'm sad for that dude's over there.' An old Palestinian man in *keffiyeh* was shuffling past them with the help of a stick. Raf nodded towards a scrappy little kid kicking a stone for a football in the square. 'That little boy? Who is he? What happened to his family?' He turned back to her. 'And when I talk to Esther, I think of her family that night in Zholkva and I think of my grandfather in Qatamon, what happened to them after they left; I think of my dad aged five packing up his satchel with his toys and his books, imagining he was coming home again in a few weeks, and I'm in bits for them all. For everyone. But truthfully, Tash, I also just feel like the luckiest schmuck in the world that I'm the one who gets to have the luxury of just *thinking* about it, when they actually had to live it. Or are still living it.'

She bit her lip. 'Okay. Point taken.'

Under the table, he trapped her knees hard between his. 'That's not what I meant. It wasn't a criticism. I *love* how you think, I love how your mind works. I love you. But . . . Look, I know I'm an incurable optimist, and maybe I really am dumb and naïve, but I can't walk around here feeling bitter about the past. Besides, I have no right to feel resentful. My family's past isn't really mine.'

'What do you mean?'

He hesitated. 'Tash. Listen. I think maybe you want me to tell you something I don't feel. And I know that's only because you're empathetic and lovely and you want to make sure you're really soaking it all up and grasping it and feeling everything there is to feel in that great big heart of yours. But it would be hypocritical of me to try and . . . I don't even know how to put this . . . to try and inhabit something that I have no ownership over. What the fuck do I have to complain about? My parents were some of the lucky ones.'

'*Lucky*? Raf. Your parents were not lucky. They were forced from their homes in the middle of the night under attack. They lost everything they had. They ended up in a refugee camp. How can you call that lucky?' She looked at him, hard. 'What is it in their story that you won't acknowledge? Why won't you, I don't know, take responsibility for it?'

'Of course I won't take responsibility for it — it's not mine to take!'

'But I mean now. It's *all* our responsibilities, now, isn't it? This whole place tells us that.'

'Sorry, Tash, but I don't think you can live your life as an imagined counterpart to your parents' life.' He motioned at the waiter to bring over two more coffees.

'So what, you just delete history?' She sat back, exhaled. 'Rafi, I'm sorry to say this, but this is the one thing about you that I just can't believe in. Your idealism is premised on the idea you can just blithely ignore history, and I don't think you can. I think that's wilful blindness. I don't believe in it.'

'Well, I don't believe in all your guilt and liberal shame, if we're really getting down to it,' he told her, without malice, as he stirred extra sugar into his second coffee. 'You think that by exhibiting endless guilt and concern about what happened — what happened to *everyone* — you somehow partake of the original injustice yourself. That's what your whole guilty liberal shtick is built on. But Tash, baby, all you've done is grow up in America, the luckiest of the lucky, and you've had everything. Just like me.'

'How do you feel about being Palestinian, Rafi?'

He balked. 'How do I feel about being *Palestinian?*'

'Yeah. How do you feel? Because I think maybe you want to have this identity, and yet you don't, and you're deeply fucking confused.'

He inclined his head. 'Do you, now.' He stuffed another pastry in his mouth. 'Clever girl. I don't know how to answer that.' He reached out a conciliatory hand. 'But I do want you always to say this stuff to me, okay? Everything you really mean and feel. Because nobody ever calls me on this stuff, and it's important.' He smiled at her. 'And even

246

though you've just been so cross and mean, I really want to kiss you.'

'You're right. You're right, of course you're right. That's why I'm cross. And I want to be having this conversation with you for years and years.'

'You can. You will. But first, you have to kiss me.'

'Raf, you're ridiculous.'

'Nope, I'm in love with you. And I just want to say one other thing, okay? You're right, my family had a tough time of it. In many cases are still having a tough time of it. But nobody in my family ever went through what Esther went through. Or Otto, or Adela, or even Frank. And I just want you to hold on to that fact over the next few days. Because there are going to be things that are hard to see. Okay? Promise?'

Without thinking, Natasha touched the locket around her neck.

After a beat, she said, 'I promise.'

16

Jerusalem! City of God, city of gold, city of David, of mirrors, of tunnels, of peace. City of heaven. City of longing. Tomorrow the familial obligations would begin in earnest; today was purely for themselves. Up early, swimming through jet lag, they walked directly from their hotel on the edge of the Old City to Damascus Gate and into the teeming wonders of the world beyond. Natasha, instantly love-struck all over again, thrilled to the polyglot shouts of the street vendors who peddled dates and oranges and *za'atar* and shoes and spices and batteries and toys and dresses and sweets and trinkets and untold other articles. The Old City was a hub of non-stop human activity, a nucleus of commerce, of social transaction, of drama and chaos and surprise. With blissful lack of purpose, she and Raf ambled through the Arabic Quarter, and the Armenian and the Jewish; stopping in front of certain buildings and landmarks, trading memories and reflections; looking more closely at something curious or intriguing or beautiful that winked up at them from the brimming streets. In the

Christian Quarter Raf bought her a cup of pomegranate juice pressed before them by a boy missing his two front teeth, to whom he chatted in rapid Arabic. At St Anne's Church, at the eastern end of the Via Dolorosa, he told her how his great-grandfather, his grandfather and even his own father, as a young boy, had worshipped here. It had the most magnificent acoustics in the world, he told her; inside, as they popped their heads into the ravishing edifice, a choir singing in Latin proved this to be the case.

When she realized that Raf seemed to be steering her toward the security checkpoint that led to the Western Wall, Natasha stopped and laid a hand on his arm. He looked curiously at her.

'We don't have to do this,' she said.

'What kind of American tourist would come to Jerusalem and not go see the Wailing Wall?' he cracked.

'You're not an American tourist.'

'I beg to differ.' He pulled their passports from his brown leather satchel and handed them to the young IDF soldier who was manning the checkpoint; fingers absently tapping on his gun as he chewed gum and flirted with the pretty female soldier in her army-issue khaki who guarded the other X-ray machine. 'Besides, I'm an architect. I get a kick out of walls.'

Raf swiftly unloaded the contents of his jeans pockets into the tray and removed his belt, and his Leica from around his neck. He walked through with something of a defiant swagger, she thought, and she followed him, mentally steeling herself for what she knew lay beyond.

She had of course been back many times since, but all these years later, she was still wiped out by it. As little girls, she and Rachel used to place written prayers into the crevices of the ancient wall. She remembered it so clearly from the year they came to visit Otto and Sara in Katamon, the last time they saw their grandfather, not long before he died. Rosalind had helped them roll up their papers really tight and squeeze them carefully into the cracks in the wall. All prayers, she told them, ascended to heaven from right here, from Jerusalem. And Natasha, even at five years old, had felt a sort of wild wonder at the thought of all those words, centuries' worth of words, packed tight into the magical stone. And she remembered feeling comforted, somehow, by the idea of a wall of words, even though the rest of that vacation had been rather traumatic. If she remembered rightly, it had been the first time her mom and dad had sat down and tried to explain to her — Rachel was too little — about what had happened to Otto and Sara, and also to their grandmother Adela, along with the unknown uncle and aunts, Daddy's brother and sisters, who'd all perished as children alongside her.

The precision of the memory slayed her. Of Ros clutching her and Rachel's hands as they hesitantly approached the wall on the right-hand side, the narrower area reserved for females. Shyly, they had prayed for their grandpa Otto, whom they knew might die soon. And for their other grandpa and grandma back at home in New York, Max and Esther. And for their grandma Adela and all the other lost members of their family. Ros had started to weep, uncontrollably, and Natasha hadn't known how to bear it. A very simple but profound understanding had lodged itself in her soul then, like a prayer being stuffed into a crack in the wall: she did not ever want her mother to feel like that again, and would do anything she could, anything, to take the sadness away.

Today it was Rafi who tightly held her hand as they approached the wall. And behind it stood the iconic mosque that his mother Amina and her family had prayed in for generations. Al-Aqsa. *This is your history*, she reflected, *you whom I love. But it's mine too.*

251

For a few minutes they stood at a distance and observed the wall and its lines of black-clad davening worshippers in deepening silence. *My family. My wall of words.* Eventually Raf put a hand gently on the small of her back and they walked away from the wall, away from the direction they'd come.

The guard at the checkpoint had told Raf in Hebrew that al-Haram al-Sharif was open to tourists and followers of other religions this morning. It was serendipity, Natasha was convinced. She had never been inside Temple Mount, and the first glimpse, after climbing the stairs, took her breath away. She could not speak: all words, all responses died in her throat as she absorbed the sheer scale and tried to make sense of the dignity and magnificence of this most ancient and sacred of Islamic works of architecture.

'I think I need to sit down,' she finally said, faintly.

Raf, Leica back around his neck, touched her cheek. 'Okay. I just want to look at something around the other side. I'll only be a couple of minutes.'

'Take your time.'

In the shadow of the Dome of the Rock, Natasha dropped to the ground and took a sip of water and tied her blue scarf a little tighter over her hair. She needed to collect herself, to straighten out her tangled mind, but it was all too much to take in, this concatenation of rock and earth and stone and metal and mosaic and paint and engineering and artistry and the divine. *And everything that it means to be a human being,* she thought simply. *There is nothing that is not here.*

Struck by a need overpowering and pure, Natasha did what she always did when she had to try and make sense of something difficult. She reached for words — or in this case, her notebook, in which, having pulled out a pen, she began to scribble.

17

'*Shukran jazeel!*'

'Thank you' was pretty much the limit of her Arabic, but she was determined to try.

'*Ahlan!*' Raf's grandmother beamed in response, as Raf poured coffee into three little brass cups. It was not long since they'd eaten breakfast at the hotel, but Maha kept going back to the kitchen and returning with trays of pistachio and honey parcels, little dishes of fresh olive oil and ground thyme, crushed green olives, sweet onions, warm flat bread. She had gone to so much trouble to celebrate Raf's visit.

Natasha sat back in her chair and took in their surroundings. She was trying to stave off an imprecise sadness that she could feel pressing in on her chest as Raf and his grandmother chattered in their musical language. Maha's house had clearly once been beautiful, but it was now in a state of near-dereliction. As Raf had led her through the Jewish Quarter of the Old City and down a dirty, cramped alleyway adorned with faded red, green and black graffiti, he'd told her that his cousins had warned him things had gotten bad since he'd last visited. But the extent of the dilapidation and the squalor had clearly been worse than he'd imagined; he had gasped when they reached the house. Mangy, skeletal cats picked at bones and other scraps scattered around the piles of broken brick and other unidentifiable detritus near her front door, and the smell of sewage was overwhelming. As he'd reached for the battered grey knocker shaped like a closed grey fist, Natasha could see the muscles working in his jaw. She'd never noticed that happening before.

'Hey.' She'd tried to reach out to touch his hand, to share a moment before they went in. But Maha was already opening the door and he was stooping to enclose his grandmother in the most loving of embraces. At the sight of Rafi, Maha had started to cry, and had held on to him for as long as she could, until he'd gently disengaged her in order to introduce her to Natasha.

Inside the house, many of the traditional patterned floor tiles, which had probably once been exquisite, were broken, as were two of the windows. Arbitrary bits of pipe and plumbing were exposed; a mad spaghetti of electrical wires dangled through one window; and a section of the roof appeared to have collapsed, exposing a luminous triangle of blue sky. While the surfaces were spotless and shining, the stench from the open sewer outside could not be disguised, even by this beautiful fragrant coffee she had prepared for them.

Maha herself was all warmth and kindness. She was dressed in an embroidered *thoub*, which Raf had explained over breakfast was the traditional woven Palestinian dress. 'It's a bit like wearing a Mets jacket,' he'd joked. 'It marks out the territory, tells people where you're from.' Now, though, there was no laughter in his eyes.

On the wall was an embroidered image of the Dome of the Rock and the Al-Aqsa mosque. Next to it were embroidered Qu'r'anic phrases in gleaming brass frames. On a low table, covered in an embroidered tablecloth similar to the work on Maha's dress, Natasha saw photographs of a girl she recognized as a young Amina and her siblings, as well as faded snapshots of the dozens of grandchildren, including Rafi. There was also a formal, sepia-tinted wedding picture of Maha and Walid, Raf's grandfather, and others that looked as though they dated all the way back to the Ottoman era, or at the very least the Mandate years.

As Natasha turned her attention back to Raf and his grandmother, inevitably excluded from their conversation, she saw that her boyfriend's face, usually so unaffected and open, was tense. Their voices were rising. At one point it was clear that Maha was trying to reassure him about something, touching his arm, but Raf was not to be consoled.

'What's the matter?' Natasha wondered, but Raf perhaps did not hear her. So absorbed was he in their discussion, he seemed almost to have forgotten she was there.

When they left, he looked deeply shaken as they walked back through the Old City. Touching his hand, Natasha hoped to transmit in that modest gesture, which was all she could comfortably do until they reached the privacy of their hotel room, that she loved him, and understood at some level that what they had just seen was devastating.

'I'm sorry,' she said, as they exited through the bustle of Damascus Gate and headed up the pale stone stairs to street level. At the top, Raf stopped and properly looked at her. For an instant he seemed almost surprised she was there. And then his face began to relax, and the jagged lines of his frown to dissolve. He ran a hand through his hair.

'I'm sorry I disappeared back there.'

'It's okay. I understand. Can you tell me what was going on with Maha?'

They carried on walking up towards Nablus Road.

'She's been applying for permission to fix up the house for years, maybe ten years,' he began. 'She doesn't want to do anything much, but my mom sent her some money just to mend the roof and do the plumbing and they ... Well, the Israelis won't grant any Palestinians in East Jerusalem or the Old City permission to rebuild or do up their houses. They won't let her do anything.'

It was the first time she'd ever heard him say something like that, *'the Israelis ... '* in that tone of voice. *They.* She steeled herself as he carried on.

'And then last month she had a visitor. Some charming young guy from the Civil Administration, speaking impeccable Arabic. And he told her that her house was worth about two hundred thousand shekels.'

Natasha, doing a basic conversion in her head, didn't know if that was a lot or a little — such an amount, a little over $50,000, barely got you a storage container in New York.

'Two hundred thousand sheks,' repeated Raf. 'And you know what he told her next? That if she sold it to them, they would pay her a million *dollars* for it. A million dollars! That's three-point-five million sheks.'

'Jesus!' Natasha exclaimed. When he didn't respond, she added, unthinkingly, 'But that's a good thing, right?'

He stopped.

'I mean, that's a hell of a lot of money.'

'It gets worse,' he said, ignoring her. 'Because when she said no, they straight-up told her they'd give her *two* million bucks for it. Two million American dollars.'

'*What?*' Natasha spluttered. 'Two million bucks for that house? What did she say?'

'Tash, they're offering her that on the condition that she renounces her Jerusalem ID and leaves.'

'Oh. But — where would they ask her to go?' Hurriedly, she corrected herself: 'I mean, not that she would ever leave . . . '

'Well no, not up until now she wouldn't. Turns out those sharks have been coming back every six months or so. And meantime the house is falling apart and she's not allowed to do any renovations, nothing, literally nothing; she lives in that . . . that *shithole*, with the drains overflowing and the roof falling in, and she's eighty-six years old. I was going to see if there was anything I could try and help fix while we're here, just some basic structural stuff, but she's not even allowed to do that without risk of financial penalty. And now they're offering her this crazy amount of cash — most of which you can bet, by the way, would get sucked up in taxes and bureaucracy and whatever — and saying they will make it easy for her to move; they will do everything to help her pack up and relocate. You fucking bet they will. And she is so stressed out by it all, she told me she's actually now considering it.'

Natasha tried to take on board what he was saying. Maha's blue Jerusalem permit was indescribably precious, she knew, to Raf's family. It was everything. Between two large extended Palestinian families, she was the only person left with the blue passbook; the sole Jerusalemite remaining from hundreds, thousands of people who had for generation after generation been born, lived their lives and died here. She knew all this was going on, it wasn't like she didn't read about it back home, but to actually see it in flesh and blood, to put a face on it — Rafi's grandmother's face — was finally to under-stand what it really meant. And it got to her. Why was this woman being kicked out of the house she had lived in all her life? Why was it fair that if she, Natasha, decided to come and live in Jerusalem she would be allowed to buy a house like Maha's right away. What happened to Maha, and all the others like her, in that equation?

'So did you try and change her mind?'

Raf sighed. 'Yeah, course I did. And then I thought, wait, who the *fuck* am I to tell her what she should or shouldn't do? Me, with my nice little life in Brooklyn! Who am I to tell her how important it is that she hang in there and stay in Jerusalem at all costs, when they're making her life unlivable, when they're . . . ' He stopped. 'Sorry, I'm going on.'

'It's okay. You know I agree with you, right?'

'Yeah,' he said quietly as they carried on up the street, past the shop selling music on ancient cassette tapes, and the hairdresser, and the hopelessly optimistic-looking travel agency, outside which a collection of old men in *keffiyehs* always seemed to be gathered, smoking sheesha on green plastic chairs and drinking tiny cups of Arabic coffee all day long, never a customer in sight. 'I do know. And I'm sorry, Tash. It was just such a shock, that's all.'

Raf took off his sunglasses and passed a hand down over his face. 'I guess I've just been kind of kidding myself that my old *jaddah*'s fine out here because she's still in Jerusalem, and that's all that matters. I now see that is not the case.' He sighed again. 'And that it's *not* the only thing that matters. Not at all.'

261

18

More than five thousand miles away, the inimitable clamour-honk of Midtown through her cell phone was like a parody of itself. She blinked, groggy and confused. It looked darkish outside beyond the curtains, but clearly not night; what the hell time was it anyway? Moving her phone away from her ear to glance at its clock, she registered 7:42pm here. So just before lunchtime in New York. Succumbing to jet lag's siren lure, they had headed back to the hotel late this afternoon to have a quick nap before going out for dinner; they must have crashed right out and missed the alarm. It took her another moment or two to decipher and digest the words that were bubbling sporadically up through the line. It sounded like:

'We'll commission a thousand words.'

'I'm sorry, can you repeat that?' She scrambled upright in bed. Next to her, lying on his front, Raf stirred under the linen sheet. He turned his head towards her and laid his hand across her stomach, nudging her body closer to him, but did not open his eyes.

'A thousand words, by next Monday?'

She'd sent the pitch by email yesterday in a rare fit of bravado after they'd returned from visiting Raf's uncle Fadi — not, in fact, his uncle but rather his father Zaki's cousin. And now her insides did a little jig as she absorbed the impact of what she was hearing. 'Are you serious . . . Really?'

After a bemused pause that could simply have been international telephony doing its thing, the editor, presumably sitting at a desk all the way down on Hudson Street, Manhattan, confirmed that yes, he was serious. 'We like it. The Last Pig Butcher of the West Bank. Quirky. We'll have to come up with a catchier title but we all think it's a really interesting angle. John has always spoken so highly of you, and I enjoyed that review you did for N+1 recently. We'd like to try you out writing for the blog.' Her throat crisped; her heart began to scud as the disembodied voice went on, 'Listen, it's a pretty bad line, so we'll be in touch again by email to finalise details, okay?'

Natasha shook her head and hung up.

'Who was that?'

'I think I just got commissioned by the *New York Review* blog!' She began to gabble. 'John Deegan, my old editor at the *Times*, he'd put me in touch with an editor there ages ago, when I first lost my job, but I never seemed to have anything right to pitch them. I just sent this last night, almost as a kind of joke. I never expected them to call back!' She gave a little shriek.

Raf wriggled onto his back and pulled her body on top of his. He held her face in his hands. '*Habibti*, that's amazing. Well done you.'

'I just can't believe it! The *New York Review*! I've wanted to write for them for, like, ever.' She kissed him.

'Smarty pants,' he said into the kiss. 'About time they saw sense, then.'

'But this is crazy!' She slumped off his body and lay on her back, grinning like a lunatic. 'I can't believe it! They want a thousand words!'

They turned so they were lying opposite each other now, foreheads touching. Raf held her close. 'A thousand words on what?'

And for a moment, then, Natasha faltered. She swallowed. 'I was going to write . . . I thought I would write about Fadi and Noor . . . '

★   ★   ★

It had been blossoming within her all week. Sitting in the archives at Yad Vashem, she'd felt a rush of something primal and urgent. A

264

sense, after so long, that she was back where she belonged: notebook open, pen in hand, her brain fully engaged, trying to wrestle and shape a world through language. And perhaps it was thanks to the few pieces she'd been writing again recently; or perhaps it was just that she felt so awake to everything around her thanks to the overtures she and Esther had been making into her story; or perhaps it was how scraped and raw and simply alive she felt being here, here of all places, with him. She felt like herself again. Since they had arrived they had been winking at her everywhere, these little observations, these arresting details, these stories that were calling her name. And then yesterday, it had simply been impossible to tamp down any longer the journalistic impulse that, when it came to it, was still as instinctive to her as breathing.

*　*　*

From the terminal on Sultan Suleiman Street, right by their hotel, Raf and Natasha had caught a 'bus' — a dilapidated service taxi, really; it only had about ten seats, their vinyl covers cracked and shabby. Natasha had tried not to let her nervousness about taking public transport deep into the West Bank show. Ros and Frank had always claimed to be 'pro' the idea of them all visiting the territories, and yet, Natasha reflected, they never really had. She had been to Bethlehem once and Ramallah twice, always for short visits, always in private cars. This was an altogether different experience. From behind her sunglasses she had watched with fascination as the final two passengers boarded: a man, and a woman in full burqa holding some tatty plastic shopping bags. There ensued a heated discussion. Natasha was so caught up in wondering about the hidden face behind the burqa, the deep brown unreadable eyes, that it took her a moment to realize that the woman was in fact directing a question, in quick-fire Arabic, at *her*. 'She's asking if you'll move to sit next to her,' Raf had explained. 'She can't sit next to a male stranger but there are no other free seats, and she says she can't wait for the next bus, she's already late for an appointment.'

The bus had trundled through the bumpy, treeless roads of East Jerusalem and out towards Checkpoint 300, the controversial crossing at the site of Rachel's Tomb, where a corridor of Bethlehem had been annexed so that it remained on the Israeli side. At the first sign of the graffiti-daubed security wall, something icy had seized Natasha's heart. It was not as if she hadn't seen it before. But the pictures they printed in the *Times*, even the sections of the wall she had seen in the flesh while driving with Adam and her family a few years ago, could not have prepared her for the experience of seeing it so close.

Her fingers itching, she had resisted the urge to pull from her bag either her camera or her notebook, but had sat still and observed out of the window the hordes who gathered noisily under the occasional umbrella by the entrance to the checkpoint, hawking oranges and watermelons and shoes and batteries and paper kites to the cars that waited patiently in line to pass through. As the bus passengers clambered off at the checkpoint, she stood on the dusty roadside and silently absorbed, too, the sight of lines of Palestinians held in stasis, waiting. She and Raf, with their navy blue American passports, were waved through without delay.

On the other side of the barriers, as promised, Uncle Fadi had been waiting for them by a battered silver car; a big bear of a guy in a brown leather jacket, despite the heat. She'd been concerned about how he might react to her, knowing she was Jewish, but he had swept them both into a giant hug with a heartfelt *Ahlan-wa-sahlan!* As they'd driven through Bethlehem, which seemed even more rundown than the last time she had been here, she'd noticed the faded, peeling martyr posters, the angry-looking graffiti everywhere, the desolate faces. And sitting quietly in the back, she had retrieved her notebook, taking it all down.

If the town exuded a dejected exhaustion, Fadi's house conveyed the opposite, as cousins and aunties and uncles gathered to celebrate Raf's return. She'd been sat next to Fadi at lunch, a gigantic feast prepared by his wife Noor: grilled lamb with rice and raisins, sumac, almonds and *labneh;* a variety of Palestinian salads plus heaps of fresh falafel; piping hot flatbread with *za'atar.* And as Fadi told her his life story, relishing the novelty of an audience who hadn't heard it before, Natasha listened, rapt. The eldest of seven male cousins, he had inherited their great-uncle's pig farm, which had been in Sarafand, close to the British army base during the Mandate, until the Israelis took the city in 1948. After being evicted, the family had bought a small plot of farmland and two pigs here in Beit Jala. The pigs duly mated, and again, and the farm had grown each year until it was profitable. After a while they had opened a butcher's shop in the village, and the farm and butchery had been passed down the generations ever since. And now, Fadi had taken some pride in informing Natasha, he was the sole pig butcher left in the West Bank.

After the meal, while Raf helped Noor with the dishes and played soccer outside with his young nephews and nieces, Fadi had invited Natasha into his study to show her some photographs. And she had been reminded of what Raf had told her in Jaffa: *talk to Fadi*. As he'd guided her through the albums, he'd told her about his butcher's shop and its colourful customers — the Muslims popping in for forbidden sausages and the brazen UN wives with their diplomatic car plates smuggling back pork chops and bacon to their expat communities in Jerusalem or Tel Aviv. Looking up from a faded shot of Zaki and Fadi laughing and up to their knees in what had to be pig shit, Natasha had asked, 'But why aren't the expats and the Christians *allowed* to come to you for their sausages and pork chops?' He'd reminded her it was illegal to take anything over the border from the West Bank. 'That's why they have to be smuggled. If the IDF search your car and find the Beit Jala bacon coming back into Jerusalem, *ya'ani*, you could be in all sorts of trouble. But they're not allowed to search cars with diplomatic plates. So the consul general's wife, this sweet, innocent-looking lady, she comes to me every Friday and buys all these forbidden things, bundles them into the boot of her big car and smiles at the IDF at the checkpoints all the way home!' Fadi had chuckled as he took another swig of the sweet wine that had been pressed from the vines outside the house. Then he'd closed the photograph albums and led her back into the living room. 'She promises me she's not starting a black market for contraband pork over there in Jerusalem, *ya'ani*, but you never know!'

★   ★   ★

On the bus on the way back, Natasha, no longer caring if she drew inappropriate glances, had feverishly written down everything she could remember of their conversation, employing the old tricks of her trade — the acronyms and mnemonics and anacrostics she'd learned to rely on whenever she didn't have a dictaphone handy.

Raf, listening to his iPod and staring out of the window as the landscape rolled past, had only seemed to notice what she was doing when they were approaching Jerusalem.

'What are you writing?' he'd asked, pulling out an earbud and turning towards her.

'Just getting my thoughts down.'

He'd peered curiously at the page. 'Thoughts about Esther?'

He'd come to visit her while she was working at Yad Vashem the other day, and they'd passed an emotional hour in the archive with the original faded fragment of Esther's devastating Buchenwald love letter to her sweetheart Emanuel. While the letter, of course, never failed to unravel Natasha, she had not expected Raf to react in the way he did. He had spent a long time staring at the Yiddish words, and when she'd finally touched his hand and said maybe it was time to go, he'd looked up, and his eyes had been liquid.

'Not exactly . . . ' she'd blustered. 'I was trying to get my head around today.'

'Oh,' he'd said. 'Right.'

'I liked Fadi a lot.'

'It's bad. Noor told me it looks like they may have to sell the shop.'

Natasha had been shocked. 'Why?'

'The Christians are all leaving Beit Jala and there's no other market for his products there, obviously. And nobody from outside Bethlehem is allowed to come over the border and buy them, so it's unsustainable. What the hell does a pig butcher do if he can't sell pork?'

'Wait. Why are the *Christians* leaving?'

'A lot of Muslims are moving to Beit Jala from places like Hebron. The Christians feel like they're being pushed out, I guess. Auntie Noor described it as an exodus.'

Natasha had never really considered the impact of the settler-driven demographic shift on the Christian community. People tended to refer to the ongoing conflict between Israel and the Palestinians as 'the situation', a cheap shorthand for all that was too difficult to express or consider. And typically 'the situation' was framed in the struggle of Israeli Jew vs Palestinian Muslim and did not allow for much beyond that.

'So where are all the Christians going?' she'd asked.

'Who knows.'

*   *   *

Now, in the hotel bed, Raf was staring at her. 'You are kidding me. For real?' Sitting up, he pawed at his eyes, scratchy with too much daytime sleep, then itched his left shoulder blade with his right hand. She watched his smooth brown skin move over his sinewy muscles, his long, slight frame so different from the hirsute varsity bulk of pretty much every guy she'd ever dated since her teens,

272

not least Josh Liebowitz.

'I'll write their story honestly and with integrity,' she said. 'I'll honour everything Fadi told me; everything you said on the bus home yesterday. I'll try and do something really ... nuanced, something that wakes American readers up to the whole Christian dimension here. Puts a human face on it. I hope you know that. You — they — can totally trust me.'

Raf folded his long limbs up off the bed with a barely concealed snort. Casting his eyes around the room, he found his boxers amid the tangled heap of their hastily removed clothes from earlier and yanked them on. 'Tash, that's completely beside the point. These people are not 'the Christian dimension', whatever the fuck that even means. They're my uncle and aunt. This is my family we're talking about. They're not subjects for a *piece*!'

'I think you're being unfair.' She tried to hold her ground, wrapping the bed sheets defensively under her arms and resting her chin on her knees. 'And short-sighted. You *told* me to talk to Fadi! This is a chance to really tell their story. And it's a huge deal. I know I haven't been working as a journalist since we met, Rafi, but this is me. You have to understand that. This is who I *am*.'

Raf moved towards the bathroom. Hovering at the door, he turned, and his eyes were splintered with anger. 'Natasha. Think about what you just said. This is my family we're talking about. Real people. *You're* talking about a job, a vocation.'

'Raf, I — '

'My family. That's *really* who I am.'

He managed not to slam the door.

19

Embarking from the number 18 bus at Al-Manara, Ramallah's bustling main junction, Raf was instantly swallowed up into the kinetic scrum that made even the mayhem of the Old City in Jerusalem feel torpid. All human life was here, playing itself out in the raw and raucous day-to-day drama of existence. Car horns blared as drivers tried optimistically to squeeze around the grid-locked roundabout; kids dashed madly to and fro; street vendors sang out their cries, peddling their wares; mothers in full burqa deftly shopped for groceries and essentials whilst juggling babies on hips and toddlers at hand; a costumed man sold tiny glass cups of tea from his red contraption to stationary drivers right before the lights changed; and just then the muezzin launched into his call to prayer, which was transmitted through the speakers strung high up above them. Energized, Raf quickened his step as he headed down one of the main roads off the Manara and down the hill, noticing as he did how things seemed to have changed, at least on the outside, in the year or so since he'd last been here. Sure, the streets were still potholed, services were probably dysfunctional, but Ramallah these days was vibrant, both economically and culturally; this morning it felt like a city confident in itself.

At Café Pronto, he chose a table on the sun-dappled terrace outside, noting all the young Ramallah-ites tapping away on laptops or gabbling on iPhones as they smoked their sheeshas or cigarettes. He ordered coffee and a fresh juice and sat down, leafing through that morning's *Al-Quds*, which he'd picked up from the hotel's front desk, but not really seeing anything on the page. The past few days had been pretty intense; it felt good just to take a moment to breathe, by himself; to reflect. He wondered now if his reaction to Natasha's New York phone call yesterday evening hadn't been a little too extreme. There was no part of him that thought she would tell Fadi's story with anything but empathy and grace. It had just been a shock to hear her discuss his family in those terms, and he still didn't know how he felt about it.

He heard a voice cry '*Habibi!*' And suddenly there was Nada, striding towards him, tall and angular, sunglasses on, dressed all in black despite the heat, looking pretty badass, as usual. Before she reached him she stopped to greet and kiss most of the other patrons of the café; she was something of a Queen Bee in these parts.

'*Kaif halek?*' She kissed him thrice and sat down. 'Welcome back.'

'I'm good. Where's Leila?' he asked in Arabic.

'She's dealing with a bug we had on the site this morning; she'll be here in like five minutes. Are we eating? I'm starving.'

Raf smiled. She hadn't changed one bit. 'You go ahead. I just had breakfast. And I need to meet Natasha for lunch.'

Nada Khleifi pushed her sunglasses up into her black hair and slowly arched an eyebrow. Then she inclined her head and said, with arsenic-laced sweetness, 'Of course you do.'

After kissing the waiter hello, ordering coffee and deciding against food, Nada immediately lit a cigarette. 'So did you get the chance to check out the site? Did you have a think about what I said?'

'I always did love your idea of small talk,' Raf quipped. 'How's your mom doing? How are your brothers? And the new job?'

When she didn't reply, he conceded: 'Yeah, I saw the site.'

'And?'

Raf ran a hand lazily through his hair and took a sip of his coffee. 'Very impressive. Very thorough.'

'So? Will you help us?' She leaned forward, fixing him with her eyes.

He let her. He'd long ago learned how to resist the Nada Khleifi Jedi Mind Trick, and in that particular game he could give as good as he got.

'There's no way,' he said after a beat. 'Sorry.'

Nada shrank back in her seat and scowled. 'Are you *serious*?'

'Yes, I am serious.'

'You saw the evidence we have already though, right? Why *wouldn't* you help us? Nobody has to know anything, where it came from. If you even *get* anything. It can be completely anonymous. What have you got to lose?'

He didn't, he felt, need to dignify this with a response. Instead, he asked, 'Does Leila even know that you've asked me to do this?'

Nada sat back and exhaled smoke in his general direction. 'No. Not exactly. But if she did, she wouldn't have a problem with it. Come on, Rafi. This is nothing. I thought you said you were going to his place tonight.'

'Nada, I'm not going to spy on Natasha's *uncle*! Look. I respect what you're doing with the site in general. But really, I don't want any part of it. I *can't* be any part of it. There's too much at stake for me now.'

'Then why are you here?'

At that moment his cousin Leila appeared on the terrace, and immediately he jumped up and they embraced. 'Wow. That really was only five minutes. I thought you'd be an hour. It's good to see you, Lei.'

'You too. So where's your Natasha?' Leila sat down and kissed Nada hello. Growing up in the same refugee camp, these two had been neighbours and pretty much inseparable since childhood. When people first met them they often thought they were sisters, and after Nada's father had died in Megiddo jail when she was fourteen, they practically were. Leila's parents Shafiqa and Ramzi had kept an eye on Nada, stopped her from getting into too much trouble; she'd even lived with them for a while. And, one crazy summer night, a very long time ago, Raf had lost his virginity to Nada whilst in Ramallah visiting his family. They'd subsequently slept together, on and off, in the intervening years. The last time they'd hooked up had been years ago, but there remained a residual charge in the air. Leila, registering it now with a quick flicker of her eyes, bummed a cigarette from Nada's pack on the table and offered one to Rafi. 'Oh right, I forgot you gave up.' She lit up. 'Isn't she joining you?'

'You'll meet her when we come to stay,' Raf

said coolly, avoiding Nada's withering look.

'I can't wait.' She took a drag. 'So did you see our new site?'

'Very impressive,' he said. 'You guys have been rigorous, as ever. Some of those pictures were shocking.'

Nada had been checking her phone. 'I've got to run,' she announced. 'I need to go deal with something.' As she kissed Raf goodbye, she muttered into his ear, in Arabic, 'Chicken.' It took him a moment to register what she'd said. He rolled his eyes at her. 'Fuck off.'

'Fuck off yourself.' She was smiling, but he knew she was unimpressed. And after doing the rounds of kisses and goodbyes on the terrace, she was off, phone already pressed to her ear, a streak of black in the bright Palestinian sunlight, leaving Raf and his cousin to catch up alone.

★ ★ ★

In their hotel bed that evening, before going out to dinner, Raf was resting his head on her chest as they got their breath back. His hand gently cupped her breast. 'I'm sorry for flipping out about your article last night,' he murmured into her skin. 'I guess I'm just finding it weirdly hard to be here.'

'Why do you think that is?' Natasha had one hand in Raf's slightly damp curls and was stroking his long, long torso with her other. His body was a daily amazement to her.

He was quiet for a moment. Then he said: 'It's not enough just to come here. Not enough to come and work for the summers, get drunk on Taybeh, eat falafel, smoke sheesha, hang out with my cousins, pretend to *be* one of them for a few weeks or a few months. It's not *enough*. Sometimes I guess I just feel like a fucking fraud. I don't belong here.'

'Raf,' she tipped up his chin with her finger so she was looking into his eyes. 'You're not a fraud. You're not.'

He rolled on top of her, and kissed her.

'What I am,' he muttered as his hands anchored her body under his, 'is in love with you a lot. Jesus, Tash, I can't believe how much I want you all over again.'

★   ★   ★

In the cab winding up towards the hilly south-western suburbs after they had made love again, Natasha was thinking how much Raf *did* look as though he belonged here. With the lowering sun pouring through the car window and gilding his magnificent profile, the land seemed very much to claim him as one of her own.

Up on Homat Hatzelafim, outside Adam's house, they paid the taxi driver and watched him disappear back down the hill, then instinctively hung back for a moment by the green wrought-iron gate. In its silky slow descent, the sun was painting Jerusalem a most unreal shade of rose gold under an enormous sky streaked aquamarine and vermilion.

'When we were teenagers, Rach and I thought Ein Kerem was the most boring place on earth,' Natasha remarked. 'A whole twenty-five minutes' drive from the city, nothing to do . . . ' Despairing today of her younger self, she breathed deeply the cypress-scented air. 'We used to do everything we could to escape with my cousin Shira. Every single night. Just to go out to some lame West Jerusalem bar that we thought was cool.'

'And now it seems like pretty much the most beautiful place on earth.'

'Pretty much.'

Adam greeted them out on the shaded patio, welcoming Natasha with a hug and shaking Raf's hand. 'Great to meet you, Rafik. I've heard a lot about you.'

'Likewise.'

Adam seemed in good spirits, if a little greyer around the temples than the last time she'd seen him in New York. He fetched drinks and a pottery dish containing enormous green olives dressed with lemon, and they sat outside making small talk about their trip; Natasha drinking a glass of Carmel red, Raf a Taybeh beer, Adam a Scotch on the rocks to accompany his cigarette. It was cooler up here among the hills and the olive groves, and Natasha soon wrapped the shawl she'd bought earlier in the *souk* around her shoulders. When dusk fell and the mosquitoes descended, they headed inside the old stone house.

Over dinner, her uncle was full of questions about the New York Bernsteins. Natasha found herself steering conversation away from Ros and Frank and instead focusing on Rachel, Esther and the West Street extension. This seemed a logical way to include Raf. Nor did she mention the commission from the *New York Review;* delighted though she was sure her uncle, a subscriber, would be at her news. Although a tender equilibrium had been restored between her and Raf this evening she still felt as though they were navigating on eggshells; and that at any moment he might lapse back into his more volatile mood.

But Raf tonight seemed somehow retuned; returned. After excusing himself to take a quick call out on the veranda, he placed his phone down on the table and started asking Adam about the cases he was working on. To Natasha's surprise, he displayed a detailed knowledge about some of them.

'Well, you have been doing your home-work, haven't you?' Adam got up and went to his drinks cabinet. Natasha watched as her uncle pulled out a bottle of single malt, then switched it for a blend. He held the Scotch glasses up to the light. 'I'm impressed.'

Raf shrugged. 'Nothing to be impressed about. I read about them. And the area you work in is something I've always been interested in.'

'Mmm. I think Ros mentioned that you'd been involved in a housing project in . . . Shu'fat, was it?' Adam lit a cigarette and slid the pack across the table.

Typical Ros. Natasha rolled her eyes and took a tiny sip of whisky. Between them they'd managed to put away almost three bottles of wine over dinner; she could already feel tomorrow's hangover inching closer. 'Wait, *Mom* told you that?'

'I was.' Raf nodded. 'Right on the edge of the refugee camp. I worked on a housing and social project there.'

'Yeah, I'm familiar with it. It's an impressive outfit. I know Jihad Abu-Zneid, who runs the women's centre there.'

Raf took a sip of his drink. 'Jihad's pretty formidable.'

'Formidable is one way of putting it.'

'And I've always been interested in what's happening in places like Bil'in and Sheikh Jarrah and Silwan,' Raf went on. 'I guess that's where most of your restitution clients are from? I used to work with a guy who was one of the original organizers of the Sheikh Jarrah protests.'

'Every Friday afternoon,' Adam explained to Natasha, 'a group of ultra-lefty Israelis march on a particular street in East Jerusalem to protest against house evictions.'

'I know,' she said, leaning forward, not quite able to judge from her uncle and boyfriend's tone whether they were coming at it from the same place.

'Unfortunately they dub it *ethnic cleansing*, which doesn't help anyone,' Adam scoffed. 'Trust me, throwing around terms like that doesn't do the Palestinians any favours. You want to say to these Israeli kids, come on, give it up, go home!'

Raf was drinking his whisky through pursed lips. 'But the solidarity movement attracts some real heavyweights. A lot of them are fiercely committed to the cause. They're down there week in, week out. Isn't it a bit patronizing to call them 'kids'?'

Natasha glanced at her uncle, who was wearing a neutral, impassive look on his face.

'Anyway, are you really saying it would be better if there were no protests, no one bringing attention to these cases?' Raf continued. 'If no one tried to raise awareness that these people are being kicked out of the houses their families have lived in forever and nobody's doing anything about it?'

'Hardly.' Adam poured more Scotch into his glass. 'If that's what I believed, I wouldn't be representing them at all, would I?'

'I don't know,' replied Raf, evenly. 'I don't *know* why you do what you do, Adam. Why don't you tell me.'

Natasha laid a hand on his arm. 'Come on, guys. What are we really talking about here?'

'Where it's possible for them to stay in their houses,' Adam ignored her, 'that's what we fight for. When it's not, I fight for better settlements, better recompense, and for restitution of assets if I can.'

'Right. Mmm.' Raf eased back on his chair. 'So that's what happening with Zainab Bakri, is it?'

Natasha was aware of a change in

286

atmosphere. She had never heard of anyone named Zainab Bakri.

'I'm very happy to talk about Zainab Bakri if you know the details of that case,' Adam replied, coolly. 'There's a woman I've been fighting for every day of my life for the past three years. I guess that's mainly while you were in New York. Not here.'

'Actually it's not really Zainab that interests me.'

'Oh. What interests you, Raf?'

'Her son, Hassan.'

Adam eyed him. 'I'm not sure what you think you're saying, Rafik, but I'd be very, very careful talking like that here. It's fine on the Upper West Side, but this is real. This is not some American kid's idea of the Israel-Palestine conflict.' Adam checked his watch, then drained his glass and stood up, patting the table with his palms.

Raf, she noticed, picked up his phone from the table and slipped it into his jacket pocket.

'And, much as I would love to continue this riveting discussion, I think we're going to have to call it a night. I still have a brief to write and some real people to protect. I'll call you a cab.'

For the first time, Natasha saw an anger and indignation that she'd never known in the usually unflappable operator that was her uncle and she wondered what had just passed between them.

* * *

'What was all that about?' she demanded, once they were outside the gate and walking down the hill.

'What was all what about?'

'Your conversation with Adam. It was weird.'

'What do you mean, weird?'

'I mean — weird. Why were you attacking him like that?'

He looked at her. 'Are you crazy? I wasn't attacking him.'

'He *felt* attacked. How do you even know about all that stuff anyway? That woman you mentioned?'

'I told you. I'm interested. I just read the papers.'

'Really?'

'It's a pretty big case, Tash.'

'Raf, I'm not stupid. I have no idea what was going on in there, but I do know you weren't just talking about what you were talking about.'

He put his arm round her shoulder. '*Habibti*, you are super-smart and perceptive. And okay, I admit, maybe your uncle dicked me off a bit. You have to see that he can be a bit pompous and patronizing?'

She hesitated. 'I guess . . . '

Raf groaned. 'Man, and he can put the booze away. I thought it was only polite to try and keep up, but this is going to *hurt* tomorrow.'

'My mom and dad call him Adam the Tank in private. He always could drink everyone else under the table.' She frowned. 'But Raf, I don't — '

'Adam the Tank, huh? That's interesting.'

He hailed an open cab, and got in. After a frustrated beat, she followed him.

20

She blinked and rubbed her eyes; stretched an arm out to his side of the bed. It was empty.

'Raf?'

There was no answer from the bathroom.

Eventually she located him downstairs, in the hotel courtyard, engrossed in his book. There was a pot of coffee and some breakfast on the table. He looked up when she appeared, and smiled at her. 'Morning.'

'You gave me a shock,' she grumbled. 'I didn't know where you'd gone.'

'Couldn't sleep. I didn't want to wake you.' Dog-earing his page, he set the book down on the table. 'Hungry?'

Natasha dropped into a chair, annoyed. Back in New York, Raf had occasionally been known to disappear before she was awake. But, laden with bagels, newspapers, juice, coffee, he always came directly and attentively back to bed.

'What's going on?' she asked.

'Nothing. I'm just having my breakfast.'

'Why didn't you wake me up? We always have breakfast together.'

'I've been up for hours. I couldn't sleep. Do you want to order something?'

'You should have just woken me up.' She knew she needed to stop sounding like a sulky child. She smiled privately at him. 'I *like* being woken up by you.'

'You looked so sweet and so asleep. Besides, I can't do that *every* morning.'

'Why not?'

He raised an eyebrow. 'Well, okay then, I will. But don't get cross with me next time I try it and you're late for work or something.'

'I promise I never will. Ever ever ever. For all our lives.' She leaned over and stole a sip of his coffee and a croissant. 'You sure there's nothing going on? Is this about last night?'

'No, Tash, it's nothing! I just couldn't sleep and I was hungry, okay?'

She sat back and signalled at the waiter to bring another pot of coffee and some juice. 'So I was thinking maybe we could go to Katamon this morning, see the house that Otto and Sara moved into after they left New York? Are you up for that? It's an amazing old Jerusalem villa, you'll love it.'

'I'm sure I would, but I'm actually heading over to Shu'fat, to see some of the guys I used to work with and check out how it's all going at the project.'

'Oh. Right.'

'Want to meet back here for lunch? Or that cool place on the roof in the Armenian Quarter?'

'Or, I mean, I could just come with you . . . ?'

He pulled a face. 'Sorry, Tash. I actually thought you were going back to Yad Vashem to do some more research this morning, that's why I made these plans.'

'If you're too embarrassed to introduce me to your friends, Rafi, you know you should just admit it.' She was grinning, hoping to pass it off as a joke. But he would know there was a barb of truth in it: all week she had been bugging him about showing her his Jerusalem and meeting his friends; apart from Gilad in Tel Aviv, he hadn't really introduced her to anyone.

'Oh, *man*. You figured it out.'

'You could always cover me up, put me in a hijab,' she suggested. 'I speak really excellent Arabic, you know. Nobody will ever guess.'

'Great. Perfect. Make sure you pack it when we go to Ramallah to hang out with all my friends tonight.' He squeezed her knee briefly. 'You crazy girl. Now stop stealing all my breakfast and order your own.'

* * *

'So Raf tells me Adam Bernstein is your uncle?'

Natasha had been talking to Raf's cousin Leila, but she'd gone outside to take a phone call and their other friend Nada had immediately started asking her questions. After Leila's concert they'd come to this bar in downtown Ramallah that would not have looked out of place in the East Village, she thought; all retro PLO posters on the walls alongside iconic — or perhaps ironic — 1970s album covers. The DJ was mixing funk, hip hop, Pink Floyd and Bowie at ear-splitting levels.

'That's right, yeah. He's my dad's brother.'

'How well do you know him?'

What a strange question. Natasha wondered if it was a language thing. She looked at Nada and repeated it. Nada nodded.

'I mean, he's my uncle. He's lived here all my life, so I don't spend that much *time* with him. But I know him pretty well, sure.'

Nada lit a cigarette. Everyone else around the table was talking in Arabic. Raf was at the bar; Natasha glanced over in his direction now. It was taking him forever to get this round of drinks in.

'He's got a good thing going on, hasn't he,' Nada said, and for a second Natasha thought she was talking about Raf.

'Adam? What do you mean by that?' She shifted in her chair. 'He's doing some great work for Palestine, if that's what you mean.'

Nada smiled. 'Is he? Is that what he's doing?'

Natasha inclined her head. *Don't even try it, girlfriend*, she thought. *Whatever your game is with Raf, I will take you on. And I will win.*

'What exactly are you trying to say?'

'I'm not *trying* to say anything,' Nada corrected. 'I'm saying it: I think your uncle is mixed up in more than just helping Palestinians. I think he's helping himself.'

Natasha stared her down. 'What are you talking about? What does that even mean?'

Nada pulled a wallet out of her black jeans and handed Natasha a business card with her name on it. **NADA KHLEIFI**. A cell-phone number, email, Twitter and website address.

'Check out our blog sometime. It's all on there.'

'Thanks.' Natasha stuck the card in her jeans pocket, knowing she would do nothing of the sort. She leaned forward and fixed Nada with her eyes.

'Listen. Just because I'm Jewish doesn't mean that I can't have sympathy or empathy for other people. And you're wrong about Adam, too. Being Jewish doesn't mean he doesn't have sympathy for Palestinians. Being Jewish doesn't mean he's not on your side.'

'Doesn't it?' Nada asked, all innocence. 'Funny. That's not the lesson we've learned living here.' She exhaled. 'Oh great, here comes Rafi. Finally . . . '

★ ★ ★

Raf was carrying a tray of Taybehs and Cokes back from the bar.

'Sorry, folks. They just had to head up to Taybeh, go pick some barley, turn it into malt, start fermenting it . . . ' He set the tray down on the table and noticed that Natasha's arms were crossed defensively over her body. Her features, usually so open, were set tight. Raf felt a prickle of concern; he'd left her chatting happily enough to Leila, who was the only one remembering to speak English, despite Raf's plea earlier that they didn't use Arabic all the time tonight. Now he realized Leila was nowhere to be seen.

Natasha rose to her feet and uttered a cool 'Excuse me.'

He sat slowly down and looked at Nada, who was, ominously, wearing the mask of self-righteous defiance that he had seen so many times over the years. Crossing borders, in bed, everywhere.

'What's going on?' he asked in Arabic.

Nada took a slow drag of her cigarette. 'Nothing's going on,' she answered sweetly, in English. 'I was just asking Natasha how she was finding Ramallah, that's all.'

'That's all?'

Nada then made a great fuss of attending to the sheesha waiter, who had just arrived by their table. Going through the rigmarole with exaggerated care, she finally prodded at the glowing rocks and proclaimed her satisfaction with the flavour of the tobacco. Then she stubbed out her cigarette, put the silver pipe in her mouth, and inhaled. Her eyes flashed.

'What did you say to her?'

Nada took another deep drag. The water bubbled. He resisted the urge to blink in the face of the apple-smelling smoke she had just blown, perhaps innocently, in his direction.

'Not much. I may have said something about how interested I was in the work her uncle does.'

Nada muttered something to her boyfriend Mahmoud that was too quiet for Raf to catch, but which sounded, in Arabic, like *fucking Jew*. Mahmoud snorted, and Nada passed him the sheesha pipe.

Raf felt sick, wondering how he could have been foolish enough to leave Natasha alone with this difficult crowd. 'What did you say to her about Adam?'

Nada rolled her eyes. 'I don't even *remember*. It was nothing. I said something about how she might want to dig a little deeper about her beloved lefty uncle and she freaked out. Go find her and ask her yourself if you're so worried about it.'

Raf slammed down his beer but at that same moment, Natasha reappeared at the table. She took the sole remaining Taybeh from the tray.

'There you are. Everything okay?'

Natasha ignored him. 'Mahmoud. Please can I have a cigarette?'

He pulled one out of the packet and passed it to her. Natasha thanked him and picked up a lighter that was on the table. Conversation resumed, in non-stop Arabic. Raf joined in half-heartedly, but could sense Natasha's rage curdling silently beside him.

He was sure he could feel the eyes of everyone around the table smirking at them, these two lame Americans, and he felt a familiar bite of shame. There had been many times like this over the years, when he'd tried to fit in here, tried to say the right thing or do the right thing, conscious that deep down his Palestinian friends and family must all be thinking the same thing: *but membership of this, of what we are, does not come so cheap.* In the end, his chance possession of Palestinian blood no more conferred morality or belonging than it did disgrace. The word 'fraud' returned to taunt him and Raf felt the stirrings of an old humiliation as he remembered how it had led him to do some pretty reckless stuff in the past with this crowd. Impetuously driving a car across the Gaza border with the girls smuggled in the back; playing along with his male cousins' dumb plots; countless other stupid things that had always felt thrilling but terrifying at the time. And secretly, what a relief it had been to get back to Dearborn after the long hot summers here, when the most dangerous thing he might do was try and buy beer with his fake ID at the local Seven-Eleven.

He became aware of Natasha stubbing out her cigarette and gathering up her jacket and bag. 'I'm going outside for some fresh air,' she told him.

Raf nodded. And then, after a moment, feeling like an even bigger dick in front of everyone, he couldn't help himself: he got up and went to find her.

She was outside on the terrace, staring at the view of the valley below. She turned to him when he said her name.

'Well, I must say, your ex-girlfriend is a real charmer.'

'My *ex-girlf* — ?' Rafi exhaled.

Natasha's eyes were slate-hard. 'Why didn't you tell me? Of *all* the fucking things to just forget. Why didn't you tell me? And I heard you guys met up this week too. That's nice. Did you just forget to mention it, or were you lying when you said you'd gone to Ramallah to meet Leila?'

'Oh, please. Leila *was* there too. And she's not an 'ex-girlfriend'. We had a couple of dumb hook-ups when we were like, fifteen, that's all. It's nothing! Her boyfriend is sitting right there at that table!' Raf ran a hand through his hair. 'Tash. You're getting worked up about nothing. Okay? I'm not Josh, for fuck's sake.'

The moment he said it, he regretted it. Her golden eyes flashed, and he realized he had seen this vulnerable and lovely girl in so many kaleidoscope moods since they'd first encountered each other last September, beginning right away with those tears in the *New York Times* elevator. But never, ever so incandescent as this.

'It doesn't matter anyway,' she said. 'I've decided I'm going to head back to Jerusalem tonight.'

'What? You can't do that! We're staying

with Auntie Shafiqa. Come on, you're being ridiculous.'

'Am I?' She eyed him coolly. 'Do you know what she just accused Adam of? The one time any of them deigned to talk to me in English, that is?'

He sighed.

'Right. Okay! So you *do* know. Well, it's fucking pathetic. And why do I have to sit here and take this? Why do *I* have to be the one who feels guilty all the fucking time about my family — about my mom's prejudice and my dad's handy moral blinkers — when your family are just as prejudiced against us! Has anyone in my family ever insulted you like your cousin and your friends are treating me tonight? And what? I have to put up with it because, oh, I'm *Jewish*, and my moral outrage on their behalf means nothing? What was it you said to me in Jaffa, about keeping in mind what my family had been through and not beating myself up? Do you have any *idea*, Raf, how many Palestinians Adam has helped over the last twenty years?'

He was amazed to see her so exercised. 'Look . . . ' he tried, more gently. 'You're right. I'm sorry. I'm sorry. They shouldn't have said any of that stuff about Adam. People just get worked up because of the normalization issue — '

' — Normalization! *Normalization*! I keep hearing that word! What does it even *mean*?'

Raf shrugged. 'Some people reckon any financial settlement is like a concession to Israel, an acceptance of the status quo. And Adam's right at the centre of that storm because of what he does. It's easy to make him a target.'

'You mean they're scapegoating him.'

'Well, no, not exactly, I wouldn't go that f — '

'Well, I think it's a fucking joke. You heard Adam yourself, just the other night. He works *tirelessly* for those people.'

Raf flinched. 'Those people?'

Natasha let out a long sigh. 'You know what I meant.' She looked at him. 'I think it would be better for both of us if I went back tonight. I love you, Rafi, and I'm really trying here, but I'm so fucking angry right now. I don't want this to ruin our whole trip. Give my apologies to your aunt. I'll see you tomorrow.'

She moved to leave and Raf seized her arm, his grip harder than he meant it to be. 'Tash. Obviously I'm not going to let you go back to Jerusalem tonight. Please, just come back inside.'

She wrenched her arm away. 'Did you

301

listen to *anything* I just said?'

'Tash. I can't leave Ramallah now. You surely have to see that.'

'Yes, I do see that! I see *exactly* where your loyalties lie. You've made that crystal clear, Rafi.'

'Well, I'm not going to let you go back to Jerusalem on your own. Not tonight,' he snapped. 'So you're putting me in an impossible position here.'

'Well, I'm sorry about that. But I'm a born-and-bred New Yorker, I'm thirty years old, I'll get a cab.'

'Natasha, I'm serious. You can't go back to Jerusalem on your own. Not tonight, it's not safe.'

Her blazing eyes met his. She held his gaze. 'Fine. Then come with me.'

He wavered for a split second, and in that lethal hesitation, he knew what she'd seen. And what she thought it meant.

She shook her head. 'Yeah, I thought not. Bye, Raf. I'll see you tomorrow.'

★ ★ ★

Adam answered the phone on the fifth ring. After the initial mad adrenalin buzz of leaving, she was feeling small needles of apprehension as she walked towards the junction at al-Maysoun, where, as they'd driven past in Mahmoud's car earlier, she was sure she'd seen some cabs waiting.

'Of course you can stay,' he said. 'But, fight or no fight, Raf should not have left you on your own tonight. Tomorrow's a big date for the Palestinians, May fifteenth; it's Nakba and there could be some trouble tonight. Where are you now? Shall I send a car to come and fetch you?'

Approaching the first taxi in the line, a battered blue car, she nodded at the driver and mouthed, 'Al-Quds?'

He muttered an answer in Arabic and she caught the word 'Qalandiya', followed later by 'Al-Quds'. She nodded, confidently.

'Adam, don't worry, it's fine. I can handle it. I'm getting in a taxi now. I'll come straight to you.'

'Okay, well take great care. It's late and you never know. Be vigilant. And call me if you need anything.'

'Will do. See you soon.'

In the car, she told the driver: 'Yeah, we can go through Qalandiya, that's fine.' They agreed a price in shekels, the driver being all of a sudden able to speak English, and he started the ignition.

They approached the checkpoint not long afterwards. The taxi driver swung into what looked like a vacated parking lot and pulled over. It was dark, and deserted. He turned the engine off. She waited. He looked at her in the rear-view mirror.

'Qalandiya,' he said. And then, slowly, '*Checkpoint*.'

'Yes. Go. *Yalla*. Al-Quds.'

He shook his head, and repeated his phrase from earlier, making a little walking gesture with his fingers. But she knew; she'd seen with her own eyes when they came to Ramallah this morning: you didn't have to walk through Qalandiya anymore. She made an exaggerated driving gesture in response. '*Yalla*.'

He gabbled some more and looked at his watch, then rubbed his fingers together in the universal sign.

She sighed. So *that* was what this little charade was about. 'You want more money? No, we agreed. Fifty, to Jerusalem.'

He raised his voice, and she made a great show of shrugging, defeated. Fine — if he wanted more money, fuck it. Tonight was probably not the night to haggle. 'Okay. I give you more, let's go. *Yalla*.'

There was a bang, suddenly, on her window that made her jump. Two young Arab guys in jeans and leather jackets stood there, pointing at her. 'Taxi?' one of them said. 'You want to go to Jerusalem?'

Thankful that they spoke some English, she wound down the window. It was late, after 11pm, and there was nobody else around, she couldn't help but notice, as her heart began to quicken. 'Yeah, I made a deal with this guy to go to Jerusalem,' she said. 'Can you please ask him what's happening? I told him I'd pay him more money, fine, but I just need to go.'

Her cab driver said something to them in an angry tone of voice.

'He says he told you,' the young guy said. 'He could only take you to Qalandiya.'

'What? No, I said Al-Quds. He knows that. I need to get to Jerusalem.'

'He said he told you he doesn't have yellow plates. He can only take you this far.'

Yellow plates? Natasha swallowed, her resolve of earlier starting to dissipate. *Come on*, she said. *You were raised on the West Side. You can handle these jokers.*

'I don't get it. He told me we'd go to Jerusalem. Now he's asking for more money. I see exactly what's happening here.'

The taxi driver started gesticulating again, and the other kid turned to Natasha. 'No, he told you Qalandiya only. He's asking you to pay him the fifty you agreed. You can walk through, over there.' He paused, and gave her a grin. Some of his teeth were missing. 'Or we can take you to Jerusalem. Two hundred shekels.'

Natasha was outraged. 'Two hundred shekels? Are you *kidding?*'

The guy shrugged, nodded towards the taxi driver, who had switched the engine back on.

'You need to give him the money. He needs to go.'

'Okay, okay.' Natasha fished in her purse for a fifty-shekel note and handed it to the driver. Then she got out of the car and slammed the door.

'You can take me? Do you have the right plates?' she asked, sarcastically.

'Two hundred shekel.'

'No way.'

'Fine. So you can just walk through and get a *servees* on the other side. Good luck!' The boys laughed as they sloped off. Her taxi driver had already driven off, and she wondered if she'd just been hustled, all this talk of yellow plates. But then it dawned on her. Of course he couldn't drive through to Jerusalem if he only had white West Bank licence plates. It wasn't like nipping between boroughs on the BQE! What a moron she was. She contemplated calling Adam to ask him to send that car to pick her up after all; but that seemed like such an admission of defeat. Then she considered phoning Raf to tell him she was sorry for losing it, and that she was now stranded in Qalandiya, and maybe he could come and get her in Mahmoud's car?

But then she remembered that she wasn't sorry, she was steaming.

In the distance she could still see the young boys hanging out, kicking a makeshift soccer ball around, and was half tempted to call out 'okay okay, take me to Jerusalem, any price'. But the other half of her, the native New Yorker part, won out. She would figure this out. She'd go through the checkpoint on foot and take the 'servees', the service taxi, on the other side. She wouldn't waste her shekels. She'd be fine.

Natasha had been wearing Adela's gold locket all throughout this trip; but now, some streetwise instinct told her to remove it, just in case. Slipping it into her purse, she approached the place the kid had pointed to when he'd told her she could walk through. Blinking under the neon strip light, as her eyes adjusted from the darkness of the parking lot, she saw that she was in what looked like some kind of concrete holding pen, divided into lines by metal rails. There were a few people standing on line, waiting, talking amongst themselves in Arabic in low voices. She noticed a trio of young guys in leather jackets and jeans; a man who looked like a businessman in an ill-fitting suit, with a briefcase in his hand; another man, standing alone, whose eyes darted up at her; and a woman with a couple of young kids, a gorgeous little boy and girl. They stared back at her when she tried to smile at them. The little boy, wearing a nubby blue sweatshirt with a faded image of Spider-Man on it, swung himself listlessly on the rail, before being shouted at by his mother. He jumped down and scuffed at the dirty floor with his foot, while the little girl rocked herself backwards and forwards on her sandals. After a moment, though, she stole a look back at Natasha, who smiled at her again. The little girl beamed, her face and her enormous eyes lighting up, and then just as quickly she looked away.

Natasha wondered how long these children had been waiting in this place. Beyond the area they were standing in, she saw lines of booths and airport-style X-ray machines with conveyor belts, but only one line appeared to be operational at this time of night. She dug in her bag and found her passport, feeling irrationally grateful for its embossed gold *United States of America* and for what those four words stood for here. She held on to it and wondered how long this would all take. It had gotten a little chilly now.

Blinking in the artificial brightness, she tried not to dwell upon what had just happened with Raf, about what — now, after this week of strange travails — this latest argument might mean. She'd think about it later: right now she needed to keep her wits about her.

A voice came barking in Hebrew over the loudspeaker and she jumped. No one else seemed perturbed. Glancing up at the bank of cameras above them, she ordered her skittering heart to be still. It was fine. *This is what Palestinians have to do all day long*, she reminded herself. *It's good for you to experience it*. And to her shame, but she couldn't help it, another little voice reminded her: *nothing is going to happen to you. You're an American Jew. You'll be just fine.*

She watched as the man with the briefcase at the front of the line walked forward and disappeared behind the barrier. Nobody else moved. People murmured to each other, but mostly there was just a taut, tense silence. She continued to wait, trying to catch the eye of the mother and her children, just for the sake of some interaction. The little girl looked her way again and burst into giggles. Then she skipped a little closer to Natasha.

'What is your name?' she asked, in broken English.

Natasha smiled, delighted. 'Natasha. What's yours?'

'Lilya,' she replied, seriously. 'How. Are. You?'

'I'm fine! How are you?'

There was a hiss as Lilya's mother beckoned her back. Ignoring her, Lilya held her hand out to Natasha's and shook it, with beguiling formality. 'I am. Fine.' Then she ran back to her mother and brother, leaving Natasha touched by the flicker of a human connection, even here.

Some more time passed. Shifting uneasily from foot to foot, she cast her eyes around, taking in the details; conscious of the notebook in her bag, the pieces she was always working on in her head now. Focusing on what she saw around her, she tried to commit her observations to her memory. As soon as she was back at Adam's tonight she could jot it all down, and maybe this experience too would somehow make its way into the piece. If not the piece about Uncle Fadi, then perhaps the one she had been formulating in the back of her mind. A piece whose scene, she thought, probably needed to be set by two juxtaposed but strangely parallel images: a girl fleeing her house with her family in the middle of the night; a boy, across the globe, doing the same. Galicia, Palestine. Zholkva, Qatamon . . .

Wait. *Qatamon* . . . Natasha was freshly appalled by her own idiocy. How could she not have realized that the Qatamon where Rafi's father's family had lived until 1948 must be the same village as the Katamon where Otto, Sara and Adam had moved twenty years later? No wonder he hadn't wanted to come and see their house.

She felt a crunch of remorse in her chest, and a sudden longing to hear his voice. She pulled out her phone. Dialled his number. Waited.

There was no answer. He was probably still at the bar.

She checked her watch. It had just gone midnight. Another Hebrew announcement came loudly over the system and one of the guys from the leather-jacketed trio moved forward. Counting how many people were still on the line ahead of her, Natasha made a quick, guilty calculation in her head and wondered if the boys with the yellow plates who'd offered to drive her to Jerusalem were still outside. Maybe they could take her back to Raf instead. At this rate, it might be another hour or longer before she even got to pass through. She dug in her bag for her purse, and, surreptitiously scanning the billfold, saw that she had plenty of shekels handy. She made a snap decision to leave. Nobody needed to know what a total chicken she was. She tried to catch Lilya's attention to wave goodbye, but the little girl did not turn around again.

21

'Would you care for the *filet*, madam, or the salmon?'

Rosalind Bernstein glanced up at the hovering waiter. 'Oh, salmon, please.'

'Good choice!' Fran Gutmann clapped her hands. 'I'm going for the salmon too. Sauce on the side, though.'

'I just find beef a little too heavy these days, don't you?' Marion Seligman agreed, from across the other side of the table. 'Plus, so calorific. That must be how you stay so tiny, Rosalind. Alan and I are really trying to cut down on our red meat intake.'

Ros managed a polite smile and quashed the rebel temptation inside her to instantly switch her order to steak. Ordinarily she never said yes to these charity things; would rather chew off her own foot than spend hours in the Waldorf Astoria in the company of this gaggle of *yentas* and *balebostes* who talked of nothing but their children's super-human accomplishments or their banker husbands' latest philanthrophic gestures to opera houses and museum wings. But tonight the charity was in aid of a charity for terminally ill children, and had been organized by a great friend of hers, Kate Federman, whose baby granddaughter had died last year. She'd contemplated sending a cheque and regretfully declining the invitation to dinner, but Kate had been so disappointed when Ros had said she might not make the event, that in the end she had agreed to go. Frank, though, had flat-out refused, so here she was suffering it alone.

As the conversation turned to expecting offspring and upcoming marriages, Rosalind was struck by a genuine incredulity that women really talked about this stuff, and like this. She of all women understood that sometimes, the thing to do, to keep everyone happy and the world in order, was to play the part — to walk through a kitchen door bearing plates of food, or *schep naches* at *shul* after your daughter got engaged to a nice handsome boy with a good job at a Midtown hedge fund. But she could not brook the possibility that conversations like this were not just a theatrical enactment of the box society felt comfortable putting them all into, but what *actually* interested these women. Nobody was listening to them: why didn't they talk about something that mattered? It was an embarrassment to womankind; it made her cross.

But she must play this part, tonight, too. Tucking into her rather bland salmon, she turned to the woman on the other side of her and put on her most interested face. 'So tell me again, what does your son do . . . ?'

She was surprised a moment or two later to hear the muffled ringing of her cell phone again. When it had first started going off in her purse under the table earlier, she'd surreptitiously left it to ring out, hoping no one would notice. She didn't receive many calls in the evening; she hadn't even thought about it. But now, as it started up for at least the fourth time, she realized she should have switched the damned thing off.

'Whose *is* that?' someone asked.

Rosalind reddened. 'Gosh, I think it must be mine. I'm so sorry.' She leaned down to retrieve the bag from under her seat and fished the phone out just as it went dead. It was almost certainly Frank, wondering where his dinner was, having forgotten that he had forced her into this purgatory alone. No doubt he would order in Ray's Pizza and be just fine.

It was as the tuxedoed MC took to the platform to give an introduction to the charity they were all so generously supporting tonight that Ros felt a discreet tap on her shoulder. She spun around and was surprised to see a uniformed member of the Waldorf staff leaning towards her.

'I'm sorry to bother you, Mrs Bernstein,' the suited man said, in hushed tones so as not to disturb the rest of the table. 'But your husband is outside. He says he needs you to leave immediately.'

The table, of course, turned out to be eminently disturbable. Heads began to swivel as the scent of potential gossip filled the air. Ros was conscious of further darts of heat springing to her cheeks.

'My *husband?*' she echoed. 'Frank's here? Are you sure — '

'He said it was extremely urgent.'

The women murmured. Rosalind stared at him for a prolonged second, unable quite to compute. Instinct got her to her feet. Moments later she was charging through those gilded Waldorf Astoria corridors towards the lobby, where her husband was standing, still in his work suit, ashen.

At the sight of his wife, Frank's face collapsed in a mess of emotions. He threw himself at her, and she could feel his body, the bulk of him, trembling. His voice, when he managed to speak, was hoarse.

'You need to come with me. Come with

me,' he said, releasing her and grabbing her hand. 'Let's go.'

* ★ ★ ★

Three miles downtown, at the Bowery Poetry Club, Rachel Bernstein was sipping a bottle of beer and contemplating the oh-so-perilous line that separated performance art from pretension. This was a big night for Skye, who, Rachel believed, was a talented performer with a pretty unique voice, and who had at last convinced some agents and managers to come check her out. But Skye's act, a blend of political poetry and rap, on which she had been working so long, was the penultimate show of the evening. At this rate there might still be hours to go. And meanwhile the ginger-bearded, heavily tattooed guy currently up on stage was the sort of tedious navel-gazer devoid of charm or charisma but endowed with a hearty sense of his own artistic genius that gave any sort of creative art a bad name. She stifled a yawn, and turned her back to the guy who had just sidled up to her at the bar.

'Hey there. Can I buy you a drink?' he asked, undeterred.

She motioned at her nearly-full bottle. 'Thanks, I'm good.'

He held out a hand. 'I'm Brady.'

She did not even bother with a tight smile, nor hold out her hand. 'Rachel.' To telegraph her lack of interest, she pulled her phone from her bag under the pretence of checking it. The thing was on silent, as usual, and it took Rachel a few beats to register the notification on the screen that was somehow telling her she had seventeen missed calls. *Seventeen.*

She stared at it, disbelieving. Then unlocked the phone and checked again. Seventeen missed calls. And all from the same number: *Dad (cell).*

Esther, she thought instantly, her stomach plummeting as she jumped up from her barstool and dashed out to the sidewalk, pressing the phone to her ear.

★ ★ ★

Skye was in the green room they provided for artists to warm up backstage. She had channelled Patti Smith for her big night and was wearing a white shirt with black braces, black trousers, black boots, her Soul-Glow Afro resplendent. She looked extremely fine, Rachel had thought earlier as she'd helped her dress in their bedroom, but now Skye was scowling at her and the effect was not a pretty one. Witnessing Skye's reaction to what she had just told her, the emotion Rachel felt closest to right now was disgust.

'I've got to go,' she repeated. 'I'm going. I only came to tell you so you didn't freak out when you couldn't see me in the audience. This isn't optional, Skye, it's a family emergency.'

Skye was shaking her head. 'Nuh-uh, Rach. You don't just walk out of here. Not now. Not like this. My show's in an *hour*.'

'Skye, this is my fucking family!' Rachel yelled. 'Something dreadful's happening. Stop being such a fucking prima donna!'

'How fucking dare you,' Skye growled. 'How dare you! You walk out that door, girl, I swear we are done, done. D.O.N.E.'

Rachel stared at her, then made a snap decision. 'Okay, listen. How about I stay until your act, and then you come with me immediately afterwards?'

Skye let out a cruel snort. 'Rach. This is the most important gig I've had in my whole career. You know how much I have riding on it. I can't go anywhere afterwards. I need to meet the people out there. How hard have I been working for this?'

'Skye,' Rachel pleaded. 'It's my family. You must understand.'

'I understand what's happening right now.

It's one hour, Rachel. You could have waited to do this, but you didn't. Because the world has always revolved around you, hasn't it? Well, I'm sorry, princess, everyone else on this planet might drop everything for you whenever you snap your pretty little fingers. But not me. Not anymore.'

With that, Skye shoved Rachel out of the door and slammed it in her face. Rachel was so momentarily stupefied by what had just happened — by everything she had learned in the past few minutes — that for a moment, she froze.

And then, her heart beating frantically as she collected herself, she tripped back out on to the Bowery and broke into a run.

22

The light, when she opened her eyes, was blinding. She immediately squeezed them shut again. A moment of indeterminate length seemed to pass, before she became aware of a babble of strange voices and the alien sound of machines bleeping, including one beside her ear. Wherever she was, it was sweltering hot. She tried to open her eyes again. Her head ached with occasional shocks of diabolical pain. *Where am I?* she wondered, and perhaps tried to ask, as a shadowy dark figure in white swam towards her, muttering in a language she didn't understand. The figure patted her forehead with a damp cloth and adjusted what she could now feel was a strange weight on her head.

'*Marhaba!*' she heard. '*Kaif'ek?*'

Natasha's mind was swimming in the strangest way. 'Where am I?' she attempted to say, but the act of trying to speak sent more excruciating shocks of pain through her head. Gradually she began to register the metal instruments, the people in white uniforms, the medley of beeping machines and wailing humans all around her. This person must be some kind of a nurse. Therefore she must be in some kind of a hospital.

Hospital?

Shutting her eyes again against the brightness, she tried to claw back through her memory for an answer. Think, think . . . Her mind circled, sluggishly, but she appeared to have no distinct memory of anything. Then an image of Raf bubbled back into her consciousness and she remembered their awful fight; her leaving him at that bar. Ramallah. And then — nothing.

Alarmed, Natasha began struggling to try and get herself upright, but the nurse gently restrained her, intoning in Arabic all the while. Natasha took in the blue hospital-issue gown she was wearing and then the solid white cast on her right arm, which she discovered, when she concentrated on it, that she could not even feel. There was an elementary-looking IV connected to her other arm, and the machine she'd heard beeping appeared to be monitoring her in some way, two jagged lines coursing along the green LCD graph. Through a gap in the threadbare curtain she made out a few other beds and some retro-looking machines offering their own contribution to the symphony of sounds.

Natasha tried to swallow but found her

throat was rasping and parched. Awkwardly and in pain, she tried to turn to see if there might be a glass nearby, and as if reading her mind, the nurse reached for one. 'Water?' she asked, in English.

Natasha accepted a plastic cup of liquid with her IV hand and gulped it down. '*Shukran jazeel,*' she managed, at which point the nurse, checking the charts around Natasha's bed, beamed.

Encouraged, Natasha muttered, 'Ramallah?' and the nurse nodded.

'What happened?'

'Wait, wait,' said the nurse, as if Natasha had any other option, and then she disappeared.

Natasha reeled. Now there was something. She remembered. She had been at that checkpoint, on her own. She had been going to Adam's house, but . . . How long ago was that? What had happened? Did anybody know she was here? Where was *Raf*?

She tried to move on to her side to see if anything of hers was nearby — her phone, her passport, her bag, her notebook, anything. But she could see nothing near her bed that belonged to her.

The nurse returned with a doctor, who had a stethoscope around his neck and a clipboard in his hands.

'Miss Bernstein,' he said, his Arabic betraying a slight American accent. 'I'm Dr Ghazi Aburedwan. I'm relieved to see you've woken up of your own accord. We were extremely worried about you.'

'What happened?' she whispered.

'You were caught up in an explosion at Qalandiya check-point in the very early hours of this morning and fell unconscious,' he explained, slowly, as if this might neutralize the shock of his words. 'How are you feeling now?'

Natasha opened her mouth. 'I . . . ' she tried. But no words came, as she attempted to comprehend what he had just told her.

'Are you in very great pain?'

Judging from the whimpering and the wailing around her, there were people in this ward facing agonies far more intense than hers. 'I don't know . . . My head hurts a bit,' she managed. 'And I can't really feel my arm. Or my right leg.'

'I'm afraid the arm is broken.' He nodded. 'A bad fracture. Also your hip. You'll feel it once the morphine wears off.'

'Oh.' *Morphine?*

'The good news is, the cranial trauma was in the best spot that it could be.' He smiled at her. 'A few inches over and that could have been it. Also, we were very lucky that you were brought to us so soon after the explosion. If you'd lost any more blood it could have been critical. But I want to assure you that we have run comprehensive brain scans and everything looks okay. It was very close. You are a very lucky lady, *alhamdulillah*, thanks be to God.'

I am a very lucky lady, she registered. *Alhamdulillah*.

The doctor was checking his chart. 'We want to monitor you for a little longer before they move you. The last morphine injection will keep the worst of the pain away, but you do have a head trauma, so we have to stay vigilant.'

'Move me?' she echoed.

'Your uncle is outside. He's requested that you be transferred to a hospital in Israel as soon as we declare it safe to do so.'

Natasha blinked. Adam was outside? So he knew she was here! But where was Raf?

'Has anyone else . . . come?' she asked.

'I don't believe so. Do you have more family members here in the Palestinian territories?'

She opened her mouth, closed it again. 'Not . . . not exactly.'

His smile was kind. 'It's not officially visiting hours, but if you feel strong enough, would you like me to send your uncle in?'

Natasha swallowed. 'Yes, please,' she said. Then added, softly: 'Thank you for looking after me.'

★ ★ ★

Weariness was etched in deep lines across his face. 'Oh, thank *God,*' he cried as he sprang towards her bed. 'You're awake. How are you feeling, sweetheart?'

'I don't know,' she replied.

Adam sat down on the white stool beside her bed, looking unusually pale. He took her hand. 'You were unbelievably lucky, Tash. Do you remember anything about what happened?'

She tried. Hard. 'Not really.'

'Well, thank God you're alive.'

She was shocked. 'Why? Did . . . did people die?'

He looked up at her, and his face softened. 'Yes, sweetheart, some people died.'

She was struck by a memory as cold and clear as ice. The little girl. 'There was a little girl . . . ' she whispered. *'Lilya.* Her name was Lilya. Did she — '

'Now, we're going to move you to an excellent hospital in Jerusalem just as soon as you feel strong enough,' Adam was saying briskly. You shouldn't have come here at all, but because your passport was nowhere to be found after the explosion, they didn't know what you were. Your head injuries were critical, so the Palestinian medics brought you to the closest hospital. And I have to say, they do all seem to have been brilliant.'

Natasha silently tried to absorb all this. *That little girl. What had happened to her?*

'They didn't know what I was?'

'I mean they didn't know who you were, whether you were a Jew, an Arab, where you came from. In fact, all they found on you was a card with the name Nada Khleifi on it, so at first they thought that could be your ID. I didn't realize you even knew Nada Khleifi. Friend of Raf's, is she?'

Nada . . . thought Natasha, confused and bewildered. *Where was Raf?*

'I've also made sure the media are off the scent so we won't be bothered on that front,' Adam was carrying on. 'And I've told the police they're to wait until you're strong enough before they even attempt to talk to you as a witness.'

Natasha tried painfully to swallow again. 'Adam, do you know where Raf is? Have you heard anything from him?' Her hand flew instinctively to her throat, which was bare. Adela's necklace . . . Had she taken it off?

'And do you know where they put my phone and my things?'

'Oh Tash, sweetheart. I don't think anything you were carrying survived the blast. You were found unconscious and bleeding with nothing on your person. Like I said, that's why they brought you here in the first place, otherwise you would have gone straight to Israel. They didn't find your passport until much later.'

His phone beeped and he checked it, his features knotting into a frown. 'Oh Christ. Six more people were just killed in another Nakba attack in Tulkarm.' He glanced up. 'Listen, you get some rest, okay? I'm going to go and talk to the doctor. And then whenever he thinks you're ready, there'll be a Hadassah ambulance with yellow plates waiting for you outside. I'll follow in my car.'

Struggling against a tide of nausea and pain, Natasha fought to stay focused. 'Adam, can I borrow your phone?' she begged. 'I really need to try and speak to Raf.'

'Come on, sweetheart, you mustn't worry about anything. Let's get you out of here and to safety first, okay?' He kissed her forehead.

Natasha tried to protest again but the morphine was doing something strange to her head. Adam slipped out of the room, and before she could help it, she was closing her eyes and dropping off a cliff.

★   ★   ★

When she next awoke, it took her a few moments to adjust to the light again. Her eyes came to rest on a white orchid on a windowsill, catching the sunlight that streamed through the glass. Disorientated, she found she was not in the same room in which she had fallen asleep. Just then she became aware of someone else nearby, and knew, with some preternatural instinct, that it was her mother.

'Oh! *Tash!*' Ros hurried to the bed. The hospital tubes and paraphernalia made the embrace awkward. 'You're *awake!* Oh honey, my sweetheart . . . How are you? How do you feel?'

'Mom,' Natasha managed, fogged with confusion. 'Are you really *here?* Wait. *How* are you here?'

'Dad and I came on the first plane, the second Adam called. Oh my God, my *baby*, just look at you. I can't believe what's happened . . . Thank God you're okay. Just thank God. Did the doctor tell you? One inch over, or if you'd lost any more blood before they could operate . . . '

'I know, I'm so lucky.' With some exertion, and gentle assistance from her mother, Natasha managed to sit up a little. In the effort and the sheer emotion of the moment, she began to cry.

'I love you so much, Mom,' she said, her voice shaking. 'Thank you for being here.'

'Oh, sweetheart. You know I love *you* so much.' Ros took her IV hand and kissed it. 'And I'm just so, so sorry we've been fighting these past few months. I hope now we can put all of this behind us. You are so brave, sweetheart. So brave. Do you need anything? Can I get you anything?'

Natasha swallowed. Her throat was parched again. 'Can I have some water? Where are we?'

'In the hospital, of course! Dad's downstairs getting some coffee. We didn't want to sleep until you woke up. You've been out cold for hours.'

Natasha frowned. 'Really? I feel like I don't remember anything. Nothing makes sense.'

'The last morphine injection yesterday knocked you right out, but the doctors assured us it was fine, that it was good for you to sleep.'

'So where are we?'

'Jerusalem. Hadassah Ein Kerem. It's a fantastic hospital. I cannot believe they sent

330

you to that shack in Ramallah . . . '

At that moment Frank opened the door carrying two takeout coffees and a plastic bag. He gasped when he saw Natasha was awake, and deposited the hot drinks on the plastic side table before rushing to her bedside. 'Oh, Tasha,' he cried, and her name came out as a choking sob. Her father's tears mingled with hers and began to soak her cotton hospital gown, a pink one now, she noticed. 'Oh thank God you're back, Tash. Honey, we love you so much, so much. I just can't believe — '

'Hey, Dad,' she whispered. 'It's okay. I'm okay.' Although the tears were streaming down her cheeks, she attempted to smile at her parents. 'I can't believe you got here so soon. You two are unbelievable.'

'We came the moment Adam called,' Ros repeated.

Natasha gulped down the cup of water her mother had handed her. 'Has anybody heard from Raf? We had this big fight, right before it happened, and I left him in Ramallah. I'm so worried he maybe doesn't even know what's happened or where I am . . . '

Rosalind and Frank exchanged a quick glance. After a moment's hesitation, Frank sat down by her bed, on the other side from his wife, and clasped the hand that was poking out of her plaster cast.

'Sweetheart, we need you to just try and focus on getting better, okay? You've been through a massive trauma and you mustn't worry about anything.'

'That's just what Adam said.' Natasha looked closely at her parents, trying to read and interpret the space between them. A slow, oozing unease was throbbing upwards through her thorax as it finally occurred to her that every time she mentioned Raf's name, somebody changed the subject. Disoriented, she realized she had no idea what time it was, what day it was; how long it had been since she had last seen him. Whether he even had any idea she was here. 'What do you mean?' she breathed. 'What's going on? What's happened to him? Where is he?'

'Shhhh,' Ros soothed. 'Dad's right. This is not the time. You need to try and relax, honey, and not worry about anything now.'

'Mom,' Natasha countered, as purposefully as she could manage through the woozy barrier of drugs, pain and fatigue. '*Where is he?*'

23

Rachel put the kettle on to boil. Esther was unusually quiet today, but she understood why. She didn't feel much like talking either. When she went back into the living room, she found her grandmother had pulled from her bookshelves an enormous leather photo album. It was spread out across her lap.

'What is that?' Rachel asked.

'It was after my hip operation, when I was so bored and had nothing to do. Carmen and I got very industrious with the old photos.' Esther showed her. 'Here, do you remember this day?'

She indicated a photograph of Natasha and Rachel in what must have been the early nineties; Natasha aged about eleven, Rachel maybe eight or nine. They were on vacation staying at one of Frank's colleagues' beach house on Cape Cod. The girls were leaning diagonally against each other, bearing each other's weight as they sat on the stone wall overlooking the sea, skinny suntanned legs dangling over the edge, twin dark heads pressed together to create the tip of the triangle; the sun, at that magical, indeterminate moment of the afternoon where it seems like the day will last for ever, bleaching their faces and gilding the crowns of their heads. The Atlantic sparkled behind them as a single seagull swooped dramatically into the gap between their bodies.

Rachel closed her eyes. 'Now probably isn't the time to get too nostalgic,' she murmured, willing her tears not to fall. 'Although that possibly is my favourite picture of all time.'

'You're right. I should be focusing on the fact that she's alive, and she's fighting, and . . . ' Esther tailed off. She too closed her eyes. 'I just can't help feeling that one of the reasons she went there in the first place was my fault. We've been working on this story of mine, and we decided it would be a good idea for her to go and do some research. And now this.'

Rachel was shocked. 'It's absolutely not your fault, *Bubbe!* It's nobody's fault. You mustn't blame yourself. I think you're just so tired. Would you like to take a nap?'

'Oh, no, no. No.'

Rachel glanced out the window. 'So maybe we should take a walk,' she said, with a forced cheeriness. 'See what's happening over at West Street? It's beautiful outside.'

Esther turned to gaze out towards Abingdon Square, and it occurred to Rachel, watching her, that her grandmother seemed strangely ageless today. Sitting in her old armchair looking out at street level at the impervious city, she seemed both like a very, very old lady who had seen it all — which she had, of course; right down to the very depths of the darkest places in the human soul and far beyond — and also the most innocent child. Rachel felt a lump rising in her throat. She had been on the verge of all-out tears ever since she'd heard about Natasha. Skye had still not called; she had no idea how to make sense of any of it. She felt truly hollowed out, scalped by everything that had happened.

She dropped down to a squat, putting her arms around her grandmother as if she were the parent, the dispenser of comfort in this equation. She couldn't remember ever seeing Esther so vulnerable. They remained like that for a few moments, simply clinging on to each other, and then Rachel pulled back and rose to her feet. 'Come on, Grandma. I really think we should get out of here.'

'Okay.' Esther turned back towards her. 'You are right, my darling. A little fresh air might do us some good.'

As Rachel had hoped, Esther did seem to perk up once they got out into the sunshine. 'Let's not talk about it for a while,' she suggested as they crossed the little square and headed down Hudson Street. As they gravitated southwest, towards the river, she started to ask about what had happened with Skye, but Rachel shot her down immediately. She did not want to talk about it. So Esther let it go, and began to tell her about the talk she'd given in Washington last fall and how a woman in the audience had brought up her Emanuel. Listening, Rachel absorbed their surroundings. The High Line, the gazillion-dollar hotels, the cocktail bars serving plant-powered infusions, the studiedly shabby cafés where people hung out across an invisible fibre-optic universe and anyone might be writing some game-changing code, some literature, a blog, or, who knew, just a status update or Tweet. As they crossed Perry Street, Rachel put an arm around Esther's delicate shoulders and thought again how astonishing it was that a single human life could hold so much. From a small Yiddish-speaking village in Galicia, to this.

And everything she had survived in between.

She glanced down at her grandmother's frail arms as they pushed the chrome frame of her walker. It was a hot spring day; Rachel was in cut-off jeans and a tank top and could still feel a long trickle of sweat inching down her back. But Esther as always wore long sleeves, even on a day like this; even as high spring yielded to summer.

At West 10th Street they veered right, passing a Chinese couple picking resolutely through black trash bags on the street, even here in this neighbourhood, and, further west, a man dressed in seersucker shorts and a flamboyant fuchsia shirt who was planting bright yellow flowers in the soil at regular intervals down the sidewalk. They exchanged a greeting, remarking on the beautiful weather, and Esther and Rachel carried on towards the community centre. Raf's magnificent extension was on schedule, and Rachel and Natasha, before she left for her trip, had been plotting a huge summer party to celebrate the combined events of Esther's ninetieth birthday and the opening of the new wing. Rachel felt a little seasick when she considered that now. Would Tash even be okay by then? Would anything have gone back to normal, whatever normal was? Would her sister be home?

As soon as they walked through the door of

the administrative office, Jorge jumped up to greet them. 'Hey,' he cried. 'How you doing?' Over the years, he had become, like so many, a sort of surrogate child to Esther, and he enveloped her now in a protective, son-like hug. 'Do we have any news?'

'Not really,' Rachel told him, over the docile whine of the power saw from the building site next door. 'Our parents are there now, and she's been moved to a hospital in Jerusalem.'

'She was just so lucky,' Esther murmured. 'So, so lucky.'

Jorge shook his head and let out a slow whistle through his teeth as he did. 'I still can't get over it. All the times you see that on the news, you know? I read online this was one of the worst suicide attacks this year. It's too much to think that Tash was right there! Anyway, listen, I got a call for you, Rachel, earlier.' He shuffled a couple of papers on his desk. 'Someone called . . . lemme see . . . Layla? Asked you to call her urgently on this number.'

'Layla?' Rachel echoed. 'I don't think I know a Layla. Why did she call me here?'

'She said . . . what did she say, she said she had been told to call this number and ask for you. I didn't think I should just give her your number without asking, you know? I know how you get those crazies wanting to call you up and ask you out all the time!'

'Thanks, Jorge. Did she say where she was calling from?'

'It was a terrible line. Lemme see, now. I wrote it all down for you.'

Rachel examined the yellow Post-it on which Jorge had scribbled:

For Rachel
Call Layla **EXTREMELY URGENT**
917 ?? 2597 217 029

She frowned. 'Jorge, this doesn't even look like a real number. It's way too long.'

'I thought it seemed kind of a weird one,' Jorge agreed, studying it now. 'You know what, I think she told me 97, but I figured she must mean 917 and I just didn't hear the 1, what with the bad line.'

'Wait a minute.' Rachel turned to Esther. 'Could this be an Israeli or Palestinian number?' And before she could finish the thought, Esther was handing her the phone.

The line rang and rang. She was about to give up when someone answered.

'Oh, hi. My name is Rachel Bernstein. I think I may have got a message to call you.'

Rachel listened to what the voice at the other end of the line was saying, and after a moment, dropped to the chair in stunned disbelief.

★　★　★

'So, not for too much longer,' he was confirming in Hebrew down the phone. 'Just a little more time for them to look into it . . . Yeah, no, no, keep it very clean . . . Okay, that sounds about right. *Toda*, Ilan. I'll call you later.'

Adam hung up and turned around. To his surprise, Frank was standing just a few metres away, outside the glass frontage of the hospital, whose lights had just begun to glow in the limpid blue Jerusalem dusk. Adam dropped his cigarette and ground the butt under his heel.

Frank raised a hand in semi-awkward greeting. 'Didn't want to disturb you,' he said.

'Not at all. How's it going up there?'

'The doctor said she was stabilizing but they need to check on something that came up on the MRI. They say she may have to have another one tomorrow. She's asleep now. Hopefully poor Ros is, too. This whole thing has been hell for her.'

'You don't want to try and get some rest yourself? Or how about something to eat?

Have you guys had anything today?'

Frank shrugged. 'I just don't think I could.'

Adam nodded. 'I can't even imagine how I'd be feeling if that was Shira in there. Well, just let me know if I can get you anything, okay? There's a pizza place around the corner, a pretty decent falafel stand down the street; whatever you need, just shout.'

'Thanks. I know I should pop back to your place and at least grab a shower and a shave and a change of shirt, but I just can't bring myself to leave. I keep thinking, even if I go for half an hour, something might . . . It's stupid, really.'

Frank glanced upwards, rapidly blinking back emotion, and Adam saw, beyond the puffy eyes and the fleshy jowls, the brilliant, enormous-hearted older brother towards whom his feelings were so mixed.

'That's not stupid, Frankie. Why d'you think I've been hanging around here so much? It's terrifying, how close she came. I still can't get over it.'

'Ad,' Frank said, quietly. 'We really don't know how to thank you. For everything you've done.'

'Please. It's nothing. As if you wouldn't help Shira in just the same way if she was in trouble in New York.'

Frank ran a hand wearily over his three-day

stubble and said nothing. Then he turned towards his brother. 'Any other news?'

Adam grimaced. 'Nothing conclusive, but it seems there's a whole back story there. Doesn't look like they want to let him go any time soon, just in case.'

'Jesus.' Frank shook his head. 'And they're sure it's really him?'

'Looks conclusive, but you never know.'

'How could we have been so naïve?'

'Go easy on yourself, big guy. This happens. And it reflects well on you and Ros that you were prepared to put any anxieties about where he was from aside and welcome him into the family.'

Frank sighed. 'Well, I wouldn't go that far.'

'In any case. Nothing's decisive yet. It may even turn out to be a coincidence. Maybe he's totally innocent.'

Frank looked at him; his eyes so broken and bloodshot. 'I just can't believe any of this,' he muttered. 'I guess I'm still in shock. We all are.' He frowned. 'I'm going to have to tell Tash, once she wakes up. Do you think you can fill me in again on exactly what you know?'

Adam opened his mouth, then closed it again. His whole life, he had wanted nothing more than to impress his big American brother Frank. In Frank's mind, Adam was convinced, Adam would always be the kid who'd wet the bed until he was eight; who'd been shipped off to Israel by his mother; whose wife had left him and whose only offspring had first gone off the rails, then married a *frummer* who did not fit into the family mould at all. Adam had never once been able to admit to Frank how life really was for him out here. Had never told him what had happened to him in the army; what he had witnessed and endured; what he had not been able to endure; what he had done. And how all that had compromised him in ways Frank would and could never understand. He had remained in the shadow of his older brother always — and for what, he wondered now? Why? What did Frank have that was so damned special?

Today, Adam Bernstein looked into his older brother's eyes and saw that for once it was Frank who was the terrified one; Frank who was flailing and out of his depth; Frank who needed Adam to look after him.

'Tell you what. You look as though you could use a coffee, if not something a little stronger. There's a place around the corner that does much better stuff than the piss they serve up there. Why don't we take a break and I'll run you through everything I've found out so far?'

'That sounds good.' Frank managed a tired, grateful smile. 'Thank you, buddy. You're the best.'

24

'So, then. Your next flight to Tel Aviv . . . '
Rachel was giving her most radiant smile to
the guy behind the counter at JFK as she slid
her passport in front of him. 'Whatcha got for
me?'

The guy finally pulled his gaze away from
her face and back over to his computer,
tapping at his keyboard. 'Uh . . . okay. Jeez,
but it's busy. So looks like the only thing I
can do is a Delta El-Al codeshare leaving
tomorrow morning, going via London.
Business. So it'll be . . . let me see . . . nine
thousand, five hundred, twenty-five dollars,
thirty-one cents.'

Rachel didn't even blink. 'Oh that's too
bad,' she said. 'The thing is, I need to go now,
this evening, on the next flight out of here.
Are you absolutely sure, Mr . . . ' She
checked his tag. '*Dwight*. Hey, that's a cool
name. Are you really sure you can't help me,
Dwight?'

'That seven pm flight's all full. And the
next one after that. I'm not seeing anything
else come up.' He looked apologetic. 'I'm
sorry.'

'Can you get me your manager?'

'Uh . . . listen, lady, I'd like to help you, I really would, but — '

'It's okay, I got it, your hands are tied. But I'd love to talk to your manager, if that's possible?' She smiled at him again. 'Please?'

After a few moments, another man appeared behind the counter. 'Can I help you?'

She repeated her need to fly to Tel Aviv on a flight this evening.

'Well, I'm sorry about that, we'd love to help you out. I think my service agent Dwight told you it would be our pleasure to book you onto the first flight leaving tomorrow morning. But there's absolutely nothing we can do tonight.'

'There's absolutely nothing I can do tonight either: I have to catch that plane. Please can I see *your* manager?'

The man looked confused. 'There *is* no other manager. I'm the manager. And if I could help, I would, but — '

'So here's what I don't understand,' Rachel said, firmly. 'I know the seven pm is full, but I don't believe *everyone* can possibly have checked in yet. And we all know that there is always a risk of being bumped off a flight if you don't check in in good time. Right? Because there ain't an airline on this planet

346

that doesn't over-book.'

'Yeah. Well, yes, that is true.'

'So here's what you need to tell me: if there are still open seats on this plane, what do I have to do to purchase one of them? So another person maybe gets bumped off. What difference does it make? Sure, you have to compensate them with some vouchers, but you get me paying you whatever you want to charge me. At some point down the chain there's a free seat. You don't lose.'

She could see the man wavering in the face of her impeccable economic logic.

'*And* what if I were to tell you this is a potentially life or death situation?' she went on. 'What do you do in those circumstances?'

He swallowed. 'In a life or death situation we would do what we can to get you on the plane.'

'Thank you.' She handed him her credit card. 'Put me on the jump seats, put me in the bathrooms, put me in your crew and I'll serve dinner. Just put me on the plane.'

★　★　★

Natasha blinked, as a look of utter disbelief spread across her face.

'What?' she whispered. 'What are you trying to tell me?'

347

Frank was holding his daughter's hand. 'I'm so sorry, sweetheart,' he said. When he'd come back up to Natasha's room after getting coffee with Adam, he'd been relieved to see Ros passed out in the little cot next door. She hadn't shut her eyes for over forty-eight hours; she was completely wiped out. He'd intended that they'd both have this conversation with their daughter, but Natasha had been awake, dozy but awake, and the first thing she had asked him was whether he'd heard anything more about Raf's whereabouts. Frank, being able to hold off no longer, had tried to break the news as gently as possible, and he continued in this vein now. 'This must be the most terrible shock. Believe me, it is to all of us. We could never, ever have imagined this.'

Natasha appeared to struggle for breath. '*Arrested?*' she croaked. 'I don't understand. Why? How? Where *is* he?'

Frank tried to take her hand but she whipped it away.

'Sweetheart. I know this is hard to hear, but you have to try and stay rational. Raf is being held at a police station in East Jerusalem while they investigate something.'

'Investigate *what?*' she wailed. 'What has he been arrested *for?* How did this happen?' She struggled upright in her bed. 'Is Adam helping him to get out? He must be helping him, right? I just don't understand, how did this happen?'

Frank sighed. Wary of causing his daughter further distress, he wondered how much detail he should go into. Adam had just filled him in over coffee; told him everything he knew. About how, the night of the bombing, Natasha had rung him to say she'd had a huge fight with Raf and wanted to come stay with him. He'd offered to send a car, but she'd assured him she was in a cab on her way to his place already. When she still hadn't turned up more than an hour later, he'd started to feel a little concerned, but this was pretty normal for these parts; short journeys could take forever. It was only when the news had started pouring in that a terrorist had blown himself up at Qalandiya checkpoint, killing an IDF soldier as well as three Palestinian civilians, that Adam had really begun to worry. Unable to reach Natasha, he had eventually gotten through to various of his contacts in the Israeli border and defence forces, and had been told there were reports of a possible American female being caught up in the blast; he had jumped straight in the car and had been allowed to come down and visit the scene.

The few survivors of the Qalandiya attack

had been rushed to the ER at Ramallah Hospital, which was where Adam had in the end discovered Natasha, who was unconscious. He'd wondered about trying to get hold of Raf, and had happened to mention to one of the police chiefs on the scene that Natasha had a Palestinian boyfriend who had left her earlier that evening; he was wondering if he'd been seen at all. And seemingly it had struck them both at the same time, the strangeness of the fact that this Palestinian guy had allowed his Jewish girlfriend to pass through Qalandiya at midnight on the eve of Nakba — the 'Day of Catastrophe' for Palestinians that marked the foundation of the State of Israel. It hadn't even been Adam's idea to run a quick background check on Rafik Haroun just to rule out any suspicion; rather, that had been instigated by a guy named Ilan Navok, from the police force. And when Ilan had discovered that Raf had a police history here — that there *was* a former terrorism-related incident on his file — an arrest warrant had been launched. It had been pretty easy to track him down: barely forty-five minutes later, Raf had walked right into Ramallah Hospital of his own accord, saying he was desperately looking for his girlfriend, a Jewish-American tourist he feared might have been at

Qalandiya when the explosion went off — at least that was the story he'd given them. And now, although nothing had turned up *explicitly* connecting him to the Qalandiya attack, nor to the Palestinian suicide bomber responsible, they were holding him while they looked into things. That was pretty much all Frank knew.

But could he tell Natasha any of that? Where would he even begin?

'It's just *such* a shock,' he repeated lamely, to buy himself time. 'To discover that Raf in any way might be . . . '

'What?' Natasha, visibly weak, had found a vocal strength from somewhere. 'What are you saying?' Her face was even paler than it had been, but her voice did not waver. 'You don't believe Raf's done anything wrong?'

Frank faltered. 'Well, no, but I mean . . . '

'Dad!' Natasha cried. 'The reason I was at Qalandiya that night was entirely my fault! I went there, I knew it was dangerous, it's my responsibility. Raf had nothing to do with anything, and the only thing that is *shocking* is that an innocent man is being held in an Israeli police station for no reason!'

'Tash, honey, just try and stay calm, okay. And rational. Nobody is saying Rafi actually played any part in the bombing. But they seem to have . . . '

'Have *what?*'

'They seem to have found other things on him from the past. They wouldn't be holding him if there was *no* reason.'

Natasha began to shake. 'They wouldn't be holding him if there was no reason?' she spat. 'Really? How can *you*, of all people, say that? Do you honestly think for one second that Raf, *Raf*, is capable of what you're saying?'

Frank let the question fall into the charged space between them. He searched inside himself. Did he? Did he really? Trouble was, his brain was in such paralysis, his heart so fraught, all he could really focus on was Natasha's health; he didn't know what he thought. He was well out of his depth here; he couldn't even begin to try and untangle the legal situation in his own head. And Adam had told it to him all so straight: *we know nothing for certain, it could still be a mistake, but this is what we got, this is what we know, and this is how it rolls here.*

'Okay.' Tash was nodding now. 'I want you to go. I want you and Mom and Adam to just go. All of you. Away from here. For a bit. I just need you all to leave me alone. Please.'

Frank was aghast. Natasha, lacking the grumpy teenager gene, had never spoken to him like that in her life.

'Honey . . . ' he tried. 'Please. I know

you're in a lot of pain and deep shock and you are exhausted. I know how traumatic — '

'Dad!' she gasped, holding up a hand. 'Seriously. I love you, but you need to get out of here. Now. Please, just go.'

Frank's over-full heart broke anew at his daughter's admonition. 'All right, sweetheart,' he finally said. 'All right. Whatever you need. We'll check in on you again in a little bit, okay?'

'Okay,' she whispered.

★ ★ ★

Here and there, he had said to her that night. *Here and there. I'm a bit of a hybrid. Much more importantly: sweet or salty?*

'Why did you lie to me?' she'd challenged him a long time later, after she'd discovered the truth about where his family was from. 'Why was it something you thought you had to hide from me?'

'I didn't lie to you!' he'd protested.

'It was a lie by omission. Why didn't you tell me?'

'I didn't lie to you.' He'd become very grave. 'I will never lie to you, Tash, I swear.'

After the longest time searching his eyes, she had said, 'Rafik Haroun. Are you going to be something I have to survive?'

He'd laughed, and taken her face between his long, beautiful hands. Kissed her with the greatest tenderness.

Are you? she wondered now, numb.

25

'*BOOM!*' With an exaggerated hand gesture, to better demonstrate his point, the driver turned around as he cut the engine. He gave her a broad smile. They had joined yet another line of near-stationary cars. 'This week, very bad bombs — *boom*!' He made another explosion noise. 'That's why we waiting so long now. Cigarette?' He offered her the pack, and she declined — but reluctantly. A smoke might be just the ticket. Her insides were shredded. She'd landed on time, and this Arab-Israeli driver Sami, as arranged by Raf's cousin Leila, had been waiting at Ben-Gurion the moment she emerged from security. But thanks to the hold-up outside Qalandiya, she was already almost an hour late to the rendezvouz Leila had suggested in the Ramallah cafe whose address she kept pulling out and checking all over again.

When she arrived, apologetic and a little flustered, two striking dark-haired girls of about her own age rose to greet her. The smaller introduced herself as Leila Masri, Raf's cousin, and the taller, skinnier one as

Nada Khleifi, a very old friend of Leila and Raf's.

'Are you hungry? We can order some hummus or fattoush or something if you'd like, but we don't have much time.'

'I'm fine.' Rachel shook her head. She had not slept a wink on the flight and could not contemplate eating anything. She asked for a black coffee and a glass of water.

'So,' she said as she took a deep breath. 'You'd better tell me everything . . . '

Leila had already explained on the phone that Rafi — along with Nada's boyfriend, Mahmoud — had been arrested at Ramallah Hospital in the early hours after the Qalandiya blast. Now they filled in the gaps. When they'd learned about the bomb, Raf had immediately called Adam in Jerusalem, who had been livid with him for allowing her to travel through Qalandiya on her own, especially given the date.

'He needn't have worried: Rafi was already blaming himself for that,' Nada added. 'I have never in my life seen him so distressed. He was going crazy, completely crazy. I have seen Rafi in some pretty extreme situations over the years, but never anything like this.'

'Adam told Raf that Natasha had been taken with the other survivors to Ramallah Hospital,' Leila continued. 'Mahmoud had to take the 443, the settler road towards Jerusalem, because there were roadblocks everywhere, but unbelievably, we didn't even get stopped. Raf ran straight out of the car when we arrived and pretty much right into the arms of the police. It almost seemed like they were *waiting* to arrest him, like he'd walked into a trap.'

'Jesus,' Rachel said, exhaling. 'And Mahmoud? What about him?'

'They separated them. Mahmoud got taken to Ofer prison here in Ramallah,' Nada said. 'But they just wanted to teach him a lesson. He's been released now.' She shrugged. 'It's happened many times before; it'll happen again. They know they've got nothing on him.'

Rachel gulped coffee, trying to make sense of the madness she was hearing. 'But I still don't understand . . . You implied to me on the phone that there was a possibility that *Adam* might have had something to do with the arrest. Why?'

'We don't know that he did,' Leila corrected. 'All we know is that the *only* person who knew Raf was heading to Ramallah Hospital at that time, apart from us, was Adam. Because he knew as soon as he told Raf that Natasha was there, Raf would go. And why would they, out of nowhere, arrest this American dude who shows up hysterical at the hospital? He's not exactly your prime suspect to be in collusion with a suicide bomber, right?'

'Right. Yeah. I do see that . . . ' Rachel conceded. 'But it just doesn't make any sense.'

Leila took a drag of her cigarette. 'Well, unfortunately, it kind of fits with some other stuff about Adam that we've been looking into.'

Nada picked up an iPad that was lying on the table. 'Let me give you some context,' she said, tapping the screen. She clicked on a tab and brought up a street map, pictures of a demolished house, a Palestinian family, some lists of Arabic names. Rachel studied the screen, but the images meant nothing to her. 'We've been collecting and collating verbal evidence from some families who were or are still fighting eviction cases — mostly in Bil'in, Silwan, Susya and Sheikh Jarrah. Many of the cases are ones in which Adam Bernstein or one of his colleagues was defending the families in question. And often there would be a blaze of publicity in the left-wing Israeli press for all the good that he was doing for these families. And then, in the aftermath, there have been many cases in which people from that same community or even family would later be taken in by Shin Bet, the domestic security service, for questioning, and sometimes end up in jail. So far there's nothing actually indicting Adam Bernstein or proving that he is playing for both sides, but he's a common denominator in too many cases where this has happened for people not to start making the connection.' She clicked open another page. 'The biggest issue is the case about this woman, Zainab Bakri, who lives in the Old City in Jerusalem. I was telling Rafi about it before.'

'Who's Zainab Bakri?'

Nada pinched the screen to zoom in on a picture of a frail-looking Palestinian woman wearing a black dress with red and green embroidered panels. 'The Israeli Civil Administration are trying to evict her from the house she has lived in her entire life by producing these fake title deeds from forever ago that claim it originally belonged to a Jewish family. Back in like, *Moses*' time. Adam Bernstein is supposedly representing her, but the whole thing has got ugly because now her family are being investigated by Shin Bet and one of her sons was allegedly tortured in a police cell a few months ago. He was twenty-eight years old and he died of a heart attack. Go figure.'

Rachel was appalled. 'But there's no

possibility Adam had anything to do with her son's *death?*'

'No, no, of course not. The issue seems more to be that he's passing on information. Winning these families' trust, and then maybe betraying them. We don't know what for; we're not even sure it's for money. The latest thing we have is this recording that somebody captured on an iPhone, of him having a drink in the American Colony Hotel with this police chief, Ilan Navok, who's a total pariah amongst the Palestinian community in East Jerusalem. The recording is not very clear but it sounds pretty definitively like Adam was offering him some inside intel on Zainab.'

'And now it has come to light that Adam Bernstein and Ilan Navok served together in the first Lebanon war, and it seems maybe Ilan saved Adam's life.'

'Wait. So . . . Adam owes this police guy his *life?* Is what you're saying?' Rachel's head was spinning.

Just then, another dark-haired woman appeared at their table. She kissed Leila and Nada hello, then seamlessly picked up their conversation. 'Although to be fair, a lot of this is still speculation.'

The woman, who to Rachel's surprise had a strong Israeli accent, held out her hand for

Rachel to shake. 'You must be Rachel Bernstein. I'm Gali Biron.'

'Gali's the investigative reporter I told you about on the phone,' Leila explained. 'She's completely trustworthy, she's up to speed with the situation, and she's going to drive you to Jerusalem.'

'Wait, you're not coming to Jerusalem too?'

Nada and Leila glanced at each other. 'Sorry, maybe that wasn't clear,' Leila said. 'Nada and I are not allowed into Jerusalem.'

'Even *East* Jerusalem?'

'Nowhere in Jerusalem.'

Rachel was embarrassed. 'I'm so sorry. I didn't realize that. You must think I'm very stupid and insensitive.'

'Don't even worry about it.' Nada waved a hand. 'So, Gali's going to take you to find your uncle and have a word with him.'

'I have to get to Adam alone,' Rachel said. 'If anyone else knows I'm here before I've spoken to him, it's game over.'

'Exactly.' A note of weary patience was in Nada's voice. 'And she's arranged through one of her contacts at the police station where Raf's in custody that you can have a few minutes with him. It won't be long, but at least you'll get to see him and tell him what's happening. Gali won't be able to go in with you, because she mustn't be seen, but she'll explain everything you need to do on the way there.'

'It sounds more complicated than it is,' Gali promised.

Nada glanced at Leila. 'Before you go, though, we do need to explain something else about Raf,' she said. 'Something you should know.'

Rachel put her coffee cup slowly down and squinted in the sunlight. 'What about him?'

'So my cousin's like, the most innocent guy in the world, right?' Leila reached for another cigarette and fiddled with it. 'Just a goofy idealist, you know, who believes that architecture can save the world and that one day we'll all just co-exist in peace and harmony, listening to vinyl records and reading poetry.'

Rachel couldn't help but smile.

Leila lit the cigarette as she continued. 'But he did get caught up in something when he was here one summer, years and years ago. It's not bad. Well, not *too* bad. But it does explain why it's easy for them to detain him in a police cell with no other evidence . . . '

★ ★ ★

'I can imagine this is all quite hard for you to take in,' Gali was saying as she opened the trunk of her car for Rachel to dump her bags.

It was overflowing with camera equipment, dog-eared notebooks, half-eaten bags of chips, a lone falafel, a broken satnav, a head torch, a flak jacket, and, rather alarmingly, a baseball bat. 'Sorry about the chaos, by the way. I spend a lot of time on the road.'

'No worries.' Rachel waved a hand. 'You should see where I live. Thank you so much for this.'

'Have you seen your sister yet? Do you know how she's doing?'

Rachel shook her head as she settled into the passenger seat and pulled on her seat belt. She noticed that Gali didn't bother with hers. 'I figured I needed to find out what was going on with Raf first. To see if I can help. This whole thing is so insane. Adam has always been pretty much a hero in our family.'

Gali nodded as she cranked the car, which had a banner saying PRESS emblazoned across the windscreen, into gear. 'Once upon a time, Adam Bernstein was a hero for that lot, too. I believe he even holds an honorary Palestinian passport.'

'He does. It's been a source of some pride in our household for a long time. So what happened?'

'I don't know what changed exactly, but I think people got fed up that he was making political capital and a shitload of money from being this great liberal Jew fighting the cause of the Palestinians, when I guess a few things just started to not add up. He has so much access to the Palestinian communities in East Jerusalem, he speaks beautiful Arabic, his legal record is impeccable, he knows a lot of these people quite intimately and . . . well, they trusted him.'

Gali was keeping her eyes straight ahead as she expertly navigated the Ramallah traffic toward Qalandiya. Rachel tried and failed not to glance sideways at her. And then Gali flickered her eyes to the right and caught her gaze.

Busted, Rachel looked away. 'But do you really think he *is* betraying their trust? Is there any actual evidence?'

'It's hard to say. On the surface, he is often achieving these big settlements for the families and he seems like he's on their side. And, what you also have to know, Rachel, is that a lot of people will automatically resent the sort of work Adam does anyway. For them, the only way you can truly represent Palestinians is by fighting the Israeli occupation per se, rather than their rights within it. They see any settlement with Israel as tantamount to accepting the status quo, and they hate it.' Slamming her foot on the brake and emitting a colourful Hebrew curse at the

364

guy who'd just cut them up in the crazy traffic, Gali went on: 'The normalization issue is a major hot potato. Stop me if you know all this anyway, or if I'm not making sense. I realize these are the sorts of circular conversations we have with ourselves endlessly here.'

'I think I'm with you, just about. But what does any of this have to do with poor Raf? Do you think it's possible Adam could have deliberately gotten him arrested? *Why* would he do that?'

'I don't think he would. But I do think it's perfectly feasible that if Adam mentioned Raf's name to Ilan Navok and they checked out Raf's background . . . there's the situation with the Molotov cocktail from when he was fifteen that Leila was just explaining about; there's a Jewish girl directly connected to him who's lying unconscious with head wounds in hospital; it's Nakba. In this climate, they can never be too careful. Why would they *not* hold him in police custody, when it's so easy for them to do so, and just buy themselves some time? Welcome to Israel, by the way.'

Rachel tried to digest all this. 'So. You think the way to play it when I see Adam is to threaten him with revealing the American Colony recording?'

'I don't believe in threatening anyone with

anything,' Gali clarified. 'But maybe, if he knows you know about the Zainab Bakri tape, and the evidence being gathered on Nada's website, plus you say you've been contacted by an investigative reporter who has a lot of background information, well maybe that will help him put pressure on Ilan Navok to release Rafi right away — without you compromising your relationship with your uncle too much. I guess who *else* you tell in your family is up to you. Maybe they don't all need to know everything. Maybe they don't even need to know *anything*. It depends on what your family's like, I guess. I know what mine are like.' She gave Rachel a knowing smile.

Rachel looked at her. 'Why would you do all this for us?' she wondered.

Gali shrugged. 'Leila's a good person. She's helped me a lot over the last year or so. Nada too, although you wouldn't know it. She's had a crazy life, that girl. She's lost so many people close to her. So Leila's beloved cousin is in police custody, clearly for no reason. And the girl he apparently told his cousin he wanted to spend the rest of his life with just before she got blown up in a suicide bomb is lying in hospital with no idea where he is. It's easy enough for me to help in this small way, so why wouldn't I?'

She looked again at Rachel, who felt her insides tumble. Perhaps because of the combination of jet lag, adrenalin, no sleep, too much coffee on an empty stomach and fear about what lay ahead. Perhaps.

'Besides, I should warn you, our little plan may not even work. There is every chance it could backfire on us. You may not even get to Adam; you may not get to Rafi.'

'But he's scheduled to be in his office until four, right?' Rachel checked her watch. 'And you made that fake appointment?'

'Sure. But anything could happen. You just have to keep your head. My hunch is you'll be able to cope with anything this afternoon throws at you.'

Rachel looked towards the driving seat again, but Gali did not turn. At Qalandiya, they fell silent. Gali held up her press ID and both of their passports, the Israeli and the US, and a cluster of male IDF soldiers gathered around their car, taking a while to go through the documents and check the trunk. They asked a bunch of questions in Hebrew before finally waving them through.

'By the way, they just did all that because they think you're hot,' Gali laughed, as she put her foot down on the slightly less potholed East Jerusalem roads. 'These guys know me well; I come through Qalandiya all the time. I haven't been stopped there in ages.'

Once again, just one more time, Rachel dared herself to look back towards the driver's seat. Where now she found Gali looking at her.

'Everything here is fucking crazy, by the way,' Gali was murmuring, a faint smile on her beautiful mouth. 'In case you hadn't noticed.'

★ ★ ★

Gali swung into a parking space on a nondescript Jersualem street, a short walk from Adam's office. She twisted her long body over to the back seat and retrieved a bag, from which she drew a manila folder marked with some Hebrew words. 'Everything's in there,' she told Rachel, handing it over. 'Newspaper clippings, police reports, photographs, and local municipal maps. Stuff about the eviction and restitution cases that are linked to the Shin Bet angle. There's a lot about Zainab Bakri's son, Hassan. Some context. Most of what you might need is in English; I would suggest going over what you can before you meet with Adam. There's a lot of Hebrew documents in there too, but you shouldn't need them. I would caution you not to get into any details, unless you have to. It's just to show Adam that you mean business.' From the pocket of her jeans, Gali pulled out a slim silver memory stick and handed that over too. 'This is the American Colony recording, in case you need it. But only as a last resort.' Then she whipped out a pen and scribbled a number down on the back of a scrap of paper. 'And that is my cell-phone number.'

Rachel nodded. She felt a little dazed. 'Gali. Thank you. You've been so kind.'

'No problem. I live for this stuff. Now go, quick, and good luck. Call me when you're out, okay? I'll be somewhere around here; I just can't stick around and risk getting seen. There might be protesters who know me outside Adam's building. You'll be fine, Rachel. Good luck.'

★ ★ ★

'Can I help you?'

Rachel was relieved to hear the secretary spoke English. 'I hope so. I'm here to see Adam Bernstein. I've booked a meeting.'

The secretary looked dubious as she clicked on something on her screen. 'And who are you?'

'My name is Rachel.'

The woman frowned at her screen. 'Well, I'm afraid he's not expecting you. He has another appointment scheduled for this time.'

'I know. But you can tell him his niece is here to see him.'

Now the secretary was polite, but firm. 'I'm sorry, but Mr Bernstein is very busy and has another appointment.'

'You can tell him his niece is here to see him.'

The woman eyed her for a long time, then pressed a button on her system and spoke quietly. 'Mr Bernstein. Your niece is here.'

There was a pause, then Adam's voice came through, sounding confused. '*What? Natasha's out of hospital?*'

'No, it's Rachel. She says her name is Rachel.'

*   *   *

She found she remembered this office from visits as a child. Adam's office was a lot less chaotic than her father's. Here the bookshelves were full but not overflowing with legal spines, and there was a stack of files neatly arranged on his desk. His many awards were positioned discreetly around the room. An air-conditioner was going at full blast.

'Rach! This is a surprise. Frank and Ros

didn't mention you were coming out too.'

'They don't know I'm here.'

Something passed quickly across her uncle's face. He came around from behind the desk and embraced her. 'I'm sure they'll be delighted to see you when they do. Please, sit down. So what brings you here?'

She took a seat opposite his. 'Well, obviously I'm in Israel for Tash. But I'm here right now for Rafi.' She watched her uncle's expression closely.

Adam's face was unreadable. 'For *Rafik?*'

'Yeah. I might as well get straight to it. I don't know why he's being held in police custody. I know he shouldn't be there. And I want to get him out.'

He clasped his hands on the desk and looked at her, impassive.

'And I'd like your help.'

She felt her uncle's eyes holding hers. Rachel took in the chrome-framed photographs of Adam on the wall. Adam and a *keffiyeh*-clad Yasser Arafat before he died. Adam and Bill Clinton, taken around the time of the Oslo accords, she guessed. Adam and Shimon Peres, more recently, wearing charity soccer shirts and big smiles, their faces red and sweaty. She was touched to also see a picture of Adam and Frank, both in Mets shirts, in the garden at 83rd Street.

Adam must have been about ten in the picture.

'I want you to get him out.'

His tone, when he responded, was disturbingly even. 'You want me to get Rafik released?'

'Yes, I do.'

'But Rach, he's not my client, I don't know anything about him. I'm not sure I can help.'

Rachel crossed her arms. 'Adam. Why is Rafi being held by the police?'

'Your guess is as good as mine. They think they found something on him, I imagine.'

She studied his cool, handsome poker-face. Either her uncle was a superb liar, or Nada and Leila had him all wrong. She pulled the manila folder Gali had given her from her bag and held it across her knees, for reassurance as much as anything. 'Okay. Let's leave the why out of it. I don't know whether you played a part in getting Raf arrested, and I don't really care. So long as he comes out.' Rachel leaned forward. 'Adam. You're my dad's brother. So I don't want this to end badly. But I think we both know what's happening here. And I *know* you can help get Rafi out.'

Adam smiled in apparent bemusement. 'What on earth are you talking about, Rachel?'

'Your whole reputation, in the world, but also in our *family*, rests on what you say you do for the Palestinians. And I've seen some evidence that what you say might not in fact be the whole picture.'

Adam's gaze flicked down to the folder on her lap and for a split second his composure seemed to waver. He opened his mouth to speak, but Rachel silenced him with a hand. 'I do not want you to tell me a lie, Adam. I do not know what the truth is and I do not need to know. I just need Rafi released.'

Adam leaned back in his chair. 'It's good of you to come all this way, Rach, and I'm really pleased to see you. But you're in way over your head, just so you know. If you're threatening me, just be aware what that means — '

'I'm not threatening you.' Her heart was racing.

'Because this won't end happily for your sister. Or her boyfriend.'

Rachel swallowed. 'I am not threatening you, Adam. I'm just saying, you should know that people know. And that *I* know.'

He leaned forward to meet her in the space between them. 'And I'm just saying: if you do what you're implying, it could have serious consequences that you don't understand. This isn't a game, Rach.'

'I know. It wasn't a game for Hassan Bakri. And it's not a game for Raf, either.'

Adam stared at her for a prolonged moment. *I will not be the one to look away,* she told him silently.

Then he nodded, almost imperceptibly. 'Okay. Okay. I will see what I can do.'

Rachel kept her voice steady, allowing no whisper of triumph to enter as she stood up. 'Thank you.'

'I'll walk you out,' Adam said.

★ ★ ★

In the waiting room outside Adam's office, Rachel felt herself doing a parodic double-take at the sight of the figure seated calmly in one of the chairs, reading a magazine. For a crazed instant she wondered if she was hallucinating until she heard her uncle's stereo gasp.

'Esther?'

She saw her uncle glance questioningly over at his secretary, who shrugged as if to say: *your family!*

'*Bubbe?*' Rachel croaked.

Esther had risen to her feet with the aid of her walker, and she gave them her most innocent smile. 'I heard Jerusalem was beautiful in mid-May. Thought it was about time I came for a little visit after all these years. Don't you agree?'

Rachel shook her head, incredulous. 'Gran, you are *something* else — '

Esther pressed a twenty-shekel note into her hand. 'Pop down and get me an orange juice, would you, sweetie? I just need to talk to your uncle about something.'

26

Frank's taxi left the cypress-shaded groves of the Ein Kerem suburbs and merged on to the 396 towards East Jerusalem. It had almost been a relief to receive Adam's text telling him to get down to the police station immediately; a relief to leave that hospital for a couple of hours. The doctors had decided to operate on Natasha's shattered hip again this morning, which meant he hadn't had the chance to speak to her since she'd ordered him out of her room last night. But Ros had been in there with her before they wheeled her off to theatre, and had said their daughter was inconsolable. With any luck he would be back up at Hadassah Ein Kerem by the time Tash came round from the general anaesthetic, and maybe by that stage there would be more news about Raf. Whether good or bad, though, who knew?

As he paid the cab driver, Frank caught sight of his own reflection in the rear-view mirror and recoiled. He looked ghastly: drawn and bearded, with dark circles under his hooded eyes. He felt utterly wretched.

Outside the station there seemed to be

some sort of protest taking place, a loose collection of people, mostly but not all Arabs, holding placards and yelling the occasional slogan towards the heavily guarded front entrance. For a worrisome moment, he wondered if these were people who had got wind of the story that an American-Palestinian citizen was being held in custody here, and he felt a twist of anxiety. Of all the things he was grateful to Adam for this week, his ability to somehow keep the whole nightmare out of the press was uppermost. He had seen a few reports speculating that a female American tourist had been injured in the blast, but there had been no mention of her name, and nothing about her relationship to Raf; or the fact that he was being detained. The last thing they wanted was the media, whether Israeli, American or international, butting in. But as he got closer, he saw with relief that the protesters' placards had nothing to do with Raf; the photograph was of an old woman, someone called ZAINAB BAKRI, for whom the protesters were demanding JUSTICE NOW in three languages. It was silly, but Frank felt almost cheered by the sight of this group yelling in support of some poor downtrodden soul. Having seen so many mini-protests like this one outside the police stations, jailhouses and courtrooms he frequented in New York City, he felt, for the first time in days, almost at home, after a period of being completely at sea. Handing over his jacket, wallet and keys to the Israeli security guard to put through the X-ray while he walked through the upright body-scanner, he wondered who this poor Zainab Bakri woman was, and what she was supposed to have done.

Adam was in the corner of the reception area talking discreetly to a police colonel in uniform. Looking up and noticing Frank's arrival, he raised a hand. The inscrutable expression of moments ago gave way to a bright smile.

'Frank!' he called. 'You're here. Good. Take a seat. I have some great news.' He moved towards him. 'We've just heard. Rafik has been cleared. He's free to go.'

It took Frank a beat to fully take this in. '*What?*'

'They've done their investigation. They're satisfied he had nothing to do with the attack on Qalandiya,' Adam said. He glanced over at the colonel. 'That's right, Ilan, yes?'

The man gave an impassive nod.

Frank frowned. His mind was spinning. 'But what about all the other stuff, the alleged . . . the terrorist connections you told me about?'

Adam sighed and rolled his eyes as if to say: *you know*. 'Oh, terrorism. Please. He was fifteen. Part of a gang of kids. One of the group — not him — threw, or attempted to throw, a Molotov cocktail at an Israeli bus in West Jerusalem. Nobody was injured. It happened a very long time ago.'

'Wait, but I thought you said there was compelling evidence possibly linking a Rafik Haroun to a recent serious offence?'

'You know how many Rafik Harouns we are monitoring on our system?' the police colonel offered in thickly accented English, by way of gruff explanation.

'What, and all of them American citizens?' Frank snapped, a bitter taste gathering in his mouth as he began to grasp the implications of what he'd just been told.

Ilan Navok snorted. 'Of course not. But you never know, with all the fake passports.' He shared a look and a few words in Hebrew with Adam, and then muttered, 'Excuse me,' and disappeared down a corridor.

Adam watched him go. Then he leaned back and rubbed a hand over his chin. He too looked haggard after the events of the past few days. 'What a cock-up. Excuse my language.'

'What the hell happened?' Frank demanded.

'Who knows. But this, at least, is one less

thing for Natasha to be worried about.'

Frank scrutinized his brother, as a flash of something he recognized from Adam's childhood suddenly announced itself in the middle-aged man's face. It vanished again almost instantly, but Frank, with an eye that was trained in such matters, had seen it. Young Adam, as well as being a somewhat wimpy little guy, had also been the most tremendous fibber, able to winkle advantage out of countless scenarios with a charming smile and the sneaky lies that were only busted much later, if at all. Frank had all but forgotten about this aspect of Adam's character, until now. Or perhaps it was just that he had not expected to encounter it in the fifty-eight-year-old version. Something stirred uneasily inside him. He almost — almost — let it go.

'So the intel that they had on Raf . . . ?' He let the question hang.

Adam turned to him. 'Listen, Frankie. Raf was just very unlucky he happened to walk into Ramallah Hospital right at that moment, with the police already there and jumpy. Wrong time, wrong place. Wrong guy. But after an incident as major as that Qalandiya bomb, nobody's going to take any chances, right? You must see that.'

'But they had *nothing* on him!' Frank

raged. 'I want to know what, exactly, was linking Raf to that incident.'

'Like Ilan said — a lot of Rafik Harouns in the system.'

'But Adam!' Frank protested. 'You told me that not only did they have a file connecting Rafik — *our* Rafik — unequivocally to one of the perps of a recent attack in Gaza, they also had a file on him going back to the mid nineties! You said there were probably fingerprints, DNA samples; that there was every likelihood Shin Bet and Mossad would have been tracking him and his family here and in the US for years!'

The full extent of Frank's catastrophic mistake, his lack of faith, the betrayal of every principle he had ever held dear, now dawned immense and inexcusable inside him.

Adam held up his hands. 'Hey, buddy. Go easy, huh? So it was a different Rafik Haroun. A mistake was made. Not my mistake; don't try and pin this on me.' He gave a sneer. 'And what, you're thinking, this sort of thing would never have happened in the good old US of A? Please. The fact is, this kid is in their system for suspected involvement in a previous incident. They're not going to take their chances. This is Israel in the twenty-first century. Nobody ever said it was pretty.'

'But Raf was a *minor* when this alleged

previous incident occurred. And what's more, he wasn't even convicted!' Frank leaped up and began pacing the room. 'It was seventeen years ago! I have to say, I just find this unspeakable. Deplorable. Your cronies here ought to be ashamed of themselves. How long would he have sat rotting in that cell if you hadn't deigned to tell them to let him out?'

'Enough, Dad,' a voice soothed. 'Adam has done his very best here.'

Frank whipped around, wondering if he was going mad. Had the lack of sleep finally got to him?

But no. His eyes and ears did not deceive. Emerging from a corridor, flanked by an exhausted-looking Rafik and — impossibly, no, surely not, his *mother-in-law* — there, somehow, unbelievably, was his daughter, his *younger* daughter, a look of dazed triumph widening across her face.

★ ★ ★

Frank wondered how much Raf knew or suspected about the murky shenanigans and obfuscations that had kept him detained in Israeli police custody for the best part of four days. If he was bitter, he did not show it. Dressed in scruffy jeans and a now-filthy white T-shirt, he wore a relieved and grateful

382

expression as the policeman showed him into the reception area. A female officer behind the desk handed him a release document to sign and passed across an old brown leather satchel containing his personal effects. He seemed cheerful enough, although there were deep grey shadows underneath his eyes — eyes which, Frank noticed now, seemed extraordinarily to be almost the exact same colour as Rachel's. According to his father's legend, his younger daughter's distinctive turquoise eyes came directly from Adela. When Otto had met baby Rachel for the first time, he had struggled to speak for a moment because his new granddaughter had his dead wife's eyes. Now Frank noticed Raf's properly, and as he looked between him and his daughter, the strangest thought struck him: that they could almost be brother and sister.

Raf held out his hand to Adam, who embraced him with easy chumminess, and then he hugged Esther and Rachel all over again. He murmured something in her ear and she laughed. Then before Frank could tentatively hold out his own hand, Raf was throwing his arms around him too. Frank felt tears spring to his eyes.

'Come on, you,' Rachel said after a moment, tears shining in her eyes too as she tugged at Raf's arm. 'There's someone else who really, really needs to see you.'

Raf slung his satchel over his shoulder and held out his hand, which she took. He offered his other hand to Esther and together they walked, the three of them, towards the door, where the dim shouts of the protesters outside could still be heard. Frank had begun to follow when he realized Adam was hanging back.

'Aren't you coming with us?'

His brother shook his head. 'I just have to deal with a few other bits and pieces while I'm here,' he said. 'I'll catch up with you at the hospital later.'

Frank called to the others. 'Hey, you guys, go see if you can get us a cab. I'll be out in a minute.'

As they headed out of the door, Frank heard Rachel gabbling about some people called Gali and Leila and Nada and Mahmoud and he shook his head in awe. He had no idea what part his younger daughter had played in all this, but he had a hunch, a crazy hunch, that Raf might have languished innocently in that cell even longer had Rachel not shown up, blazing with purpose.

'Quite the crusader, that one,' Adam said, as if reading his mind.

'Always was.' Despite the draining emotion

of the past hour, day, week, Frank suddenly felt overwhelmingly proud — of both his daughters. He dabbed at his damp eyes with the heel of his hand.

'It's all been rather emotional, hasn't it?' Adam agreed.

'I'm sorry, Ad,' Frank said. 'Sorry I yelled at you. It's not my place. Not my country.' He paused, gathered himself. Then he said, 'I'm sorry for everything.'

A moment passed between them. But Adam picked up his line at face value. 'Well, I'm afraid it's an occupational hazard for all of us in this line of work. Hated by everyone! By the left and the right; by the Palestinians and the Israelis alike.'

'Who was it said, so long as you're hated by both sides out here, you're probably doing something right?'

Adam gave him an indulgent smile.

'But I just need to know one thing,' Frank said softly. 'I need to know, Ad, that when you told me Raf was being held here, there was no doubt in your mind it was justified.'

Adam looked appalled. 'Frankie, I swear to you. Of course there was no doubt.' He paused. 'I swear on my 1968 World Series baseball card collection.'

And just like that, Frank was shuttled back to that morning upstairs at West 83rd, the morning Otto, Sara and Adam had emigrated to Israel. How he had finally lured a pyjama-clad and protesting Adam out of his room with those precious baseball cards. Denny McLain. Hank Aaron. Mickey Mantle. The heroes of the hour. With Adam distraught about leaving New York City and his beloved Mets, Frank had earnestly promised his little bro he'd send a pack of baseball cards out to the new address in Katamon every single month. Every single month. For how long had he stuck to his word, he wondered now?

'If I'd had any hint of police nonsense,' Adam was carrying on, 'any hint whatsoever, of *course* I would have fought to get him released immediately. But from what I was being told, and from the intell I'd seen on the file, things looked like they might add up. I had reason to believe there was a chance he might be a threat to Natasha, a threat to my family. And I could not risk that. Not for anything.' After a beat he added with a certain weariness, 'It grinds you down, you know? This place. It grinds you down.'

Frank looked at his brother long and hard then; searched that open, appealing face for any flash of possible deceit. But he found no trace. What he did see, there behind the broad, handsome planes of Sara's bone structure, was the shadow of Otto, of their father, and his wholly noble spirit.

Or maybe he just saw what he needed to see. Either way, he was flooded with relief.

'Well, that's good enough for me.'

'I'll catch up with you later, okay? Now go get that poor kid up to Hadassah Ein Kerem as quick as you damn well can so he can be there when Natasha comes round.'

Frank went to embrace his brother then, but before he got there Adam punched him lightly on the arm. Without missing a beat Frank instinctively dummied him, a reversal of an old brotherly routine; one they hadn't done in years, maybe not since that morning in 1968. They embraced, and in his arms, for maybe the first time since that very morning, his brother was no longer that weeping twelve year old. Adam was fine. His brother was fine. Frank felt a great, leaden weight lift from his heart.

27

July

The centre was alive with people: talking and laughing and moving between one another. Everybody had come. Esther stood alone for a moment at the darkened side of the makeshift stage and glanced through her notes. The words moved treacherously on the page and she wondered if she might even be nervous. She couldn't remember feeling like this in years, maybe decades.

Some thread in her mind pulled taut, and suddenly she was back in the camp, and she was turning nineteen. There had been so many people there that night, and she remembered this same sense: of bodies packed close, of hungry human beings intimately bound, their destinies pressed together. But it had been so cold, their breathing frozen and the moon made of ice and casting a pale light over the room. And then, when they sang happy birthday, they sang in a strange and quiet ghostly-murmured Yiddish for fear of raising the guards. And Emanuel was not there. She had felt such a terrible, eating sorrow; a sorrow that had no end inside of her but was empty and boundless. By now they knew what was happening. What their destiny would likely be, both collectively and individually. They knew.

That night in the camp she had wondered if she would ever see another birthday.

And now: ninety. Esther realized it was not her nerves that were making the words swim; it was something else. It was the very opposite of that terror. Here she was, alive, alive in New York, in the twenty-first century, surrounded by all these people she loved. And ninety years old. She knew what she was feeling: it was joy. She was full; she was full of joy.

Esther looked out over her party, suffused with warmth for all these people. There were sweet Ned and Emily, ferrying the platters of Rosa's food, back and forth among people; the daily miracle of abundance and her daughter's generosity. And Jorge behind the bar, Valentina with her trays of drinks; she'd told them both to take the night off but they had laughed and insisted they wanted to help.

She heard the piano start a new song and her eyes went to her dear friend Joey, sitting at Leo Zimmer's Steinway. He was accompanying everyone who was providing the music tonight: from the Polish Klezmer band Rachel had discovered in South Williamsburg to her own Sunday-afternoon Sondheim-and-shtetl crowd, via some of the more musically inclined clients from the centre. And right now, delivering a rendition of 'At Last' so spine-tingling it was as if Etta James herself had dropped into the party, was Audra, the woman with the long grey dreadlocks and the miraculous voice, who had started coming to the centre last November after explaining that a woman on the subway had given her the address on a scrap of paper.

It was nearly time. Esther scanned the crowd for her family. And ah yes, there ... *there* was her daughter, deep in conversation with Rafi's parents, who had flown in from Michigan for the party. Esther smiled. All that tumult, she thought, and so beside the point. The things that beleaguered and obsessed Rosa today would pass, she knew, tomorrow. Hard to believe, but from ninety, the sixty-year-old self seemed so young; so much still to learn. And at her daughter's side as always: Frank, dear Frank, testimony to the truth that there are as many different ways to make a good marriage as there are good people. And he was a good person, her son-in-law, a good man, no doubt about it.

She found Rachel, that beautiful girl, standing beside the Israeli reporter she'd introduced them all to earlier. Gali, her name was. Out of both grandchildren, Esther felt she knew Rachel least well, yet was most like her. She smiled wryly at the secret pleasure she knew Rachel had taken in surprising them all today when she had presented her new girlfriend. At least Rosalind could now relax that one of her children was with an Israeli Jew. Though whether her daughter had absorbed that particular irony was another matter.

And now she saw Natasha, her dear Natasha, lately more than just a granddaughter: now her confidante and biographer. They had almost finished working on her story; Natasha was writing it up into book form and they were even going to see about taking it to a publisher. She was standing in a group of friends with her crutch, leaning against Rafi, wearing the new necklace he had bought her after Adela's had been lost. After all they had been through, those two, and everything they'd fought for, in the end, all that had mattered was that Tash had survived and that they were together. And wasn't it interesting, Esther reflected, that in the end, it *was* possible for love to transcend tribe. She hadn't always known it would. She should have had more faith that it must.

Through the large warehouse window, the lights of Jersey were glittering across the Hudson, and now Esther was thinking again of the miracle of America, and of the specific miracle that was New York, when she saw that people were pointing in her direction, calling out something to her. Their chants of 'Speech!' were rising, threatening to drown out even the sounds of the peppy nonagenarian who had replaced Audra at the piano and was now working his way through 'My Funny Valentine'.

So the time had come. Esther folded up her notes and carefully stepped forward onto the stage. 'All right, Sammy, enough!' she cried, depositing a kiss on the old man's cheek. She had had her hair done earlier and was wearing a new blue dress, purchased by Rosa especially for her birthday party. Sammy gave her a wolf-whistle and pulled her into his arms for a little twirl before he exited the stage.

Earlier, Jorge had set up the microphone so it was standing at the right height. Esther tapped it, then gave a dramatic pause. 'Ladies and gentlemen . . . It gives me *such* pleasure to see you all here tonight.' She raised her little glass of Manischewitz and beamed, as drug addicts and homeless people unwittingly turned to clink glasses with high-up officials from the mayor's office, the New York Coalition for the Homeless, even the Senate. 'Today, in case you didn't already know, is a *very* special day.'

There were loud claps and cheers around the room.

'Now, many of you probably don't know this,' Esther continued. 'But today is the anniversary of — '

'Your birth!' one bright spark near the front yelled out. Petey had been coming here for at least fifteen years, always in the same threadbare Yankees jacket that he wore tonight over his dinner suit.

'Very *good*, Petey. Today is indeed the anniversary of my birth. Well done you. Yes, sixty whole years ago, if you can believe it, my beloved mother, God rest her soul, gave birth to me!'

After a beat, there was laughter, followed by a cry: 'But you don't look a day over fifty!'

'But seriously, now. This day,' she told them, 'this *very* day, in 1945, was also the day that I arrived at Ellis Island. Like so many, I arrived with nothing. Less than nothing, really, for on that day I was barely a human being, barely a soul. But I was very, very fortunate. As lucky as I had already been, I was about to be even luckier. By a remarkable twist of fortune, I was found by a very special man whom I had known in Lvov before the war, and who, along with this wonderful city, gradually nursed me back to health and happiness. And over the course of that time, you know, I got to understand something pretty incredible. New York didn't care what I was, or what I wasn't. She let me be all the things I ever wanted to be, and over the course of the past seventy years, almost, as those things have evolved and shifted, she's always stayed cool. I'm willing to bet that while I may be the *oldest* person in this room, I'm not the only person to whom New York has given that gift. And I can't tell you, you just can't *know*, my darlings, how I only wish the whole world could learn from New York's fine example.'

Esther took another small sip of her wine.

'You know, I had a little look at the guest list earlier,' she confided. 'And by my calculation, although I'm afraid I never was very good at math, there are nearly thirty different nationalities represented in this room. We're like the United Nations, *nu?* Except we're throwing a better party!'

There was another cheer. Esther held up her hand.

'But you know what?'

She hovered around the microphone,

waiting, until, '*What?*' everyone chorused.

'Thirty nations, thirty schmations. We are all New Yorkers! And just at the moment, when it feels most dangerous to say that — when there are people out there trying to run this country who might never have let someone like me into that harbour in the first place, and by someone like me I just mean a *goddam human being* — I am proud, *so* proud, to call each and every one of you in here tonight my brother and sister. So *sei gesund!*' She raised her glass again. '*Cheers!*'

Gleefully, the crowd called '*Cheers!*'

'*Sei gesund!*' Holding up her hand, she began counting down on her fingers. 'And *l'chaim, saha, sante, yiamas, kipis, ganbei, kampei, skol, iachidda, slainte, prost*! I can't say it in all thirty languages, but I learned as many as I could. Thank you so much for being here tonight. I toast you all, your very good health, each and every one of you.'

More applause; Esther silenced them, again.

'Now, there are many individual people I need to thank, including those who are present only in their absence, but always,' she said. Away from the mic, she uttered something quiet and private in Yiddish, before coming back to them. 'I'd translate for the rest of you but I wouldn't want to kill the mood. Now, of course, I wouldn't be here tonight without my family: my beautiful daughter Rosalind, my always inspiring son-in-law Frank, and my gorgeous grand-daughters. Don't they scrub up well?'

She watched Natasha search the crowd and find the eyes of her sister. Rachel, standing with Gali on the other side of the room, raised her glass and Esther noticed how the two sisters shared a small, secret smile.

'But none of us, *none* of us would be here tonight if it wasn't for the vision and commitment of one man,' Esther went on. 'Well, two men, in fact. Firstly, can we all please raise our glasses to Leonard Moishe Zimmer, who sadly is no longer with us but who gave us such a gift when he only *went and bought us the next-door building!*'

More claps and whoops.

'And to a young man who I know is in here somewhere.' Esther's eyes went directly to Raf's; of course she knew exactly where he was. 'Ah yes, now there he is.' She held up her glass to Raf; he kept one hand around Natasha's waist but raised his beer bottle triumphantly towards the stage. 'What you are about to see next door is the vision of this man, this architect of such lyrical and humane imagination, Rafik Haroun, who's almost become like a member of the family since we began this adventure together.' She leaned forward to do a conspiratorial stage whisper into the mic. 'And who knows, I'm hoping he might *officially* get to be a member of my family one of these days!'

People clapped and whistled and Esther saw poor Natasha flush bright red.

'You're incorrigible!' Raf called out, laughing as he shook his head.

'Incorrigible,' Esther agreed, then re-addressed her crowd. 'We all owe Rafi so much. *I* owe him so much. And I only hope he knows how grateful I am, because I couldn't possibly find the words tonight. I've drunk far too much Manischewitz!'

Everyone laughed, as Esther said simply and warmly: 'Thank you, dearest Rafi.'

Now she nodded to one of the musicians on the stage for a drum roll, and cried out dramatically: 'And, so ... The moment you've all been waiting for ... Jorge! Scissors, please!'

A beaming Jorge passed her the giant scissors. And as Esther moved towards the red ribbon that had been strung up across Raf's beautiful sliding glass door that would for always now connect this room to the Leonard M. Zimmer Wing, she looked around at her life's work and thought about what it meant.

She knew better than anyone the theatre and spin of it all. But she also knew this: that there was a building. Where all people could come, and rest, and eat. And today, that building was a little bit bigger.

And then on her ninetieth birthday, in front of her family, her friends, the myriad New York souls she had befriended along the way, Esther Goldfaden, nee Loew, who had so nearly perished at nineteen, went to cut the ribbon. As she did so, she rolled up the sleeves of her new dress.

Author's Note

As I embarked upon the daunting adventure that is writing a second novel, if you had told me I would end up with a story that dwelt upon the Israeli-Palestinian conflict, I would have looked at you in utter bafflement. I had mapped out a book about four young women set in Hackney in the 1950s, and had got happily stuck into researching that period — the history, the food, the fashions. But I had recently moved from London to New York City, and after a few months working on my post-war Hackney tale, I kept being distracted by an altogether different idea that was making itself felt somewhere deep inside me — at first gently winking at me from the wings of my subconscious, and later jumping up and down on centre stage like a boisterous toddler who will not be ignored until it gets its own way.

I'm sure there will be people who understandably wonder what qualifies an agnostic Londoner such as myself to broach the subject of the Middle East conflict — the 'vortex of our age', as Esther describes it. It's a tricky one to answer, because this subject above all is so freighted; and held so close by people who rightly feel it is 'theirs'. Part of what it is to write a work of fiction, I hope readers understand, is to exercise a giant leap of imagination and empathy with humans whose experiences are not one's own. But in many ways the question 'why am I writing about this?' also goes to the heart of one of the chief concerns in my book. I kept wondering: who really owns the narrative of their own family identity, especially if they inherit it many decades later, in totally different circumstances? Whose tragedies are these? Who has the right to tell? What does it mean to be one thing or the other, or to be many things all at once?

When I sat down opposite the proverbial blank sheet (which was a screen, predictably) and started to write what was eventually to become this novel, I had certain voices ringing in my ears. I had been travelling to the Middle East regularly since 2004, and the idea of a love story that crossed the divide was something I'd first been struck by when I began working with young people of both Jewish and Palestinian heritage. What if they became best friends? I wondered. And what if they lived fifteen minutes from each other, as the crow flies, yet were not legally allowed to visit each other? What if they fell in love?

In this story there are various loves that cross boundaries — not only the love between Natasha and Rafi, but between Amina and Zaki, Rachel and Skye, Josh and Kristen. And while no character is based on a real person, everything that takes place in the Middle East chapters — from Maha's house to Natasha's experience at Qalandiya — reflects a real-life human incident that has been revealed to me over the course of my research on the ground in Jerusalem, Ramallah, Bethlehem, Jenin and Tel Aviv. I am extremely grateful to the interviewees who so generously shared their stories, anecdotes, and at times emotionally distressing personal histories with me.

In case you're interested, here's a little background about how I came to be interested in all this in the first place. I have been fascinated by the Jewish side of my family — my mother's — ever since I was about six years old and my grandfather Lewis showed me an ancient letter written from his father to his mother. My great-grandparents Abraham and Sarah, who lived in the Øódź ghetto, had the foresight to flee the ongoing persecution against Jews like them just before the First World War. One day, they packed up what belongings they could, boarded a boat going somewhere else — anywhere else — and eventually, by chance, washed up in

Cardiff. So Abraham and Sarah were some of the luckiest Jews of the twentieth century: they escaped to Wales before the Holocaust would have made their lives perilous. As was the case for so many millions, other members of our wider Jewish family did not have such luck.

I was always struck by the Jewish notes in our history, then, even as I grew up in a decidedly unreligious household in west London. My violin teacher Rodney Friend used to say my Jewish blood came out when I played music, and it's true that I always felt an atavistic and deep stirring when I thought about that element of our family's culture and narrative. I never stopped wondering (or trying to imagine) what it must have been like for Abraham and Sarah: to have had to uproot everything they knew, everything they owned, their friends, their families, their books, their language — and step onto a boat going to a place they had never heard of into a completely unknown future.

At least they ended up having a future.

So, that was where my personal interest in Jewish refugee history originated. And then, just as I arrived at university, the second *intifada* broke out among the Palestinians in protest at the ongoing military occupation by Israel. As a curious and quite politically engaged ninteen-year-old I began to pay much more attention to what was happening in that part of the world. I started reading widely around the foundation of Israel, its conflict with the Palestinians, the vexed question of refugee right of return, and the recent history of the Middle East. What I learned terrified me, intrigued me, disturbed me, gripped me. The horrors and the waste of the conflict were disturbing; the seeming legitimacy of claims to land and history on both sides irreconcilable; and the stalemate and deadlock despair-inducing.

In my final year of my English degree I read a lot of contemporary and contemporaneous Israeli and Palestinian literature for my Tragedy paper, and my interest in the human element of the Middle East conflict — the real people living out their brave grand ordinary lives in circumstances unimaginable to most of us — only intensified. Not long after I graduated, I received an invitation to participate as a violinist in a Bach festival taking place in Israel, the West Bank and occupied Palestinian territories. I jumped at the chance to visit a part of the world which had held such fascination for so long.

That was the start of regular trips to the region, in some cases a few times a year, and the making of many important friendships.

The intervening decade has been a process of constant education and re-education for me, and the witnessing of much that is cause for distress, but much that is cause for hope, redemption, and ultimately, perhaps, tentative optimism about human nature too.

With 'the situation' as it is today, however, my heart breaks for those on both sides, Israeli and Palestinian. It is my fervent if faint hope that in our lifetime we will see peace. I am not holding my breath.

CBH. London, autumn 2013

Acknowledgements

Thanks beyond thanks to the following:

John Harte and Michael Stevens for that very first trip to Israel and the West Bank, almost a decade ago, and everything in between. Tim Moore for the magical nocturnal adventure around Jerusalem's Old City on my first night there. Also to Nicholas Collon, Andy Staples, Sam West, Graham Ross and all the musical folk who have been such a vital part of my Middle Eastern experiences over the years.

For quietly changing my life in profound ways they may not even be aware of: Ramzi Aburedwan, Al'aa Shelaldeh, Mahmoud Karzon, Fadi Basha, and all the staff and students at Al-Kamandjati. Also to the Awartani family in Ramallah for the spontaneous jam session; and to Aziz, the pig butcher in Beit Jala who so generously opened his house, extended his hospitality, recounted his life story and patiently answered my questions. On that note: I owe a debt of thanks to so many people who have shared aspects of their lives and their histories with me: many heartbreaking, many humbling. It would be impossible to thank each and every one of you, but I hope you know who you are and how indebted I am.

I also must extend special thanks to Anita Lasker-Wallfisch, who may not even remember. Esther existed as a character long before I had the privilege of meeting Anita, but it was deeply moving for me to talk to someone in 2013 who is the living and breathing proof that you can survive the unsurvivable and live out your life with strength, humanity, and compassion. Our meeting was one of the life-changing mornings of my life and I will never forget it. Thank you.

If only there were stronger words than 'thank you'! If there were, I would extend them mightily to maestro Daniel Barenboim and all the Israeli and Arab members of the West-Eastern Divan Orchestra, especially my room-mate Meirav Kadichevski and my sometime stand-partner Yamen Saadi. Thank you all for being such extraordinary musicians, such brave people, such welcoming friends and for enabling me to open my eyes and my heart. I believe — I hope — you have made me a better listener; and thanks to you all, I understand why that matters. Everything is connected.

For sticking by me, with apparently tireless patience and great good counsel through times both light and dark, I must thank

406

Rowan Lawton and Mary-Anne Harrington, the loveliest agent and editor anyone could wish for. You are both wonders. I am also deeply appreciative of the fantastic teams at Headline Review and Furniss Lawton.

For yet more fine translations of Rilke's poetry I would like to thank Emily Speers Mears. For their insights, advice, conversation, random acts of kindness, book recommendations and other gems that have been either directly or indirectly invaluable along the way I am most grateful to David and Harriet Zimmer; Nicholas Confessore of the *New York Times;* Ollie Cooke; Simon Schama; Tchaik Chassay and his team at Chassay Last; Tim Botteril; Susan Wagner; Peter Florence; Peter Kosminski; Joe Schaffers; Amber Sainsbury; Helen Brunner; Rodney Friend; Ursula Macfarlane; the staff at Soho House and the London Library.

For their great hospitality I thank my parents-in-law Eli & Lawrie Geller; Alexandra Reeve Givens; and John & Kate Edwards who once looked after me so well in Sheikh Jarrah.

A devoted shout-out to my family, always: my mum Gillian; my dad Humphrey; my brothers Perry and Elliot; my sisters-in-law Lisa and Katey; Robert and Stacia Hill; and all the glorious nephews and nieces: Elodie,

Carys, Jagger and Hunter. I love you all very much.

I have dedicated the book to the memory of my great-grandparents Abraham and Sarah Hauser, whose own refugee journey from Øódź to Cardiff whispered its way into my blood and imagination. I would also like to acknowledge the wondrous man that was their son, my mother's father, my grandfather Lewis Hawser, QC. Grandpa, you led by example when you proved that love could trump tribe. But for so much more, you were and are an inspiration. You defined what it is to be an empathetic, intellectually elegant, curious soul and not a moment goes by when I don't wish you were still here. If you only could have lived to Esther's grand old age, we would have been the very best of friends, I know. And listened to a lot of jazz on vinyl along the way. I miss you every day.

But most of all, above and beyond everything, and anything I could ever hope to get down in words, this one's for you, James Roscoe. And you know why. Thank you.

We do hope that you have enjoyed reading this large print book.

Did you know that all of our titles are available for purchase?

We publish a wide range of high quality large print books including:
Romances, Mysteries, Classics
General Fiction
Non Fiction and Westerns

Special interest titles available in large print are:
The Little Oxford Dictionary
Music Book
Song Book
Hymn Book
Service Book

Also available from us courtesy of Oxford University Press:
Young Readers' Dictionary
(large print edition)
Young Readers' Thesaurus
(large print edition)

For further information or a free brochure, please contact us at:
Ulverscroft Large Print Books Ltd.,
The Green, Bradgate Road, Anstey,
Leicester, LE7 7FU, England.
Tel: (00 44) 0116 236 4325
Fax: (00 44) 0116 234 0205

THE MOON AROUND SARAH

Paul Lederer

Born with the ability to speak, but not the inclination, Sarah lives in silence. She is surrounded by the noise of her bickering family, who are gathered to discuss the selling of the family homestead. There is no room for sentiment and a young selectively mute girl is not a burden any of them wants to shoulder. Escaping from this madness, she befriends a young man who finds her silence eloquent. If they are to understand each other, and escape the shadow of her family, they must learn a deeper form of communication.

THE SKINNING TREE

Srikumar Sen

During the Second World War, nine-year-old Sabby lives in a Calcutta family where sophisticated British habits such as bridge and dinner parties co-exist with Indian values and nationalism. But when he is sent to a boarding school in northern India, that world is soon forgotten; and Sabby is subjected, with his fellow pupils, to the teachers' draconian regime. The boys themselves take on their educators' cruel traits, mindlessly killing animals and hanging their skins on a cactus, before their thoughts turn to even more sinister schemes. Conspiratorial whisperings and plans of revenge spiral into a tragedy engulfing Sabby, in an engrossing novel exploring human nature's darkest facets.

EVERY PROMISE

Andrea Bajani

When Sara leaves him — broken by their inability to conceive — Pietro reverts to a younger self, leaving the dishes unwashed and the bed unmade. Soon after, Sara confesses that she is pregnant from a casual encounter, and comes to rely on Pietro's mother for support. This leaves the three of them in an uncomfortable limbo, unable to move on. Into all of this falls Olmo, an old man haunted by memories of war. When he asks Pietro to travel to Russia on his behalf, to right a wrong from his past, Pietro sees a chance for a new beginning.

ENON

Paul Harding

The Crosbys had lived in modest bliss in the small idyllic town of Enon for generations. But after the tragic loss of his thirteen-year-old daughter, Charlie Crosby finds himself the last living member of his family. Paralyzed by his loss, Charlie allows his relationship with his wife to rapidly disintegrate. His despair spreads like a disease and he finds himself living in squalor with a heavy dependence on pain killers. Unable to lift himself out of his misery, Charlie embarks on a dreamlike form of remembering, wandering the forgotten paths of the town, and of his history, in an attempt to make sense of his loss.

A THOUSAND PARDONS

Jonathan Dee

Separated from her husband, Helen and her twelve-year-old daughter Sara leave their family home for Manhattan, where Helen must build a new life for them both. Thrust back into the working world, Helen takes a job in PR — her first in many years — and discovers she has a rare gift: she can convince arrogant men to admit their mistakes, spinning crises into second chances. Faced with the fallout from her own marriage, and her daughter's increasingly distant behaviour, Helen finds that the capacity for forgiveness she nurtures so successfully in her professional life is far harder to apply to her personal one . . .